Daughter of the Hills

Novels of the Thirties

Call Home the Heart by Fielding Burke. Afterwords by Sylvia
J. Cook and Anna W. Shannon
Daughter of the Hills by Myra Page. Afterword by Deborah S.
Rosenfelt
Rope of Gold by Josephine Herbst. Afterword by Elinor Langer
The Unpossessed by Tess Slesinger. Afterword by Janet
Sharistanian

Daughter of the Hills

A Woman's Part in the Coal Miners' Struggle

A Novel of the Thirties

MYRA PAGE

With an Introduction by Alice Kessler-Harris and Paul Lauter and an Afterword by Deborah S. Rosenfelt

THE FEMINIST PRESS
at The City University of New York
New York

To John Markey and sixty years together; and to our family, May, John-R, Ann, and Stefan, and our grandchildren, Lili, Johnny, Ethan, Debi, and Andrew

Printed in Canada
89 88 87 86 5 4 3 2 1

First Feminist Press edition

Library of Congress Cataloging-in-Publication Data
Page, Myra, 1897–
    Daughter of the hills.

    (A Novel of the thirties)
    Reprint. Originally published: With sun in our
blood. New York : Citadel Press, 1950.
    I. Title.   II. Series: Novels of the thirties series.
PS3531.A235W5   1986   813'.54   86-9866
ISBN 0-935312-59-5 (pbk.)

This publication is made possible, in part, by grants from the Division
of the American Missionary Association, United Church Board for
Homeland Ministries, and from the AT&T Foundation.

Cover design: Lucinda Geist
Cover art: Self Portrait in a Red Blouse (c. 1900) by Gwen John, the
Tate Gallery, London. By permission of Sara John and Ben John.

Contents

Introduction

The first phase of the women's movement, so the historical tradition goes, ended in the twenties. Its passion spent in the successful campaign for the vote, its remnants torn apart by divisions between those who wanted equality at once and those who insisted on retaining hard-won protections, the movement was stifled finally by a depression that mocked individual ambition. But if one kind of feminism ended in the twenties, another emerged in the thirties. Largely overlooked by historians, its existence is documented by the literature of the period.

The old movement that ended in the twenties declined in the affluence of that decade. After the vote was won, activist women set out to translate their political success into the economic equality it seemed to promise: Alice Paul's Women's Party pushed for an Equal Rights Amendment; coalitions of women's groups supported the Sheppard-Towner Act to provide maternal and well-baby care; the Women's Bureau successfully defended the rights of wage-earning women to minimum wages and shorter hours. The prosperity of the twenties made room for ambition, nurturing the talents of such writers as Edna St. Vincent Millay, Katherine Ann Porter, Zora Neale Hurston, and Anzia Yezierska. For a while it seemed as though the women who flooded into arts and letters as well as into banking and insurance were merely the vanguard of a new generation of self-confident and fulfilled womanhood.

Then came the Depression, and widespread unemployment put an end to illusions of economic equality for women. The crisis of the thirties revealed the extent to which women's ambitions had relied on the opportunites offered by an expanding economy. With 25 percent of the work force unemployed by 1933, the picture changed dramatically. State and local governments tried to drive women, especially married women, out of the work force. Private industry took advantage of socially sanctioned discrimination against women to undercut the wages of poorly paid men. Opportunities for promotion and advancement shriveled.

To return to the home was no answer for most women. Families doubled up. Husbands and fathers lost their jobs. The home reflected the poverty and insecurity of unemployment as women and their children coped with the psychic tensions of maintaining family life and the economic pressures of insufficient incomes. Young women postponed marriage to help their parents survive, and they avoided pregnancy for fear of its economic consequences.

But women did not abandon the search for women's rights. Rather, as the crisis exposed their vulnerable positions, they began to question the degree to which the ambitions of the twenties were circumscribed by social reality. There would be no freedom for women at work while millions were unemployed; no genuine partnership in the home while clothing and food remained luxuries; no equality of opportunity for male or female children who grew up without medical attention or education. To women of the thirties, poverty and the social conditions that fostered it seemed as much women's issues as individual advancement had seemed in the twenties. To fulfill their own thwarted ambitions, women were required to connect themselves with the larger struggle for social justice. They would rise or fall with it. In this new generation, women who might earlier have been called feminists became social activists of a broader stamp.

As the old individualism gave way to concern for eliminating unemployment, preserving home life, and collective survival, women began to turn to available political movements for answers. Some moved into New Deal agencies, hoping to find a cure for despair in government social programs. Others chose to organize workers into the newly militant trade union movement. Many turned to the socialist and communist parties of the Left. Here, in an atmosphere of revolutionary possibility, they introduced questions of equality between the sexes, of women's education, and of reproductive and sexual freedom.

Left-wing groups like the Communist Party, USA, welcomed women in their ranks. They provided increased opportunities for women to act in the political arena, but they remained ambivalent about specifically women's issues. Though leftist ideology in the 1930s recognized the "special oppression" of women and formally espoused sexual equality, in practice, the Left tended to subordinate problems of gender to the overwhelming tasks of organizing the working class and fighting fascism. Both ideology and practice opposed feminism, fundamentally on the ground that it drew working-class women away from their male working-class allies and into the orbit of bourgeois women. Women constituted a formidable proportion of most left-wing groups, and Unemployment Councils, neighborhood groups, and even the emerging CIO relied heavily on them for leadership and support. By the end of the decade perhaps 40 percent of the membership of the Communist Party, USA, was female.[1] If the Communist Party did not provide a comfortable haven for women, if it subordinated women's questions and often refused to challenge sexual segregation on the job or rigid gender roles at home, its language of equality provided women with opportunities for debate, and its political programs opportunities for organizing and leadership experiences. The Left offered a forum and more

serious attention to women's questions than any other group of
the decade. It also provided women with a community of
shared experience.

Female voices, primed by the rhetoric of equality, resonated
on the printed page. A remarkable number of politically active
women wrote. Their poems, stories, and songs, as well as their
novels and essays, give us access to some of the issues seldom
addressed in political practice, even on the Left. If the nature
of women's participation in political action limited the issues
about which they wrote, it also provided depth and insight into
the critical social and personal conflicts that underlay activism.
Their political views help clarify why most of the women writers of the thirties and in this series worked in a variety of forms:
each form had both an artistic and political motivation as well as
a particular audience. Fielding Burke, for example, had published many volumes of verse under her real name, Olive Tilford Dargan; Josephine Herbst was an active reporter
throughout the thirties, as well as a critic; Mary Heaton Vorse,
whose novel about Gastonia was a rather crude and obvious effort, wrote some of the decade's best books and articles about
the developing labor movement. These writers strove not only
to perfect the forms in which they wrote but to choose the
forms most appropriate for the various political tasks in which
they engaged.

We have chosen in this series to begin with fiction because it
seems to reflect most closely the unfettered consciousness of
women in the decade. The books in this series are part of a long
tradition of literature about working-class life. Because they
are written by women, these novels do not sit comfortably inside most accounts of that tradition, nor do they conform pre-
cisely to theories of "proletarian fiction" produced in the
thirties. Yet the ways in which this women's fiction differs from
that of men alert us to the particular qualities of some of the
best female writers of this century, including Agnes Smedley
and Meridel Le Sueur, and provide the most important reason
for The Feminist Press to undertake this series.

In the 1920s, literary rebellion, in the words of Jack Conroy, "was directed principally against the fetters of form and language taboos."[2] By the thirties, literary theory had provided a systematic alternative to the modernist emphasis on formal experimentation, ironic distance, and linguistic complexity. Its major breakthrough, particularly for the work of left-wing and working-class writers, was to validate the experiences of working people. In her speech to the 1935 American Writers' Congress, Meridel Le Sueur made the point this way:

> It is from the working class that the use and function of native language is slowly being built. . . . This is the slow beginning of a culture, the slow and wonderful accumulation of an experience that has hitherto been unspoken, that has been a gigantic movement of labor, the swingdown of the pick, the ax that has hitherto made no sound but is now being heard.[3]

"Proletarian Realism," Mike Gold's widely adopted phrase, would thus deal in plain, crisp language with the lives and especially the work of the proletariat, optimistically urging them on "through the maze of history toward Socialism and the classless society."[4]

Though this is in fact a rich and complex aesthetic, it presented immediate problems for women who took their own experiences seriously. Less than a quarter of all women and fewer than 15 percent of married women worked outside the home during most of the 1930s. If the workplace was to be a major focus for art, as it was for Communist Party organizing, then, as "workplace" did not include work done in the home for the support of the family, only small fractions of women's lives would find their way into art. The rest would be ignored, subordinated once again to the demands of male politics. More important, since proletarian fiction, by the definition of the times, rested upon the central distinction between the experiences of the working class and those of the bourgeoisie, it would underplay, even deny, the relevance of other distinctive group experiences. Blacks, Hispanics, women—as groups suffering their own persecution—would have no place in it. In denying the commonalities of female experience, the vision of the proletarian aesthetic undermined such crucial issues for women as the uneven division of household labor, the sexual double standard, and male chauvinism within the working class or the Party itself.

Women writers who perceived such problems were placed in a certain dilemma: theory maintained that their work should be based upon the experiences of the working class; yet the experiences of one half of the working class—males—were clearly of more significance than the experiences of the other half of the working class. Where did that leave distinctly female experiences, like childbearing, or those, like the nurturance of children, which continued to be primarily women's tasks? And where in that theoretical framework could one find a place for the strengths and ambiguities of love, of rearing children, of family life, of the problems of control over one's body, the struggle to find emotional and sexual fulfillment?

Women writers of the Left chose to flout male convention and to write about themes that fell outside the frameworks of their male peers. But so strongly masculinist was the cultural theory and practice of the Left that it remained virtually immune to the feminist implications of their themes. The cultural apparatus of the Left in the thirties was, if anything, more firmly masculinist than its political institutions. It is not that women writers were ignored. Josephine Herbst was a "guest delegate" to the Kharkov conference of the International Union of Revolutionary Writers in 1930. Tillie Olsen and Meridel Le Sueur were among the (few) invited women speakers at the American Writers' Congress in 1935. The Communist Party's book club, the Book Union, selected as its representative "proletarian novels" Fielding Burke's *A Stone Came Rolling*, Clara Weatherwax's *Marching! Marching!*, and Leane Zugsmith's *A Time*

to Remember. Herbst, Le Sueur, Zugsmith, and Grace Lumpkin, among others, were active reviewers for *The New Masses*
and certain other Left journals.

But women were often, in fact, tokens at major conferences.
Accounts of the John Reed clubs, (the Communist Party's cultural association), of the editorial boards of magazines like *The
Anvil, Blast,* or *The Partisan Review,* and of other Communist
Party and Left cultural organizations hardly acknowledge the
existence of women—though many did, in fact, work in such
groups. The hitchhiking Wobbly style of life extolled by such
writers as Jack Conroy left room only for the rare Boxcar
Bertha, while the hairy-chested polemics of left-wing critics
like Mike Gold placed women's issues squarely in a male context. The worker-poet was inevitably male, his sexuality "evi-
dence of healthy vigor"; his comrades, cigar-smoking talkers, in
from the wheat fields or the Willys-Overland plant. In a *New
Masses* editorial announcing the advent of "Proletarian Realism," Gold pictures the new writer as "a wild youth of about
twenty-two, the son of working-class parents, who himself
works in the lumber camps, coal mines, and steel mills, harvest
fields and mountain camps of America. . . . He writes in jets of
exasperated feeling. . . ."[5] Women writers were recognized on
the Left, indeed occasionally puffed, just as women's issues
were recognized. But the values and outlooks *institutionalized*
in magazines, editorial boards, conferences, and theories of the
Left were decidedly masculinist.

At the same time, there appear to have been few distinctly
female cultural groups or networks of support among women
writers on the Left. Meridel Le Sueur mentions in her American Writers' Congress speech a group of "a hundred and fifty
women from factory and farm" who "wrote down their great
proletarian experience." Myra Page, novelist and reporter, recalls the way experienced women took newcomers under their
wings, but notes that women "felt that the general issue was the
most important thing: depression and unemployment."[6] Sup-

port among women was directed at achieving the larger goals. Women intellectuals in books like Tess Slesinger's *The Unpossessed* and Josephine Herbst's *Rope of Gold* seem, from the perspective of the 1980s, strikingly isolated from one another. While there were female-centered cultural institutions during the 1930s—the YWCA, for example, supported a Women's Press—they were not of the Left. In fact, they were likely to be noted by the Communist Party, if at all, with suspicion. In short, there was little institutional support on the Left that might have validated any distinctly female culture, and much that discouraged it. Not perhaps by design, but effectively for all that, any female—much less feminist—tradition was submerged.

Within a few years, the entire world of left-wing culture was ploughed under by the attacks of McCarthyism. It is not always easy now, thirty years later, to perceive how successful the campaign was in silencing and burying writers on the Left. One good indicator is that copies of books by the writers with whom we are concerned are absent from libraries and used book shops. After the thirties, some of the women turned away from "political" subjects; some fell into silences; others continued to write but could find no publisher; many, like Tillie Olsen, were subjected to public attack. That happened, of course, to men as well as to women. But, in addition, women were confronted with that hostile ideology we have come to call "the feminine mystique." More profoundly, perhaps, the concern for working-class life and for understanding the relationship between gender and politics were suppressed in the fifties as anti-communism, suburbanization, and consumerism controlled the environment. As the cultural soil dried up, writers lost their audience. The run of stories, novels, poems, and songs that had established for an audience certain expectations, artistic conventions, and ideological perspectives, came to an end.

When the writing of the thirties began to be re-discovered twenty-five years ago, critics persisted in denying its feminist proclivities. In his comprehensive book, *The Radical Novel in the United States*, for example, Walter Rideout suggests that "the explicit linking of political revolution and sexual freedom rarely appears" in left-wing novels of the thirties "as it did in *Daughter of Earth*."[7] In fact, however, sexuality, personal liberation, and radical politics are closely intertwined in Fielding Burke's *Call Home the Heart*; sexual politics are at the center of conflicts described in Tess Slesinger's *The Unpossessed*; personal and sexual relations provide the critical counterpoint to emerging political differences in Josephine Herbst's *Rope of Gold*.

Female writers who accepted the central class division of socialist realism nevertheless paid attention to women-centered issues. In Tillie Olsen's *Yonnondio,* as Deborah Rosenfelt argues, "the major transformation is based on human love, on the capacity to respond to beauty, and on the premise of a regenerative life cycle of which mother and daughter are a part." For feminist proletarian writers, these issues are not separable from the capacity to effect a successful political transformation. As Rosenfelt tells us, "Women's work in preserving and nurturing that creative capacity in the young is shown in *Yonnondio* to be an essential precondition to social change."[8] Such themes, ignored by male critics, are not peculiar to Olsen. Both in her story "Annunciation" and in her novella *The Girl*, Meridel Le Sueur focuses on the regenerative power of pregnancy and birth. The action in Leane Zugsmith's *A Time to Remember* concerns a department store strike, but the emotional conflict that constitutes the dynamic tension of the novel comes from the attempts of strikers and their families to cope with the social reality of women's subordinate positions.

The books in this series demonstrate the substantial and vigorous tradition of women-centered literature. We find in these books women of intellect and strength—like Victoria in Herbst's *Rope of Gold*—seeking work that is politically meaningful and yet consonant with their need for personal independence. We encounter in Slesinger's *The Unpossessed* many of the same conflicts between ostensibly progressive politics and real chauvinist behavior that helped generate the women's liberation movement of the late 1960s. With Ishma in Fielding Burke's *Call Home the Heart* we experience the contrary appeals of full-time, heroic but often grubby, work in a movement for social change and of the rich, green pastures of the hill country. These books present women (and men) in varieties of workplaces—including the home—participants in strikes and demonstrations, observers and reporters of what seemed a growing, international revolutionary movement. Their steady grasp of sexual politics illuminates the inner contradictions and struggles of movements for change. These writers are the sisters and comrades of Agnes Smedley, Meridel Le Sueur, and Tillie Olsen; their work asserts the richness, as well as the continuity, of the traditions of left-wing feminism in the United States.

Certainly all the female authors of the thirties did not write in ways that distinguished them from men. But some of the best works written by women addressed the distinctive experience of both working-class and female lives. Women in that decade produced a body of writing with qualities that overlap but are not identical with those of the male writers of the period. This literature—we might now call it "socialist feminist"—is only beginning to be explored by scholars with an eye to what it tells us about the complex factors that encouraged women to write both as activists and as critics. In presenting these books as part of a series, The Feminist Press hopes to underline the need to reconstruct the cultural context that helped shape them.

That process will require us to re-examine questions around which debate swirled in the thirties. What is the function of art in a revolutionary movement? Do we cast aside as merely absurd the notions of some socialist critics, who suggested that art was a "weapon" in the class struggle, that writers must under all circumstances convey a sense of "proletarian optimism," and that they must write only in language plain enough for plain people? Or are we to understand the criticism of the Left in that period as a creative effort to confront issues with which the artists themselves were struggling? Are there ways to resolve the tensions between the slow, sustained discipline that the artful rendering of experience demands and the more immediate requirements of writing hitched to the needs of a political movement? How can a writer bring alive the vision of a triumphant socialist future, which no one has seen or fully imagined, with anything like the power to evoke the struggles and devastation of capitalism in decline? Just who is one's audience? And if the audience for socialist art should, at least in part, be working-class people, what functions does art serve in their lives, and are these different from its functions in the lives of the traditional audience for writers?

The writers in this series largely avoided the more formulaic demands of thirties criticism. Their endings are not always unambiguous and hopeful as "socialist realism" theoretically required. Their heroines, like Ishma in *Call Home the Heart*, share both the virtues and the profound limitations of their class origins. They portray retreat as well as triumph; confusion and ambiguity as well as possibility. But struggle was never simple. Together these books provide another piece of the puzzle that illustrates how women have come to consciousness over the years. In publishing this series, The Feminist Press calls attention to the varieties of feminism and its expressions. The fiction of the thirties is part of our common heritage. We hope it will be useful in conceiving of our future lives.

Alice Kessler-Harris
Hofstra University

Paul Lauter
State University of New York,
College at Old Westbury

NOTES

1. See Robert Shaffer, "Women and the Communist Party, USA, 1930–1940," *Socialist Review* #45 (May–June 1979): 90 for this and additional information on women and the Communist Party.

2. Jack Conroy, "Introduction," *Writers in Revolt: The Anvil Anthology* (New York, Westport: Lawrence Hill, 1973), p. ix.

3. From "Proceedings of the American Writers' Congress," New York, 1935, reprinted by West End Press, Minneapolis, 1981.

4. Edward Seaver, "Socialist Realism'" *The New Masses* 17 (23 October 1935): 24.

5. "Go Left, Young Writers," *Mike Gold: A Literary Anthology*, ed. Michael Folsom (New York: International Publishers, 1972), p. 188.

6. Interview with Alice Kessler-Harris, 1 December 1982.

7. Walter Rideout, *The Radical Novel in the United States* (New York: Hill and Wang, 1956), p. 219.

8. Deborah Rosenfelt, "From the Thirties: Tillie Olsen and the Radical Tradition," *Feminist Studies* 7 (Fall 1981): 398.

Preface

It is customary nowadays to preface a novel or motion picture with the safeguard that people in the story bear no relation to actual persons, living or dead. This book, on the contrary, acknowledges its debt to Dolly and her brave Hawkins clan, and to John Cooper.

Dolly Hawkins Cooper was my friend. We came to know one another as few humans may, feeling as close kin as sisters; yet it has proven hard for me to get her down in writing fully, as she lived and dared.

During a long winter that we spent together, then summer, planting, weeding, digging up taters, gathering oversized berries in the woods, Dolly told me her story. "But this can't be lost!" I said. "It must be written down, passed on. Would you mind?"

She didn't hesitate. "If you want, why not? It's all God's truth."

A remarkable thing about Dolly: she never thought of

herself as out-of-the-ordinary. What she did, she told me, was what any woman would do, in her place.

Dolly grew up in the Cumberland Mountains of Tennessee, a coal miner's daughter, then miner's wife and mother. She took a leading part in events that may seem reckless, almost beyond believing, especially to those who have grown up in our cities and have no way of knowing, first-hand, what it is like in the coal pits and hollows of Appalachia. Or what it meant to be Dolly, love John Cooper, face what happened, and, together, come through.

Little known beyond the Cumberlands, Dolly's father, Jim Hawkins had a way with men, and with women. A dare-devil Irishman and a born leader, he passed on to Dolly his gifts—and a fiery temper. Both gave rise to more than one legend in the hills that bred them. John Bunyan and his American half-brother, Paul, would find them good company; Mother Jones, John Henry, Martin Luther King, and the logger, Abe. They have a native wit that Chaucer would relish: folk imagery and language rhythms that bring to mind Irish writers: Synge, Yeats, O'Casey.

The Hawkins were pioneers who followed Daniel Boone's trail through Cumberland Gap into Appalachia. Once small farmers in Tidewater, Virginia, they were forced off their land by the big slaveowning planters, as were many others. In the hills they joined mountaineers fighting British Redcoats; for instance, the famous battle on King's Mountain that proved crucial to Washington's winning in Yorktown.

Dolly's people, with good reason to hate slavery, had a station on the Underground Railroad, so that runaway slaves could "follow the drinking gourd" (the North Star) to Canada, and freedom. During the Civil War the Hawkins had sided with Lincoln, as had most of Appalachia. The few who volunteered for the Confederacy caused shoot-outs in the hills, as well as the Hatfield-McCoy feud.

As railroads expanded west after the war, the demand grew for Appalachia's coal. Dolly's father and hundreds of hill farmers became miners. They took their long-honored tradition with them into the pits, a tradition of standing together and organizing to get their rights. Dolly tells how her father joined miners throughout the Cumberlands to rid their hills of "penitents," convicts that mining companies took from state penitentiaries to mine coal, throwing free miners out of work. Dolly and other miners' children helped in the fight which began in 1890 and took ten years to win.

In our country each region has a growing sense of pride in its history. There are none more proud than the people of Appalachia. For a hundred years coal miners and their families have struggled to win a good life for themselves and their children: in the Alleghenies, Black Mountains, Cumberlands, Blue Ridge, and Great Smokies—wherever coal lies deep in the earth and miners risk their lives to get it. Even now, the struggle goes on.

Miners have a fierce love of their mountains, their kinfolk and their work-mates. Those who had to leave Appalachia in the fifties, because of the sharp drop in demand for coal, went to Detroit and other cities to find work. But the mountains keep pulling them back. On Memorial Day weekends they make the long trip home, to visit their people, to catch up with friends at a union picnic, enjoy a square dance, and maybe go hunting. When someone they love dies, they bring him back to Appalachia and bury him in the family plot, "where it's pretty and restful."

Now that coal, a key source of energy, is in demand again, mining families are leaving the cities and returning to their hills.

Since Dolly's time changes have taken place in Appalachia, some for the better, some not. Through their union, the United Mine Workers of America, with 277,000 members, miners have won better pay, better working conditions, and pensions. They have seen to it that boys of thirteen and younger no longer work in the mines, but are in school. Modern machines have replaced the old pick-and-shovel down in the pit. Many young miners are now high-school graduates, and take an active part in their union.

But coal mining remains a dangerous trade. Through their long experience miners have learned to rely on their organized strength and an aroused public opinion to get more safety in the mines, to put an end to so many being crippled and killed from mine cave-ins and explosions, and from Black Lung, a fatal disease that many get from constantly breathing in coal dust down in the pit. There is a method of preventing so much coal dust in the mines, a system known as rock-dusting that is used in Wales, Scotland, and other countries. As yet, few Appalachian mines have an adequate system of rock-dusting. Why? Miners point to the big oil and gas corporations that own the mines. "They don't know us miners. They live far off. Don't seem interested in us, just how much coal you load." Delegations of miners kept traveling from their hills down to Washington to get Congress to enact better laws on mine safety.

Just as Appalachia's mighty chain of mountain ranges form the backbone of a whole region of our land, from

Maine to Alabama, so miners have proven the enduring backbone of the American labor movement. During the thirties, the UMWA, led by John Lewis, started the drive soon joined by the AFL which organized millions of workers in steel, auto, oil, and other industries into the powerful AFL-CIO.

In Jim Hawkins' time, coal mining was a man's trade. Miner's had a saying, a woman below ground's bad luck, sure to bring a rock slide or cave-in. But today, as the demand for coal grows, women are beginning to work in the mines. Dolly would have liked this.

She's gone now. But for me, Dolly Hawkins will never die: a woman who "sassed fate," and by defying it, for love of John Cooper, Dolly was able, against odds, to win.

MYRA PAGE

Yonkers, New York
June 13, 1977

. . . . . *chapter* **1** . . . .

A storm was bearing down on our Cumberlands, sudden and ravenous. My skirt tucked around my waist, I hurried my brother's clothes off the line and in by the fire, then stepped outside to watch. There was a kind of almighty glory in it, blowing fit to swallow the earth and our hills atremble, fighting off then giving in to meet it.

"Dolly, quick!" In the wood near me Tobey, a neighbor's child, was garnering acorns. He dropped his treasures and ran toward me. "Outlander's acoming up the trail!"

I flipped him a piece of sassafras root from my pocket. "Get along with you." And what was bringing a stranger so far back in our hills as Toewad mine patch? Only Turtleback Creek and a twisty dirt road stretched between us and the world beyond our Hollow.

My hair ablowing free, I stepped to the ridge for a look. By the stride of him the man climbing toward us

was a newcomer to our parts. Pick and fiddle over his shoulder he came aswinging up the trail, a rare whistling under his breath. I let down my skirt.

From the mist of High Top I saw an eagle dart out. Thunderbird my Indian Granny named him, foretelling the gale. She said his coming bode a man good or ill according to his lights.

Tobey scampered behind a gum tree for a lookout while I gathered pine knots. I needed a roaring fire in our cabin to finish drying the clothes. As I dragged logs I was ahumming to myself, a bit excited like always at the fresh smell of pine and earth the windstorm was raising. Another few hours and my brother Clyde would be home and relaying pranks he was up to below ground on their mule-driver Ike. Seemed like Clyde, my Dad all over, was never growing up. Any minute a cavein might start, rotten props give way and him playing tricks!

Tobey from his hideout was waving me signals about the stranger mounting our path. I tossed my head and kept to my work. Dolly Hawkins was not giving any man a second glance. Beyond our cabin Limpy's cars, loaded with slag, were jangling up the tipple. I had hearkened to them since a child and took a kind of pleasuring in it, like sunup over High Top and the steady tramp at nightfall of our men from the pit. Down the ravine I spied freight cars reloading coal for Memphis.

I was toting a backlog, half carrying half dragging it, when close behind me I heard a man saying, "Easy there, missie! I'll give you a hand."

Even before I turned something about his voice warned me. It held a teasing laugh ready to spring when

you least expecting it. And looking down on me was a
man big as my Dad had been. His thick mane of chestnut was amuss from the blow and black eyes adancing.
His cheekbones were high and sharp pointed like Ma's,
bespeaking Indian blood, only his had laugh wrinkles.
By the bits of coal pockmarking his neck and cheeks I
knew him a miner, like my own kinfolk.

When I faced him his look quick-sobered.

"I wasn't expecting this." He spoke like to himself. He
was bigger than my Dad, and like him I saw at a glance,
full as a mountainside of life.

"Expecting what?" I could feel my own face turning
warm.

He did not answer me, just whipped off his cap and
handed it to Tobey who had come alongside me, then
held out his arms for my log.

"My name's John Cooper, miss. And I'd be counting it
a pleasure to be toting your log?"

I was half a mind for letting him have it when something in the teasing look he gave me or thought of the
Thunderbird made me step fast by him.

"Thankye, but it's not a Hawkins girl that's needing
help with a backlog!"

Tobey laughed and after a bit I heard the man joining
in. "Hoity toity!" He was speaking with little Tobey but
distinct like, so I'd not miss. "Well lad, I rather fancy it."

I quickened my step. For what made me act as I did
was nothing so close to the surface as he thought. Mine
was a way come by early, through suffering no outsider
might fathom. There was a curse resting on me. My Dad
it had struck down in the height of his manhood, then
taken Ma.

Resting my log near the grate, I turned back for Tobey since his Ma had left him in my care. I found the boy with the stranger agathering more logs and stacking them by the door.

"Maybe I could be putting the wood inside for you?" the man asked, eager like.

I shook my head. The sky was darkening fast, thunder rolling along our hills. I caught the smell of danger about him.

"But it don't make sense!" He braced himself against the wind. "Letting firewood stay out here to get soaked."

"Lotsa things don't make sense." My heart was thumping painful like. I was alone in the house. Once inside my door I might never be rid of him. I hurried my line of clothes inside and bid Tobey come in by the fire. But the man kept astanding there, like waiting some word. The damp wind had pushed up his mane of chestnut till it stood on end, waving like a kind of signal over his forehead and eyes.

"Come on, Johnny Cooper?" The lad had hold of the man's jacket. "Rest inside till the storm's past." He turned to me. "He can, can't he, Dolly?"

I made no answer, my hands aching to wallop the boy. John Cooper kept astanding there, his eyes fastened on me like they'd never let go. It had begun to drizzle in earnest. I could feel my shoulders getting damp.

"If you could see your way, miss?" he asked. "I've come a long way for a fact."

"It ain't proper that I should," I said, "but there're plenty down the line who'll give you shelter." All of a sudden the wind had taken my breath. Back of the man the storm was closing in on us. I could smell it coming, clean and hard. The sky had gone a foreboding yellow, turning our pine woods black.

"I don't know how it is with you, Miss Dolly? Being I'm a newcomer to these parts." John Cooper went on, just as if he hadn't heard a word I had been saying. "Back in Kentuck where I hail from, a body feels himself beholden to give the stranger welcome."

"Tennessee Cumberlands ain't behind Kentuck's!" I felt my dander rising. The man was playing for time. "But with us, young girls left alone don't take in strangers!" My Ma had taught me plenty about that. Wasn't that how wicked Parasidy had started?

"Beholden especial like," he went on, kind of teasing but meaning it too, "in times of storm."

"There's plenty down the line, I told you, who'll give you welcome!" I crossed to our door. Behind our cabin the great oaks were lashing and groaning from the wind. "And you better get going before the storm breaks!" Backed up against our door I beckoned Tobey inside. The lad hung back. I could see his jacket was soaking wet.

All of a sudden, eyeing me, John Cooper's laugh rang out. I grabbed Tobey's hand to push him inside, close the door in the man's face. The storm was right over us, ready to break, the wind so high I could not hear my own voice.

As I reached for Tobey a bolt of lightning shot downward. With a crackling flash it descended behind John Cooper, cut short his laugh. I saw a gum tree back of him split in two, shoot up in flame. Before I knew it I had both the man and Tobey inside and slammed the door fast.

Now came the rain, hard as a landslide, blacking out the sky. I leaned against our doorframe trying to get my breath. John Cooper was looking at me, kind of triumphant. He knew nobody could turn a man out into that. All at once I hated him as I'd hated nobody in my life, except the lowdown traitor who shot my Dad.

I drew myself up and returned the newcomer's stare. "It will soon be over!"

Grinning, he shook his head. "Not for hours."

Without answering I went over by Tobey, crouched on the hearth and shaking himself like a soaked pup, ashedding water right over my clothes.

"Tobey, you quit that!" I caught hold of him. The lad's teeth were chattering for certain. In no time I had him out of his clothes and wrapped in a gunny sack till I could fetch some of brother Clyde's things.

"Here, I'll fix him!" While I lit the lamp and put on the kettle, John Cooper started giving the boy a good rubdown, all the while jollying and pounding to get him over his chill. He already had my fire going and my line of clothes I'd dumped into a chair, spread out for me, careful like, to dry. "I used to help Ma," he said, "before—" He broke off. For a minute his teasing look left him, and I was not fearing him so much as I had. I began wondering what sort of woman his Ma had been . . . and if her kind could ever understand how it had happened between that witch woman, Parasidy LaRue and my Ma and Dad.

I made tea while John Cooper helped Tobey get into brother Clyde's things. "The saints preserve us!" He clapped his knees, doubled up with laughing, for the little fellow did look comical in his mansize pants.

Tobey, quick to act up for the stranger, began cake-walking antics around our grate, and the man laughing and looking to me to join in. Keeping my eyes to myself, I brought over the tea. John Cooper had his jacket off. His shirt was clinging to him, damp through. Underneath I could see his chest, thick like an oak, rising and falling. I hurried back to my stove. Thunder was rumbling overhead, the rain pelting on our pine log roof. The air was thick with smell of pine and drying clothes. How was it I ever thought I liked storms!

As I turned to pick up my kettle, a sight brought me dead in my tracks.

"*Whose is that?*" I pointed to the jacket dripping over the back of my Dad's chair.

"Mine." The man came by me. "You wanting I should move it?" Provoked, I made some excuse about needing the chair. Truth was, it had set me crazy for a minute, thinking it the old man's. *Dolly, if you could go back to those days, to before it happened.* My old sorrow and puzzlement came over me, and my dread of this man. I began hurrying supper, trying to drive off the cold going through me, thinking the sooner the meal done, the sooner Clyde and Old Harry home, their noses aquiver for a draught of my stew.

"Now, Miss Dolly—" I felt the stranger behind me, his breath hot on my neck. But his tone was kindly. "Hadn't you better be changing out of your wet things?"

"It's nothing to bother over, a little damp!" Try as I might, I could not keep my voice steady.

"But you're wet through!" He put his hand on my shoulder.

"You leave me be!" I moved off.

"But you're ashivering!"

So I was, but not from damp. Why couldn't the storm pass, let this man go as sudden as he'd come! Outside it was raging fit to tear the earth apart. The place his hand had been burned like a fresh-branded token on my shoulder. I reached up to rub it off. Instead it ran clear through me.

"*You leave me be!*" I was ready to spring on him. I had on others for less than he'd done. But at the look on him I turned and ran into my room. Shaking like from ague I took off my wet clothes and rubbed dry. I might have stayed to myself all evening, but a woman's work can't be laid by so easy. Tobey was calling that my stew was aboiling over, and he wanted more tea.

When I came out John Cooper turned from the fireplace, on his face the same queer light he had when he first laid eyes on me.

Tobey whistled. "Whew, Dolly! You sure look purty in your Sunday-go-to-meeting frock."

John Cooper moved toward me. "That she does, Tobey."

"Tobey's a young fool!" I said, mad to think the stranger might be getting the notion I'd dressed up for him, but too proud for explaining that I had no choice, since every piece I owned besides this I had on was by the fire, adrying.

"Tobey—" John Cooper went on, again just like he hadn't heard me— "Did you ever know a girl's eyes could be as blue as the morning?"

The lad, busy over a jacknife he'd lent him, wasn't listening. I pretended the same.

He moved closer. "And hair that shines like a field of buttercups?"

"Don't be abusing your welcome!" I turned full on him. "And I'll be thanking ye not to be putting silly talk in the boy's head!"

The man dropped back. "I'm sorry, Miss Dolly. It wasn't what I meant."

For a time everything was quiet by the fire. Tobey and the man gulped down their tea. I crossed over to the window that Old Harry had cut last spring in the side of our cabin. There was no sign yet of the storm letting up.

"Things come on some of us, sudden like." John Cooper was talking, like to himself. "With others—" he shrugged— "it works opposite. That's all."

"And don't be talking in riddles," I said. "I don't fancy such."

"I'm not," he said. "All I'm saying, lass, is what's to be is to be. Like that storm outside." He was looking straight at me now. "What's the use of fighting a thing strong as that?"

Tobey looked up from the stick he was awhittling with John Cooper's knife. "Dolly don't fancy any man's talk," he said. "I been telling John Cooper that myself."

"Tobey!"

"He asked me and I told him, ain't that all right? No sir, I told him, Miss Dolly ain't spoke for by nobody."

John Cooper's eyes were full on me, with a dare in them I made pretend not to see.

"She don't so much as look at a man," the boy finished, "excepting her own kinfolk."

Once more John Cooper's laugh filled our cabin. My

face aburn I grew busy over my stove. Behind me I heard Tobey talking on, though most of what he said was blurred by the storm. "Dolly's old man got shot dead, he did . . . in a feuding . . . my Ma says . . . her ain't been the same since."

I called Tobey over. "Go fetch me some kindling *and quit your blabbing!*" I whispered, *"or I'll give you a wallop for fair."* From then on I kept Tobey by me, busy at this and that, away from mischief and this man's prying. After a time, when he couldn't mess around with the fire any more, John Cooper took out his music box and began tuning her.

His was like none I'd seen in our valley, and we had plenty. Somebody had carved and polished its cedar body to a shining darkness. It was shaped like a great pear with strings and notes somewhere between a guitar and a mandolin.

> *Down in the valley*
> *The valley so low. . . .*

When John Cooper started plucking at the notes and humming, the light from the fire on him, it was the same as if his fingers had reached in and got ahold of the fibres round your heart. All my life I'd never thought to hear anybody who could handle a music box like this. Our mountains were full of fiddlers; folks came from miles around every fall for our fiddling contest and it was something to set your ear to. But none of them could touch John Cooper.

> *. . . . The valley so low*
> *Hang your head over*
> *Hear the wind blow!*

Little Tobey crept back to his place by the hearth, and I let him go. I was the same, quick to catch fire when music was stirring, me who couldn't so much as carry a tune clear through to the end. But sometimes, I was thinking, in those of us where it's buried deep it outlasts in others what comes easy to the tongue.

The newcomer kept on singing and rain apelting down and my stew boiling friendly like on the stove. He had come to one of the songs my old Granny used to sing me as a child. *Oh cruel Barbary Allen* who killed her own true love, then died herself of sorrow.

I pushed my footstool far back in the shadow and sat down to listen, carried back to those blessed faroff days when I was a little girl, "knee-high" my Dad used to say, "to a grasshopper." And I was lying out in our clearing, astaring up at High Top and clouds aclimbing her sides, the same as the coal cars that old Pegleg was driving up the Tipple . . .

John Cooper's music kept acoming, drawing me back to days long past. And it was Halloween and Dad had rustled a few crabapples from somewhere and set his young'uns abobbing for them in the big tub Ma used to fill for him each nightfall to rid him of soot when he came home from below ground. Digging smack up against the coal face he was pure black, only his eyes ashowing through. I could see Ma and Dad laughing at our antics around that tub, all six of their Hawkins brood abumping heads over the apples: Tim and Caleb, Herbie, Hallie, and little brother Clyde and myself. . . . Of them all I had one left. Tim and Caleb had made off to Alabam after their fracas with the laws. Herbie, our jolly one, next older than me, caught two winters back

in a mine blast. . . . And Hallie had married a stick-in-
the-mud farmer down on the plains. "I'd do anything!"
she'd told me. "Anything to get outa this stinking mine
camp!"

So I had my brother Clyde left. And Unc Harry. The
old man had been with us that Halloween night by the
fire, and it would perk anybody up to see how plumb
happy he was to have a roof over him and human folk
once more to call his own. But a fortnight before, Dad
had come up our trail, sootblack like always, and slumped
by the grate, not bothering to pull off his boots. Outside,
wind and hail were having it out. We young'uns grew
quiet, for we knew better than cross the frown puckering Dad's forehead. Ma poured an extra kettleful of hot
water in the iron tub she kept waiting for his washup,
then turned her back on us as she filled his tea cup, but
the way Dad smacked his lips and drank it off we knew
she had put in a nip for good measure.

"Sue," Dad said, handing her the cup for a refill. "A
wicked night for sleeping at the pit."

"That it is." She lingered by him, knowing what was
on his mind. Old Harry, grown too lame with misery in
his back to mine coal, was living like a homeless beast in
a worked-out alleyway down the shaft. Dad was having
Ma fix him extra snacks to take along for Harry, and
other miners the same, for who else was there to see
the old man didn't starve?

"Sue?" Dad knocked a finger across his nose. "Reckon
you might fix up a pallet and corner for Old Harry to
sleep?"

Ma looked around, afiguring. "I reckon." Clyde and I,

being the youngest, began wondering was it our corner
she was going to clear out.

"Bring him home with you tomorrow." Ma turned off,
sighing. Dad was a man for toting in stray dogs or
mountain cat, not minding that Ma had no scraps to
spare them when her brood got through.

Dad fastened up his jacket. "I'm going down now."

"Jim Hawkins!" Ma's words snapped like twigs underfoot and she thinking his eye wandering after Parasidy
or some other slip. "Jim, you ain't going back down the
hill this night!" Ma stood between him and the door.
"Listen to the storm! Old Harry's slept there all these
months and not froze." Her conscience made her falter.
"Reckon he'll last out one more night?"

Dad put his big hands on her shoulder. "Sue, I ain't
much of a Christian, to your way of thinking. But I'd
not sleep a wink in my bed this night, feeling Harry
down there ashivering."

Without a word more, Ma began getting things ready.
Clyde she doubled up with Herbie, put me alongside
Hallie.

"Sue," Dad called back from the doorway, "reckon
you might hunt up the old man a shirt? Ain't nothing in
hisn but seams."

Ma nodded, then hurried to her goods bag to rummage
the makings of another throwover, for even with door
and window barred fast the night cold found its way
through cracks, and our pallets were thin against the
floor boards.

Unc Harry soon earned his welcome by our grate. He
proved jolly company with his ghost yarns and vanish-
ing tricks learned from his Pa who had followed after a

circus, before our hills pulled him back. And the time came, though none guessed it, when he was to repay Dad's friendship in full. It could warm me yet, remembering . . .

Love, oh love—oh careless love!

John Cooper began singing an old ballad of ours, with a mean teasing look at me.

Love that will not let me be!

I jumped up. Listening to him aplucking his strings I had near forgot what time of the world it was. Through the howl of the wind we heard a sudden tramping outside our door. The music broke off. Clyde threw open our door, dripping like Old King River himself. Unc Harry followed, his brown walrus whiskers soaked and drooping, his small wiry frame with its one-sided miner's stoop like shrunk with rain. Only his tiny sharp eyes that stayed screwed up in his pock-marked face peered out at us, same as always.

"Dolly me love, I got rats in me belly!" Clyde flung off his jacket. "How's the—" He broke off, taken aback at sight of the newcomer on our hearth. I put in a quick word of explaining while John Cooper stood by, his music box laid aside, waiting.

It was something to see, the two of them, Clyde and John, sizing up each other. My brother was smaller by half a head but with a pair of arms that could out-throw any man in our valley. And he hadn't come by the carrot hair and snub nose of the Hawkins for nothing. None of us had.

It was Clyde who first moved to shake hands. "You're right welcome with us, stranger."

"Thank ye. The name's John Cooper."

Clyde grinned, showing the wide gap in his front teeth, then turned to wipe the rain off his pick ax and stand it in the corner back of the door. I was helping Unc Harry off with his boots and wet clothes and scolding him plenty for being outside on a night like this. With no job down the pit, blest the man if he didn't go, rain or shine, to hang around the mine hole. Just in case. And we'd be lucky if he didn't come down before the week was out with that powerful misery in his back.

The old man pushed me and my fretting aside. Mumbling to himself, he got into dry things, all eyes and ears for the stranger. He drew his chair near him by the grate. "Umph! And it's a bad night you chose, lad, for testing our welcome."

"Oh, I dunno as I mind." John Cooper slowed down his talking to grin at me, hurrying the stew on table. "Miss Dolly and Tobey here been making me right welcome."

At his words Clyde, busy scrubbing the soot and damp off his face, turned to look at me over his shoulder. I felt my cheeks growing hot.

"I had no choice!" My tone was sharp. "The storm saw to that."

Laughing to himself, Clyde drew off his boots and spread his stocking feet toward the blaze. Just the same as my Dad might have done. "Dolly, hurry! On me word I'm that hungry, I could eat a bear fried in spit. And we got company besides!"

Little Tobey was astraddle John Cooper's lap.

"Whew! Just listen to that!" Harry nodded toward the rumbling outside. "Like all hell's broke loose—and Dolly asking me whether it's letting up!" Unc chuckled and the others joined in—but I didn't fancy the look John Cooper stole at me in the middle of his laugh. Did he think me playing some silly flirt game?

"It's a stinking gale outside." Unc Harry sighed with comfort and drew still closer to the fire. I knew what he was thinking, how once he had slept out in such gales as this.

During supper Clyde, in the way of our mountains, drew the stranger out. "What part of Kentuck you say you hail from?"

"Buck Eye. A camp 'tother side of Piney Creek." John Cooper's eye kept following me as he spoke, while I moved about taking care of their needs. "Miss Dolly, this is first-rate stew!"

Clyde held out his dish for a second helping. "And where you heading?" he asked.

At his question I stopped short in my tracks, a painful thumping in my chest.

"Oh, I dunno." John Cooper set down his soup dish. The room grew quiet. "I kinda thought if I liked Toewad," he said, "and Toewad liked me, and there's work to be had, I might be resting here." He looked at Clyde as he spoke, but I knew his words were meant for me.

So I answered right out, not caring what Clyde might think. "You said you were heading West!"

John Cooper turned around to look at me. "Did I?"

"Yes, you did!" I stared back at him with foreboding anger. "Leastways, so Tobey said you said."

"Well—" John Cooper kept a steady glance on me. "So

I might have. But I've changed my mind. I'm astaying right here."

I felt my blood rising. "You can't stay here!" There's no jobs to be had around these parts!"

Clyde, who had been listening in, spoke up, a curious smile on his face. "Stranger, don't mind Sis. You swing a good pick? Then maybe I can get you taken on our shift." He reached behind him to pinch me on the arm. "Dolly, me own, ain't there another batch of biscuit abrowning in the stove?"

Those biscuit had scorched, and Clyde laughed still harder at my discomfort and took his pipe over by the fire. Feeling good with the stew under his belt, he and Old Harry took to swapping yarns with John Cooper, each one vying to see who could top the rest. Little Tobey sat between them, his eyes batting from one to the next, as he tried to take it all in and keep awake. I stayed to one side, dawdling over my cleanup work and wishing the long night over. With morning and a clear view of High Top, the stranger would be off. So I told myself.

"Unc Harry," Tobey begged. "Tell the one about Old Bob, the fish you tamed? No! . . . First, Clyde, it's your turn. Tell about how you and Dolly rode the coal cars with Pegleg up the tipple? And one broke loose and bashed in the side of your house! And Dolly—"

I crossed over to the fireplace. "Clyde Hawkins, don't you be telling any such nonsense!" He saw I meant it. "John Cooper's right handy with his strumming. No more than right he give us a tune, before I hustle Tobey off to bed."

Soon the newcomer was astrumming while Clyde and

Unc Harry kept time with their feet. Tobey curled up in my lap. My chair drawn back in the shadows, I was free to travel once more to the good far-off days, when Clyde and I as young'uns were riding the tipple cars up to the sky. . . .

. . . . *chapter 2* . . . .

Living close under a mine tipple might appear to some a kind of misery, but my brother and I found it luck. Like wild squirrels we roamed our forest for persimmons, walnuts, and berries in season, waylaying a green garter snake to tease, or black widdy spider, then let our fingers search under the falling leaves for trailing arbutus. And it was an off week that a mine car didn't break loose from the donkey train mounting the tipple and start bounding down in our patch. Old Peg, its driver, would cup his blackened hands and start yelling. "Watch out below! Car's acoming!"

Womenfolk left their washtubs set out in the clearing and ran for shelter. Not Clyde and I. We broke free of Ma and dashed out to whoop and jig at the looney car making it lickety split and headfirst at us, ashoveling up earth and gnawing trees as it fell. There was more fun in this than fox-o'er-the-gulley or other games—a live

car achasing us like a mad bull! We would jump and
catcall and guess on where the duffer might land, and
jeer at Pegleg yelping himself hoarse.

School out, I was aiming for a ride in Peg's cars up the
tipple. Ma warmed my bottom for it plenty. "Wanta
get yourself killed!" I'd run off to hide in the wood near
our place, and lying flat on a rock, stare up at High Top
and wait my chance. From wee bugs climbing blades of
grass near my eye to buzzards circling over the spruce,
everything around me was amoving up with the clouds
—up toward the sky. In time it seemed clouds, mountain
and coal cars grew all of a piece. Come eve'n, I was relaying it to my Dad. Sprawled in the sun like mudturtle
on rock, I fell to longing for him. He would find new
things to see. The sun warm on his face, gone pasty with
years spent burrowing like a mole, he would start his
tongue quick-moving with tales of things far-off. When
the sun made ready to drop below our ridge I ran to
meet him, safe back with us. His red head was easy to
spot above the rest, for he stood out like a great oak in
a wood of maple, not being like some, minebent. With
a whoop Dad hoisted me to his shoulder, then Clyde.
Seeing us fill the doorway, the rare glad light came up
in Ma's eyes. "Supper's ready!" She'd call sharp. "Get
washed, the lot of you!"

Ma was near me now, bent over her tub set out in the
clearing. I watched the sun glint along her black hair
and her wet brown arms amoving fast, coaxing mine
soot off her men folks' things.

"Dolly, you good-for-nothing!" Carrying her pails to
fetch water from the creek, Ma sighted my yellow frock
in the bush. "What's come over you?" She pulled me to

my feet, staring at me puzzled like. The same look I'd seen her give my Dad. "Go fetch that kindling afore I show you whatfor!"

As I moved off I heard her talking to herself, "Can't make the chit out. One minute into the devil's own mischief, the next blinking like a day-struck owl!"

I lingered over my wood-gathering, for a flock of swallows was swooping low over me, then high. My arms full of kindling, head back, I was following them and wishing me aboard—when my brother grabbed my knees from behind. "Varmit!" Knocked flat, I made a reach for Clyde, doubled up with his laughing. We wrestled in the leaves, then set off on a run for Peg's train.

"You Dolly!" At Ma's call, my brother and I ran faster. Scampering along the underside of Buzzard Roost, where the mine vein ran, I felt free as the wind and twice as happy. Soon we would be heading skyward with Peg.

We found the coal train, loaded with slag, standing outside the mine exit, ready for a climb up the tipple.

"Off with you!" The old miner astride the front car blew out his cheeks and thumped his wooden leg at us.

"Aw, Peg! Just this once!" Clyde and I danced on the tracks, blocking his path.

"Off, I say!" He shoved down the brake and signalled us off the rails. "Make way, Dolly. I'm aletting her go!"

With a whoop we ran to climb aboard.

"Get down, you stinkbugs!" Peg turned on us, his sandy whiskers twitching at both ends. "No passengers! Them's my orders."

"Aw, Peg. Just this once?"

His eyes screwed up, Peg worked his plug around in

his cheek. "There's no getting shet of you Hawkins' brats." If bossman Carson spied us, he'd send him gadabouting quick as a whistle. And what if some car broke loose and went scooting down the tipple dump into the valley?

Clyde looked at me. From our coal patch to sight a car break loose was one thing, another to be aboard her.

"We ain't afeard!" I told him. Up here in front it wasn't likely our car would break loose.

"With these lumber-busts anything can happen. Couplings so gol dern thin." With careful aim Peg spat into the car bins, then wiped baccy juice from his whiskers with the back of his hand. "What you want! Me having the death of you on me soul the rest of me days? Clear off!"

"We ain't ascairt!" I winked at my small brother and pulled the old man's arm. "Not with you adriving her, we ain't."

Grumbling to himself, with a quick look-round to make certain no bossman was near, Peg yanked us aboard. With his blackened hands he scuttled out a kind of nest in the dumpings and threw a gunny sack on top to spare our clothes. "Lay low! Keep your heads under the sack, or I'll lam you flat."

With a low whistle he let go the brake. We peeped from under the gunny sack. Our train was climbing with a jerk and a rattle. Clouds were setting astride High Top kind of restless, siddling down our half the mountain like dumpings from a giant mine car, then slipping into our valley like slate that rumbled from the tipple into our backyard. The sun was moving fast, or so it looked, in a hurry to get some place he wasn't and dragging the upper side of clouds after him like a line of donkey cars. And we too were riding high and mighty, as I had planned. Not that we dared ever get so far as High Top. No human body went all the way up her, so far as our valley knew. Most days you could not make out her summit for mist and clouds. Above the line where her trees left off there were canyons deeper, so they told, than ten wells, and boulders larger than a man's cabin. In between rocks, rattlers and copperheads were lying in wait for you, and the prettiest mountain daisies a body might hope for. I had a hankering for those daisies, and for a look at Thunder Bird's roost. Maybe I would catch sight today of the eagle with a young'un by him on the crag.

Since the day I had wandered up the foot trail leading to High Top and been lost all night in the wood, Ma had forbid me to go near the mountain. My old Granny had told me, before she passed down the valley, about a peephole High Top had poked in the sky. Through it a body might see all the places tother side our hills, the Mississip and mile on mile of cotton bolls. If I rubbed my sight clear, Granny said, I might see plumb from ocean to ocean, watch boats sailing without aid of sails and trains a lot bigger and faster than Peg's donkey cars. I'd see towns with folk aliving in houses stacked one top of the other, a good nine stories high. Houses lit with lamps that had no wicks nor kerosene, and cared for by stoves that burned without kindling or wood. And there was much more I would be seeing, so Granny told me, once on the mountain top.

How Granny knew so much without going up, I never found out. She had talked once, she claimed, with the

only man who had. Besides, my Granny had the gift—
a Seeing Eye.

Riding up the incline with Peg, I kept promising myself our donkey train was traveling on till it took ahold
of the track of clouds and we'd land next the peephole
High Top had pricked in the sky.

"Dol, you're the mascot of this here train." Peg gave
us a knowing wink. "Plague if you ain't!" Peg had set me
in front so I had a view as far as eye could reach. He
kept this place for me. I had a high color and sassy
tongue on me that set Peg's risibles going till he's twist
up with chortling and clump his wooden leg on the
car's rim. Though I was never a big mite, in this taking
after Ma, I was uncommon sturdy, and Peg fancied
that. My red hair was sun-bleached in front till nigh
straw color, and in spring wee freckles came out on my
pugnose thicker than dandelions in our mine patch.

"Mascot?" I asked. "What's that?"

The old man lifted his cap with his miner's light on it
and scratched the place where his sandy hair had worn
thin. Peg kept his lamp on, though he had no call to use
it for many a year, not since a horse-back had caught his
right leg down the pit and they dug him out. I had
heard my Dad telling Ma, when they were hacking him
free, he saw the injured man was whispering something.
My Dad bent low. "Gimmee a chew, Jim," his pal asked.
And he gnawed down on it while they finished hacking
him free.

Peg was gnawing still. "What's a mascot?" he said.
"That's one of these here figures they put on front of
ships. Sitting here, Dol, with your hair ablowing, you put

me in mind." All at once he grabbed my arm. "Drat
you, missie, keep your head inside the car!"

As we trucked up the incline, my brother and I were
craning our necks to see back down into our valley.
Miners' shacks clung to the hillside like tickbugs to a
log. Dull for want of paint, they had no shine in the
glare. But there was sparkle of gushets, full and running
toward Turtleback Creek. In the middle of our company
patch we spied our house, and Ma hanging out wash.
Further off our playmates were dragging a lad feet first,
Rescue, we called it, gas down the mine and us the rescue crew. Clyde, being the littlest, got plumb worn out,
he said, being the man dragged out feet first.

"Quit leaning out thataway!" Peg yanked us in, but we
kept craning to see back over the way our coal train had
mounted, far down and over the hill where our Dad went
every morning, to the dark spot that marked Chumley's
mine. Groundhogs, some folk called our miners. My Dad
was below adigging on his knees, and with him brother
Tim, going on fourteen and Caleb the next younger, and
Herbie. Ma was dead set against her boys going down
the mine. What with caveins and horsebacks, she said
it was no fit place for a man, let alone a boy. I had seen
her pray and tonguelash Dad and weep over each of
my brothers as his turn came. But the lads and Dad were
in cohoots. They let no boys under twelve down the
pits, but it was common practice to take them down before, and my Dad figured like the rest, once a lad was
pushing eleven, time he earned a bit of his salt.

Ma, who could not read or write her name, was hell-
bent on getting us schooled. Come snow or hail, she
hustled us off to the one-room school made of Cumber-

land pinelogs our miners had raised. School ran four months a year and Ma saw to it we went regular as to preaching, first and third Sundays at Beach Grove.

Riding up the tipple, I was seeing Ma the sunup she had packed Tim's first mine bucket, her tears dripping in the pail, her lips asking prayers over him like he was going off to war—and Tim's face ashine. In my heart I was envying him.

Our train was nearing the hump of the tipple. I chuckled to think what my Dad might say if he could sight his Dolly riding the cars toward High Top. I looked down, far down below us, over top of the woods, then up. Seemed like the whole earth was rising with us.

The cars gave a shudder. "Drat the beasts!" Peg was overlooking his trainload, a worried frown puckering his eyes. "You brats clear out of here!" Clyde and I stuck fast. The cars quieted down. The old miner let out a sigh and bore down on his plug.

"Pegleg," I told him all of a sudden, "something's gona happen. I feel it in my bones."

"Git along with you!" The old codger sent me a sharp, on-guard look. "And mind how you keep craning over the carside. Your Ma'll spot for you hellcertain."

"*You Dol-ly!*" Ma, hands cupped to her mouth, was yodeling up the valley. "*Dol-ly!*"

"Now you git!" Peg shoved us over the far side double-quick, for he had no more taste than the next for Ma's tonguelashing.

Maybe it was the jostling as he pushed us out that started it. A worn coupling gave way. Our car broke loose. Peg was sent flying through the air, us after him. We landed atop him, half buried in slag. The car was lumbering down the hillside, spraying dumpings and tree parts and yanking out roots as it fell.

"Peg, you hurt bad?" We helped him dig out. He clambered to his feet and tried to shout a warning to our patch. Clyde and I took up the yell. "Car acoming!" It was like screeching into a gale. By now everybody had seen the car and run for shelter. Except Ma. She was climbing up the hillside and waving her arms as if she meant to stop the car singlehanded. I knew she thought us aboard.

We began running downhill and yelling to Ma to jump clear. She couldn't hear us. The car was bounding off rock and pine like the Wrath of God descending on our patch—and Ma heading straight for it.

Pegleg slid down the mountainside and us after him. Everything in the wood around us was yelping and running for the brush. We tried to kick up racket enough to make Ma hear. The noise we made was like nothing beside that car. It was charging like a mad bull at Ma, and she at it.

"Ma! Ma!" Clyde and I were crying and sliding as fast after Peg as we could.

The car hit a boulder and rocketed in the air. Ma ran after it, waving her arms.

Danger over, Clyde and I rolled on the ground, laughing and shouting with all our might. The car with a last fillip had landed next to our house. After Ma had scotched us plenty, and lashed out at Peg, we hurried down to see what harm the loony boxcar had done.

"Sue Hawkins!" Our neighbors came running. "That car's done stove in the side of your house!"

I saw the tight skin over Ma's cheekbones quiver, her

eyes spark. Saying not a word she strode homeward, Clyde and me by her. Peg stumped behind. We found the car had knocked off the side of our cabin, and turned on its side, was resting peaceful and contented, endways against our iron stove.

Everybody had another good laugh, except Ma. She was tearing into Peg and the mine company and everybody in sight. Peg started off toward his donkey train, aswinging his body as he had to, because of his bad leg. Ma stopped to draw breath, womenfolk went back to their tubs. In the quiet Clyde and I heard a whimpering. At our cries Pegleg turned back.

"In the name of the Saints!" Ma and the women came running. "What is it, you brats?"

We pointed under the car. Spot, our new collie, was pinned under a wheel.

Pegleg stooped down for a closer look. Spot's leg was caught. "Only way is to lift the car." He looked around. Not another man in sight.

"Oh hurry, Peg, hurry!"

Bending on his good knee, the old man shoved with all his weight. He had powerful shoulders still. The car did not budge.

Ma and some of the women took hold of the far corner, as Peg directed. With a shout Peg and all of them heaved. The car shifted, fell back. I caught full sight of Spot, pinned by one leg. He was bleeding. Spot saw me and tried to move.

On the next lift of the car I made a reach for our dog. Peg yanked me back. "Little fool! You want your back broke!"

Peg waited for breath. "Just a little more," he said. "Another good man and we'd make it."

My brother tried to edge his shoulder under the side, next to Peg's.

"Go away, lad." The miner gave him a gentle shove. "Just in the way." Once more he gave the signal, everybody heaved. The car raised no higher than before. "Just a bit more," Peg gasped. Nothing budged. In a flash I had my shoulder under the other side. When Peg gave the word, I heaved with all my might. I reckon it was Spot lying there acrying that did it. Anyhow the car rose. Clyde dragged Spotty free.

Ma took the dog with her toward the house. "Don't cry son, we'll mend him."

I started to follow, but Peg held me back. Everybody was looking at me.

"It ain't right," Peg said. He felt my shoulder, flexed my arms. "It ain't right for a girl child to have such strength. What's it mean?"

For weeks after the donkey car fell into our kitchen Ma was after Dad, making him ask the mine boss to haul off that lumberbust and mend our house proper. Like all cabins in the patch, ours belonged to the company.

"You'd best move out. Place ain't worth the fixing," Carson, the mine boss, told Dad.

Ma said it didn't suit us to move. We had tried pretty nigh every house in the patch. The stove here drew well, and being close to the mine tipple was not so bad as to sit at table or lie in your bed at night and hear men blasting under you. And a body never knowing when the ground might give way under you.

So we stayed along with the donkey car lying next our
stove, and wind and rain and God's little critters. Dad
laid a few boards across the gap between the top of the
car and our roof, and we found the bin handy for kindling. Field mice made a nest in one end of it and I a
hideout in the far side. I could lie here and stare up at
High Top and the clouds without Ma coming on me all
of a sudden.

"Mighty convenient, spare room like this! How come
the comp'ny ain't charging you extra?" neighbors said.
"Guess we'll fix it with Peg, get us a car dumped by our
shack!" But nobody had our Hakwins' luck. . . .

> From this valley they say you are going
> Come and sit by my side for awhile. . . .

The music was still going. Little Tobey, his head
thrown back, mouth open, was snoring deep and even
in my lap. The fire had burned low, a chill was creeping
over the room. Old Harry's head had fallen forward on
his chest.

I looked across at my brother Clyde sprawled in his
chair opposite me, listening, maybe living over those
days, too, his feet stretched out like my Dad's used to
be, close to the dying heat. Clyde was a grown man now,
and I a woman grown, and old Pegleg this many a winter under the sod. Yet somehow I knew that Clyde would
be riding those coal cars the same as I up the tipple
toward High Top, so long as he drew breath.

A last piece of log fell into the embers, to burn a fiery
gold. A blaze shot up, lighting the men's faces for awhile
before it died off. John Cooper, his song ended, called
softly,

"Miss Dolly?" He leaned to peer into my corner, for I was sitting back in the shadow. "Couldn't hardly tell," he said, "if you are still there."

I lifted Tobey to my shoulder. Overhead the storm was still pounding, like on my own flesh.

"And, sure, she's there!" Clyde turned to me. "Those were some times we had with Peg, eh Dolly?" I nodded, trying to answer, for the words didn't come.

Clyde leaned over to knock the dead ashes from his pipe into the fireplace. "And here's a song, John Cooper, you might be picking out on your strings?" My brother started humming, John picked up with a few chords, thump-thumpety-thump and Clyde was off:

> *Oh a tipple car's*
> *a mighty fine place!*
> *You ride straight up*
> *and the wind in your face!*

(Come on Dolly, join in?)

> *But watch out boys*
> *should the couplings go!*
> *The she-devil's pitching you—*
> *Satan waiting below!*

"That's a right smart song," John Cooper said. "You got more?"

"A few." Clyde pulled my chair nearer his. "Come on, Dolly, let's show him what Toewad's like."

"Not tonight." I stood up, little Tobey against my shoulder.

John Cooper put aside his music box and rose to his feet. "You want I should carry the little fellow for you?" It was like a favor he was asking. I shook my head, brushed past him. Over my shoulder I told Clyde, "We'll spread our company a pallet by the fire." At my door I turned, like Lot's wife, for a backward glance.

"I couldn't imagine a better spot." John Cooper was standing by the hearth staring down into the embers, a half smile on his face. "I've not been so happy since Ma—" He broke off. "I know I'll sleep well this night."

God grant I do, I thought. I hurried with Tobey into my room, took off his shoes and loosened his clothes and laid him on my bed. With such a storm it was lucky the child was staying the night with us. Overhead it was drumming and moaning worse than ever. Would it never let up?

When I came back with pallet and comfort for the man we'd given shelter this night, John Cooper was waiting. Old Harry was already snoring in his corner. Clyde had stepped outside on the porch, fastening things up for the night.

As I spread the pallet, John Cooper stepped alongside me. "Miss Dolly, I'll never be able to thank you for taking me in." Before I knew it, he had gripped my arm. "Or tell you all this night has meant." In the half light his face and whole body loomed over me, powerful and strange. A trembling had seized hold of us. "If it takes a lifetime, lass—" He pulled me toward him.

I flung off his touch. "Oh, can't you leave me alone!" I was close to sobbing.

"Dolly!" He moved nearer, a rare pleading in his voice. "Dolly, I—"

I moved off, steadying myself on the back of a chair I'd put between us. "You wanta please me?" I kept my voice low, in case Old Harry should stir or brother Clyde come back.

John Cooper rested his knee on the front of the chair. "You know I want that." He leaned forward, a glad hungering light in his eye. "Dolly, I—"

I spoke quickly, while there was time. "I ask you one thing. Clear out of our valley tomorrow."

His hands dropped. By now the fire was so low I could not see his face. I was glad for that.

"I'm asking it, John Cooper, for the sake of us both."

As I turned to leave, my brother came in.

"Good night, Dolly," he called.

"Good night, Clyde." I walked into my room and slipped down on my pallet holding my arm fast, like it had a wound where this man's grip had been.

Long after all were asleep I lay staring up at the dark pine logs overhead, listening to the storm outside. What right had this man to barge in on us, seize hold of my life, so careless like! Easy-come, easy-go, I knew his kind. The conceited high-blooded, singsonging fool. Quick to take, and quick to leave, like as not. Let him clear off! I'd had love and sorrow enough for one lifetime. . . . More than all else I wanted to be let alone, in peace.

The smell of damp pine was thick in my lungs. The ache in my arm where he had gripped it was spreading through my body. Around me the storm drummed. When I could stand it no longer I took my blanket and went over to stand by the window. Outside all was dark and driven. Our pines were lashing and moaning, the earth drinking up the rain.

For a time I forgot my anguish, as since a child I had found a way of doing, by watching the storm. I could feel our hills fighting off and giving in to meet it.

When lightning pierced the dark it lit up High Top standing over us, on guard like always, shaken but never budged by the storm.

I looked toward the spot where we had lain my Dad and Ma, there on our hillside, after it was over. I knew they were better off, as things stood. But what of us, their children they had left behind?

The rain kept beating, beating.

Did I fancy it, or was it there, what I saw in the next flash of lightning—a giant Thunder Bird circling down from High Top toward our place? My trembling seized hold of me afresh. Was it Ma trying to send me warning?

My Dad had taught me to scoff at omens. "Thunder Bird me eye!" he'd said. "Dolly, that's the Eagle of Liberty you see overhead. The same my Great Grandpappy fought the Redcoats for at King's Mountain in '76." I could hear him telling about it yet, his full voice coming to me through the storm as it used to when we were little ones and he gathered his brood around him near the grate. My Dad was a true Hawkins, forever hankering and lusting after things beyond his sight and touch. All his life it gave him no rest. Was I the same?

And was it John Cooper or myself I was most dreading? How was a girl of eighteen summers to know. . . .

Pressed up against the window ledge I found myself praying. "Send him away, Lord. Don't let it happen to me, the same as Ma and Dad."

. . . . *chapter 3* . . . .

A fiery oversize Irishman with red beard and hair, my Dad was a man revered and cursed alike in our hills. Fightin' Jim, his mates called him. His temper was quick as a trigger but his laugh as ready, bounding joyful to meet you like our pup, Spotty, welcoming us home. His nose had a rollicking uptwist, and from under his red eyebrows, which shot up at the end, his blue eyes leaped out at you in love or anger. And you felt what gave my Dad power over men. And women.

"You are strange like him," Ma would tell me, and I knew she meant not alone his blue eye and fiery hair. "You are his Spittin' Image." It was like a heartburn coming from her, and a warning. For bitter and wrong was the end my Dad came to, though no man could lay it in full at his door. And we, his children, had to stand by and watch it happen, with no way of knowing how to stop it. Nor hinder the fury in Ma.

His day at the pit over, mine boots off and toasting his feet by the coals, Dad would draw on his pipe to get it working right, then begin his tales of the brave Hawkins clan. His was a bold story, man fighting man and both fighting nature. From the day the first Jim Hawkins had crossed the Big Drink, love of freedom and fortune in his veins, right down to our own time, our folk Dad said had been an adventuring go-ahead lot. I reckon the feel of it got in my blood.

My Dad's Dad had crossed the Great Smokies into mid-Tennessee. By now everybody was hankering after gold or maybe a homestead for himself, the days of Young Man Go West. Our Hawkins clan never got further than half way. "And some might figure," Dad said, "that's where we are yet. But it's our country, young'uns, never you be forgetting it."

Dad was a hill farmer whose cotton patch dried up on him. What they call erosion had set in on our toplands, after lumber companies began cutting down the forest. They offered Dad a handsawing job but he told them he'd sooner be shoveling up coal for Satan than have any part of stripping our hills. Well over six foot in his bare feet, he had to stoop to get through our cabin doorway, and down the mineshaft the same. "Dern company's too cinchy to build mansize!" he said. "Ain't enough we go crawling on our bellies after their coal, we must stoop and sidesweep to get inside their blasted grocery. Even in our homes." Many a time I'd seen him near butt his brains out, standing upright like a Cumberland man should.

Ma was another sort, as full of sad singing about her work as Dad was of teasing. A tiny slip of a thing and straight as an arrow, she could stand under Dad's arm and not touch. Yet even as a child, I'd seen him walk in fear of her. When the mood was on her, Ma had the bite of a rattler. She was pretty in a way, or so I thought, her black hair roped low on her neck, her eyes dark and shining till you couldn't see bottom. Her clear brown skin was pulled tight over high cheekbones, bespeaking her Indian blood. Ma's Granny had been a Cherokee. Our folk hid this—till oil was discovered out Oklahoma way, then they fell to bragging on Ma's Granny and putting in land claims along with the rest. Nothing came of it, except my getting ragged about being a half-breed from other Toewad brats. On her Dad's side Ma came of Low Dutch stock, the kind that cling to a piece of land or a notion, beyond all heeding.

Borning us one after tother, ahustling to keep soul in our skinny bodies and our nakedness from cropping out, Ma's prettiness began slipping from her. That is, the kind most people have an eye for. And my Dad was no different than the rest. Seeing this and knowing herself three years his elder, Ma turned jealous-hearted as a cat. Let a red-cheeked girl come near our cabin, whatever my Dad said or did, in Ma's eyes it was never right. All he had to do was wink or crack a joke, and Ma was off. Being the tease he was, Dad would sometime bait her for the fun that was in it. But the time soon came when the fun was used up. We young'uns could see it, and Ma too, looked like she couldn't put a stop to herself, even when she tried. She knew Dad, a true Hawkins forever yearning after things beyond his grasp. In her too were things ahungering, nagging at her peace. And fear of losing Dad. This made her indrawn, and to my child mind, strange. When Dad and she would make it up and be like I remembered them as a small child, our cabin became a happy frolicsome place. As we grew bigger the making-up times grew fewer and longer between. And Dad, once they had words, would reach for his shotgun over the mantel and take himself off for a day's hunt in the wood. Or so he said. Sometime he'd stay two or three. We young'uns came to know his wandering by another name.

Clyde and I made Toewad smartalecs eat their words in dirt about our Dad. True, Dad might be off hunting him more than a cotton tail rabbit. He was after peace with himself. For by now his roving eye was caught by Parasidy LaRue. Everybody in our part of the mountains knew it. Even Ma.

Parasidy was a tall buxom woman with thick golden braids. Hair like hers was not so easy to come by in those days as now. Her eyes were the color of pine and her laugh ran quick and free as spring gushets into Turtleback Creek. Even we young'uns who had no call to like her, found Parasidy a right winsome critter to the eye.

Her folks had her christened Paradise, but somehow her name got twisty, like herself. There were some who named Parasidy a light o' love, or worse. Others stood by her. Hosie LaRue, her man, had his neck broken down the mine. She had to get along, they said, the best she could. A lone woman in a mine camp with no kith nor kin, what was there for her to do but take in wash, boarders or such? I don't reckon Parasidy LaRue ever washed many clothes, or heaved for long over a stove. But let square-dancing time come, there was nobody so fast and gaysome as young Parasidy. With a piece of red silk fastened around her throat and sprig of mountain laurel in her hair, her green eyes were sparkling for all who had a mind to see. And Dad was one.

Hearkening to the talk about the LaRue woman, Ma had spoken her mind to whosoever cared to listen, and Parasidy knew better than come over the mountain any more to square dance at Shamrock, let alone Toewad. For Sue Hawkins was not one to let things rest with talking.

Since the night Parasidy had teased Jim Hawkins into grabbing her round the waist to swing a pigeon-wing, the she-witch had held him fast. Dad fought against his feelings as he would the devil himself. But these were low idling times in our hills. He who'd marched and fought with the best, helped clear our Cumberlands of convict labor, had to sit by now and watch things slipping downhill. For his Knights o' Labor that he'd taken such store in were breaking up, and so far nothing else among our miners to take its place. Work at the diggings was scant. We heard talk that beyond our hills, far off in the cities it was the same. So the old fighting light had gone out of my Dad's eyes, and another kind coming up. And we children, puzzled and fearful of we didn't know for sure, were missing the old times by the fire, with Dad abragging over the great Hawkins clan while Ma portioned out black walnuts and hickories we'd gathered and laid by for a winter's treat.

Dad, I reckon was sore missing them too. Once, before making off, he stooped down by me. "Dolly?" I ducked my head, for I'd been crying. He lifted me astride his broad knees. I stared down at his hands, scarred and blackened from the pit. I worked my fingers as I'd done since a baby, hunting under the curly red hairs on his wrists and forearms for the darm pockmarks a miner carries with him. Dad held me tight. I felt his stiff bristles and warm breath on my neck, and the hungering loneliness running through him.

"Dolly," he whispered, "You're not holding anything against your Dad?"

I threw my arms around him. "Oh no, Dad. Not ever." It was true. No matter whatever he might do. I loved him with my whole heart. And so, God pity her, did Ma.

Dad fought to stay hearth-bound. But let Ma's ragging begin, he'd reach for his gun and go off by himself. Before he was done, he'd find himself fifteen miles tother side our mountain passing the time of day on Parasidy's stoop. We might not see a thing of him till next nightfall.

There were plenty more, so the talk ran, who found time to wander over to widow LaRue's stoop. Among them was George Taylor, a turncoat who had gone over to the laws and spied on our miners plenty, the one chance he'd had. Now he wore a Federal badge and a swagger that made Dad's or any honest miner's blood rush to his face. Talk was that George had been Parasidy's steady till Jim Hawkins had come on the scene. Now her eye was going both ways.

Nasty rumors were circling about as to what George Taylor had boasted he'd do if he caught Jim Hawkins in Parasidy's cabin again—and how Dad had laughed when they told him, and what he answered that sent the miners off, guffawing till the rafters shook.

In our cabin there wasn't much laughing now, even

among us young'uns. Ma and Dad were having it night
and morning, that is when he was home. All that
brought him, he told her, was his young'uns. . . . When
they started in, I'd sneak off to the woodhouse to get out
of hearing, sick at heart.

Once, when her whalloping tongue went too far, Dad
laughed outright. "Sue," he said, "you're talking big. But
if I did bring Parasidy up here as you dare—why, one of
her legs is so big you couldn't roll it down the hill with
a spike!" Ma was that little.

"You bring that bitch near here!" Ma whooped at him.
"I'll roll her whole carcass down the hill!" And Dad
saw she meant it.

Parasidy's cabin was quite a piece over the mountain,
but she sometime visited Marge and Newt Graham's
place close by, near enough for Dad to stop off of an
evening after his turn at the mine was done.

Parasidy aimed to keep her whereabouts quiet, but
somehow Ma got wind of it. I came on her polishing off
a shotgun she'd got from some place (Dad kept his hid
from her), and going off to pray. I did not know which
way to turn. My Dad was down at the coal face, far
underground. I was starting off to wait by the shaft for
him, to give him warning, when Ma called my sister
Hallie and me to come fast.

"Young'uns," she said, "I got a task for you to do for
your Ma." We were going over to Newt Graham's place
and spy that woman out. Hallie and I were to go ahead
and she to follow close behind, but out of sight. We
were to knock on Newt's door and ask for Mrs. Parasidy
LaRue, polite like, say a lady wanted to hire her out.

If she was there, Ma said, we were to bring her along or hurry back double-quick.

Hallie and I were scared to go, but more scared to stay. Ma had a will like iron. Her eyes burned into us. Hallie and I started off.

Ma hid the gun under her apron and lagged behind us. Everything was fresh and green after the rain, larks and catbirds singing fit to kill. It was late spring. Hallie and I lagged, looking back. Ma's face was white and tired, the skin over her cheekbones pulled tight, but her jaw set and her eyes like on fire.

When we came to the clearing before Newt Graham's place, Hallie and I hung back. Ma shoved us. "Go on! Do as I tell you." Still we hung back. I looked up at Old High Top, wishing for a sign. Today there was nothing, no Thunder Bird, not even a cloud the size of your hand.

Hallie and I walked up the slope to Newt Graham's fence. We knew Ma was watching us from behind the sycamore. Hallie was sniffling, but I told her hush. When we came to the yard gate their dog started barking. Newt's old woman came to the door.

"Howdy, Mrs. Graham," we said. But we couldn't go on.

"Howdy," she answered. "Something you want?"

Somehow we got it out. "It—is Mrs. Parasidy LaRue astaying here?"

The old lady looked at us hard. "She was here till this morning," she said, "but she's gone. Who are you anyhow, and why you wanting to know?"

Hallie was near crying. "A lady was wanting," I spoke up, "to hire her out. But thank you, thank you kindly."

We started off. Behind us we heard a voice mighty like Parasidy's asking, "Who're them brats?"

Hallie looked at me.

"You didn't hear nobody," I told her.

When we came to Ma we told her, "Parasidy's gone." I reckon she was by then.

Home from work, Dad came after Hallie and me proper. "Spying, are you?" He took off his belt. Dad who'd never so much as laid a hand to us. "I'll lick your hides off."

"Don't you lay a stroke on them!" Ma put her little figure between him and us. She threw back her head and stared up at him, eyes burning. "I sent the young-'uns," she said, over-quiet, letting her words sink in. "If you got to take it out on somebody, lay a hand on me, your lawful wife."

Dad turned without a word and left the house.

I went off up the mountain, shamed through. Not so much for myself. . . . What was it coming to? I loved Ma. But God forgive me, I loved my Dad more. This was the only time he had lifted a hand to me.

Sitting on the hillside, I gazed up at High Top half covered with clouds. Where would it end? Turkey buzzards were circling over the trees, on a hunt. I was longing to go back to the days when Ma and Dad were laughing by the fire at my baby antics learning to cut a pigeon-wing. . . . I wanted to climb High Top, never come back.

Maybe Hallie and I had done wrong, not to tell Ma that Parasidy was still there. Maybe with the witch woman out of the way, there'd be peace in our house. . . . Yet, if Ma had done as she had a mind to, what then?

The laws would have come after our Ma, taken her off.
City folks didn't understand our hill way of reckoning.
. . . I grew heavy-hearted, brooding, not able to make
things out. So much sorrow and evil-doing in the world.
I wanted to climb old High Top mountain and just keep
on going.

Then, just like High Top herself was aspeaking to me,
an idea came. Better if I paid off that witch woman myself, got Dad and Ma shet of her for life?

I thought it over a long time, then dragged back to
our house.

After work was done at the mine, Dad dressed himself up. Manlike, he made his excuse. "Susie, I got to go
down to the store. Got to get me a shovel."

For once Ma was too broken up to answer. We knew
Dad was only waiting till after dark so he could travel
the road, unseen, over to Parasidy's house.

Dad did not come back this night, nor the next. We
had grown used to his going off. He had carried his gun
and no doubt was hunting him a squirrel or a hare—so I
told Hallie and brother Clyde.

Come Sunday morning, Ma dressed all her children
in their best and took them with her down to church
meeting. She wasn't letting anybody pity her, nor her
Hawkins' brood. . . . And while we were sitting there
in church and I praying for courage for what I aimed
to do, Dad was sitting by Parasidy's hearth, all unknow-
ing, awaiting his fate.

Dad was sitting astraddle his chair, his back to the
fire and Parasidy facing him and giggling over some
story he'd been telling her—when Dad spied the gun slipping under the door. (We learned all this afterward,

when it was too late.) Dad recognized the gun. Without speaking he nudged Parasidy and she turned around. She paled and jumped up.

"Come on in, George Taylor!" she called, trying to make out as if it were a joke, that sneak-thief easing his gun in like that. He had my Dad covered. "Just come right in!" At Dad's nod, she went over to unfasten the door, pleasant-like on the surface, looking fast from one man to the other.

George came in, his black moustache working, holding his gun cocked. "Jim Hawkins, I hear you been bragging you gona shoot me on sight."

Dad's gun that he carried for hunting was lying over on the table, out of reach. He kept his place astraddle his chair, his back to the fire, smiling that hard teasing smile of his and looking George Taylor full in the eye.

Parasidy grabbed George's arm. She knew his temper better than my Dad.

"George Taylor!" She yanked at his stiff arm. "You put up this gun! Can't you see Jim ain't armed?"

George pushed her aside. He kept my Dad covered and stepped nearer.

"Don't take on, Parasidy," Dad said, playing for time. "Take it easy. And you too, George. Suppose you sit down?" He pushed a chair forward with his boot. "Sit down and I'll tell you what I did say, man to man."

"I ain't listening." George kept his gun leveled. "Not to the likes of you!"

"George Taylor, you'll listen to me?" Parasidy locked her hands round his arm. "Come, set down for a friendly cup of tea."

George shook her off.

"Now, see here!" Dad, still grinning, made to hitch his chair nearer the table.

The coward officer, thinking Jim Hawkins was aiming to recover his gun—or so he told—let go the trigger. He emptied both barrels into my Dad's chest.

Without a sound Jim Hawkins fell backwards, into the fire. Parasidy screamed and ran out of the house, George Taylor after her. Maybe he meant to shoot her down, maybe take her off with him. Nobody ever knew. The hate she turned on that man drove him off. Nobody in our hills ever saw him again.

Parasidy kept running. Then it came over her, my Dad had fallen backwards into the fire. He was burning. She ran back, dragged him out. It was too late.

"Oh Jim—Jim!" She moaned and wept over him. She was carrying his child. . . . I never saw the child, but those who did said it was enough like me to be my twin. "You were always your Dad's favorite," they said. But Parasidy's child was born with the mark. Some claimed it was scare over the fire and pulling a dead man out, others said it was justice aworking itself out. . . . For Parasidy's child was given to fits. . . . Many a time I fell to thinking of the child. It was a hard law, God's or man's, that would make a generation unborn pay for what its forebears had done. . . .

When Ma came up the mountain with her brood from church meeting, her feeling quieted down and refreshed, she found John Clark and Dad's brother, Uncle Phil, waiting for us.

Phil Hawkins kept his eye turned aside. John Clark beckoned to Tim, oldest of our brood. John and Phil were too angry at Ma to speak directly to her. They somehow figured her nagging ways were to blame for what had come down on us all.

"Tim," John Clark said. "Your father is dead."

We did not need to be told how or why he had died. We knew even before they said, it was the witch woman's doings.

Ma turned on us, dry-eyed. "Now hush, every last one of you!" We were crying. She stood stiff as a poplar, her eyes dead ahead. "I don't want to hear a sound out of you."

Then John Clark asked her direct. "Shall I bring him home?"

Ma kept her head high. "No. He died with her. Bury him with her."

We wept all the stronger.

John Clark was staring at Ma. "You're hardly a woman, Sue Hawkins."

Uncle Phil came over to us. "Young'uns, you want a last look at your Dad?"

We dropped our heads, not able to hold back our grief. Our Dad was gone. Dad who had led the march of our miners on Chumley Hollow, set the burdened penitents free. Dad who had given honest labor a chance to make a fair living again. How could such as this come down on our Dad? He had shown us how to whittle blow pipe and dance the jig, told us stories no end; worked his hands off for us, and taught us to walk. . . . It was hard believing our Dad was gone.

"Sue Hawkins!" John Clark faced Ma, swaying like a young pine in her tracks. "These children want to see their Dad. It's their right. I'm abringing him home."

In the graveyard Ma broke down. Long afterward she

told me Dad was the seventh man killed over that witch woman, Parasidy LaRue. And more she told me . . . how no woman could put her trust in any man.

Dad's kin held his death against Ma. They even suspicioned her of informing on him to George Taylor. I knew Ma could never do a thing like that.

For the brood Dad had left behind, our salt proved grit in our teeth and scant even of this in the house. Dad's brother stopped Tim and Caleb on their way home from the diggings. A sour grin on his face, he looked them over, then turned to Clyde, big enough now for toting a shovel. "Reckon your drippings these days make poor pickings for the crows."

Before she would take nary cent from a Hawkins, Ma said she would lead us over the hill to the Poor Farm.

Young as I was, I felt burdened down with a sorrow I could not name. More for Ma than Dad, though missing him mighty. And more than all, sorrow for the way we are. . . .

Through the storm beating down on our roof I thought to hear the strong breathing of the stranger by our hearth. My hot face against the window, I strained for a glimpse of light breaking over High Top. With day the stranger would be gone.

chapter 4

Our hills were green and shining under the early light, and things so quiet I could hear the woodpeckers already hard at it in woods back of our cabin. Greedy robins were jumping about in our clearing, pecking for worms in the loosened soaked earth. Beyond High Top the fresh-washed sky gleamed through clouds still rosy and drifting off as day broke. It was a morning to set your heart to, and only the new gullies of water running downhill and our gum tree charred and split asunder to remind us of the violence of last night.

"Dol, what's aholding you?" Unc Harry rattled the stove. "Got your fire going."

As I came into the kitchen I found my buckets filled with newdrawn water from the spring and the stranger, his back toward me, looking at a cross-stitch piece Ma kept hanging by our fireplace, signed "Dolly Hawkins, age 12" *God Bless our Home*. I had embroidered it to surprise her, the last Christmas before our trouble started with Parasidy.

Not long after sunup my brother left for the mine and John Cooper with him, leaving behind him a merry laugh for Tobey, and I left standing with a stiff thankye for my portion, awondering if this was the last I might see of him, and wondering more if this how I wanted it.

Tobey put on his dried things and I sent him scurrying home, then let my ironing stand while I climbed the hillside, breathing in smells of woods washed clean. Wet bushes dragged my skirts, worn full and long. When I dodged under a pine bough or a squirrel jumped from a branch overhead, a shower came down like cooling fingers on my hot flesh. The storm was gone, but the fever had not left me.

I wandered up the hillside until I reached my Dad's resting place, and Ma's nearby. Now was the time to weed the damp earth, transplant new ferns and wood violets onto their mounds.

The noon sun hot on my back, my arms loaded with fern and daisies, I came back to our Hollow and set about my work, humming maybe a bit offkey but with a will, and uncommon eager for Clyde to be home with news from the pit.

When he came, smelling of underground and sweat, he told me he'd got John Cooper a place on his shift.

"*Then he's staying on?*" I filled the iron tub for Clyde with boiling water, then poured in the cold, my hands shaking. *So he wouldn't leave.* My heart gave a bound.

"Dolly, what's the matter?" Old Harry peered. "Ain't you feeling well?"

"I'm first-rate!" I put down the emptied kettle, my

heart pounding against my ribs like a pick ax on the coal face. Clyde was splashing and mumbling something unkind about my lye soap.

Old Harry followed him to the table. "I calculate you did a welcome thing, adding a fiddler like him to our Toewad patch."

Clyde looked up at me, a maddening grin on his face. "What you think, Sis?"

I tossed my head. "To me it's all one, whether he goes or stays."

My brother laughed, sucking in his breath between the gap in his teeth. He was a mean tease, the same as my Dad—but did he think he was up to something beyond this? Maybe he noticed I had little need for supper.

Unc Harry pushed back his chair with a sigh that came direct from his refilled belly, loosened his belt a notch, then reaching for a twig he had whittled clean and kept behind the clock on the mantel for the purpose, he worked it around his few stubs of teeth. " 'Tain't often we get a newcomer from far off as Kentuck!"

Since it was a clear evening Clyde and Unc took their pipes outside for a rest on our stoop, and my dishes soon done, I joined them. Stoops along our path were filling up, low talk drifting in the dusk and smoke rising from old corncobs held in miners' blackened fists. Nightfall was a restful time in our patch.

The color had almost gone from the sky, and the moon rising behind the clouds over High Top looked pale as a pat of butter from my churn. Katydids were droning in the alder bushes. From farther off came the bull frogs' hoarse chorus. I watched the day fade with troubled spirit. *His staying on, what did it mean?*

In a wild cherry just beyond our house a Caroline warbler began running trills, broke off, waiting for his mate to answer before he took off again in clear high notes, rising till they were beyond our hearing. Stoops grew quiet, listening. It wasn't often such a pair made their way to our Hollow. Near me came the low puff-puff of my brother's pipe and Old Harry's, and the soothing pull of their lips on the stems. There must be downright comfort in a pipe. I fell to wishing I was an old woman, old enough to be granted her smoking rights. Old enough to sit in a corner, not caring. . . .

The dusk settled down on us, letting through the stars. The moon had turned orange. A question kept running through my head, but I daren't ask it. As in answer the rollicksome music came, strummed out on a box the likes we'd never heard till yesterday:

> *Oh who will shoe your pretty little foot*
> *. . . when I'm gone?*

Unc Harry stirred. "That's Johnny Cooper for a fact!"

I strained to catch where the music was coming from. By my best judging it came from the Campbells' stoop. . . . Well if they'd seen fit to take the stranger in, that suited me. It was far off from our place. Seth Campbell was a good lad, as lads went, though I had no taste for his wooing, and the old folks jolly—but their girl, Sally Campbell, a shameless flirt.

So much the better!

Maybe now she'll be leaving my brother alone. So I told myself.

Love, oh love, oh careless love
Love that will not leave me be

They were singing now, the lot of them. I could make out John Cooper's voice and a young girl's rising above the rest. Why did they have to choose this ballad? Old Harry was swaying his body, keeping time.

See what love has done for me!

There was laughing when they finished and a few hands clapping along the stoops. I could see Clyde beginning to fidget, hankering to be off. I slipped my arm through his, aiming to keep him by me. Sally had started in again, this time all alone:

Oh meet me tonight on the mountain!

That girl was shameless, calling him the same as the bird in our tree yonder was calling his mate. Or was she making up to the newcomer?

I tightened my hold on Clyde's arm. "I was fixing to make you a batch of taffy. Might as well, with molasses handy and the fire still going."

Clyde was already on his feet. The music was getting livelier now, Unc Harry beating time with his foot. "Betcha there'll be dancing in the clearing tonight!"

By the clapping and whoops it was already starting. Clyde pulled me up. "Coming along, Sis?" I shook my head.

"Go along, Dolly!" Old Harry nudged me, his little eyes gleaming. "Ain't fitten for a girl child like you to be hanging back."

I planted my feet firm. I had work waiting inside.

"Go on with you and your work!" Old Harry spat joyously. "Blest if I wouldn't swing you myself, but for this plague-take-it misery in my back."

Since Clyde wouldn't let go of me, I walked with him a way, then as we came opposite the Campbells' stoop and he started over to them, I slipped free and ran toward Granny Morse's place. Granny and I were cronies from long back. Something about her put me in mind of my own Granny and her seeing eye. From her stoop I could watch the dancing without being over-pestered to join in.

"Come on boys, git your pardners!" the fiddler sang out, and fellows in their mine boots were reaching for the first girl handy. There in the clearing, High Top looking down, her head in a mist, they began swinging *Ocean Wave* and *Doesi-doe* and *Pigeon Wing*, and old and little folks beating time with their hands and feet.

> *Swing your gals, boys!*
> *Treat 'em right!*
> *We gona dance here*
> *Till broad daylight!*

I saw brother Clyde swinging by with Sally, her eyes shining wild and her hair tossing in his face. I knew he would not be home till morning. If then. The whoops and rhythm of heavy boots near drowned out the music. I felt the sweat break out of me, and I had to dance, yes or no.

I left Old Granny and edged nearer the circle. Just then John Cooper gave over his fiddle to another and started over, spying me—or so I'd thought. Instead he made for Sally Campbell, who left my brother readily enough.

As the two of them stepped into place, waiting for the figures to be called, I stepped up to Clyde. "Come on, do this one with your Sis?"

He gave me a rewarding look and we swung into line, just as the fiddling started. The moon had reached above the pine and our clearing in the midst of the dark ringing woods shone like day. The caller sang out the numbers and men swung all girls hand over hand. . . . Till it came John Cooper's turn to swing me.

"Hello, stranger!" Before he could say more he had passed on to the next and Sally had him back, doing with him as she had my brother, tossing her hair and lips in his face. And was he giving her the warm knowing look, the same as he'd greeted me?

Sashay folks! . . . . Now back to back!

The caller kept calling and watchers beating time and egging us on, and sweat pouring from us as the fiddle sang. When it ended I sank on the nearest stoop, with the others, fagged, breath coming hard and blood pounding till it hurt. But not alone from the dance.

Sally Campbell was half leaning against John Cooper's shoulder. Laughing, he shifted to give her a fuller resting place. I turned and ran back toward our house. All I thought of him last night was true. Easy-come and easy-go, and thankye kindly. And which girl was it his turn to swing next?

Dolly Hawkins was not one to be waiting to find out.

There was dancing in our clearing every night, for the moon was at the full and working her witch magic, and always there were some blades with strength to hold out after all day at the diggings. Sometime I would join in the fun. More often I would keep behind a scrag pine and watch. Not that I wasn't light on my feet and easy to swing to, or so the boys said. Though Young Seth and the others kept after me, and John Cooper too, I held off. . . . It was going on seven years, still I couldn't get the picture of my Dad swinging partners in our clearing out of my mind. And poor Ma's wretched eyes. The time it had come my Dad's turn to swing that witch woman, Parasidy, and him from then on never able to let go. Not till death shook him free.

"Dolly, you're a chip off the old block!" my Dad had told me many times over, "Never be forgetting that." I was remembering, though not in quite the way Dad meant. Yet when John Cooper and his music started, I had to drop my work of an evening and come out to watch.

"Beats the devil!" Old Harry nodded across the way from our stoop where the fiddling was rising. "I never saw the likes of him! The way that Kentuck fellow handles a few strings. Eh, Dolly? And gathers folks round him." Come nightfall, that's how it was. Old Harry screwed his eyes up, threw back his head. Rain clouds were settling along the ridge. There was a mist over the moon. There'll be a downpour tomorrow, he said. Then the dancing must end.

"A welcome change!" I told him. "Folks catch up on their sleep, get over acting so crazy like!" I was breathing in smells of azalea blooms and honeysuckle heavy on the air. The music kept coming at us. "Enough to tear your guts out," Old Harry said.

Clyde dropped down by us on the stoop, all slicked up. "That music?" he snorted. "Fit to raise the dead." All the same he couldn't keep his feet from jigging with the tune, his eye wandering to Sally cutting capers with another man.

I gotta gal, and you got none
Li'l Liza Jane!

John Cooper looked over from our neighbors' yard and waved a hand.

"How come?" Old Harry rocked gently, crooning to himself. "How come he don't visit our stoop, eh?"

Clyde shrugged. "Ask Sis."

Angry words rushed to my lips. So my brother was holding it against me, that I'd not made the stranger welcome, thrown him toward his girl instead? I held the words back, made some excuse about work I had waiting, and went inside. I wasn't quarreling with the lone brother I had left over that strumpet, or any man.

From the window I saw Clyde stroll across the path of moonlight between our pines to join the crowd. With a mixture of hopes and fears I could not fully make out in myself, I watched for him to make his way to Sally, claim her in the next turn for his. As she turned from John Cooper and lifted her arms for my brother to catch ahold of her waist and they swung in and out of the shadows cast by our wood, then back into the white glare of the moon, I felt myself atremble with relief . . . and downright shamed, for it wasn't Clyde uppermost in my thoughts. And if the vixen was to fasten her hold on any man, by all I held dear shouldn't it be my brother beyond any other I wanted kept free? All of a flash, leaning out of the window, I saw myself. Not to want a man, not let anybody else have him—*for such a dog-in-the-manger, Dolly, I got only contempt.* . . . Clyde was my own flesh and blood, that man naught.

For a solid fortnight the downpour kept up, not hard not gentle, just dripping down to aggravate men's souls. Night and morning our men tramped to the diggings through the mud. Once down the mine, Clyde said, who gave a goldern hoot whether it was rain or sunshine above. I knew what he meant. Though but once down a pit, being a girl, like every miner's kid I'd got the feel of it from the time I could crawl. It was in my Dad's pock-marked face and Ma's start when the mine blast came out of turn.

Crouched on his knees up against the mine face aswinging his pick, dim figures alongside, lamps on their caps throwing spots of light in the pitch dark on the coal vein and long shadows, little my brother cared for rain or sun pouring down on the earth a quarter-mile above! Gas pocket or warning rumble in the tons overhead was something to pay your respects to, or your lamp that sputtered or flared up, warning mine gas— not a few drops down your jeans.

Still the rain kept up and folks at the end of a day went on grumbling and hugging their fires. Clyde, Old Harry and I were sitting by ours trying to coax our sodden feelings to rise by relaying some longstanding tales we kept handy and replenished for long evenings such as this, when there came a knock at our door.

"Who's there?" Clyde walked over in his stocking feet

to pull back the wooden bolt from our door. John Cooper
stood there grinning at us, maybe a little unsure of himself. Rain was sliding from his cap as he yanked it off
and made us a bow. "Good time for comp'ny?"

Unc hurried forward. "Welcome, stranger!" Clyde
mumbled something and pulled another bench over by
the fire. John was looking directly at me. "How about it,
Miss Dolly? You feel like welcoming company tonight?"

I dropped my eyes. "And why not?" I kept my voice
light and hearty as I could with my breath cut off. "Unc
Harry speaks for us all."

"Well, that's fine now." John took off his wet jacket
and came over to shake hands. When his fingers gripped
mine I knew it was the same with us as three long weeks
back, the first night he had come. Like he had never left
and taken up at Sal Campbell's place.

My brother, seeing how it was, began joking with John
and our cabin filled up with laughing, like the time before.

"Don't tell me you left your music box behind?" Unc
Harry peered around him.

John wiped the rain off his high cheekbones. "I did for
a fact. No night for a fiddle to be out. Or a man either."
He took a place on the bench near my chair. "Truth was,
it's a lonesome night."

"Lonesome?" Unc Harry chortled and bit a chew from
his plug. "Don't make sense, all the crowds I bet down
the Campbells' place."

"That's right, Uncle." John reached in his shirt pocket
for his pipe. "Funny thing how a body can feel by himself in a crowd?" He gave me a studying glance. "Could
be it's the storm."

I jumped up and went over to our pot-bellied stove to poke up the dying fire, making excuse about the molasses pull I had promised Clyde. While Unc and the boys traded yarns I hovered over the simmering pot. I was wishing Tobey here curled in my lap keeping my arms busy, his eyes round with taking it in.

"Sometime back when I had more getup in my bones, I was galavanting plenty. With Dol's Pa." Unc waggled his finger to call me by him. "Lemme see, two winters afore you were born, Dol." He ducked his head and squinted around at our caller. "Your Pa and me first spotted elephants in our hills."

John, not disappointing him, threw back his head and let his laugh break free. "Pink ones or green?"

Unc wagged his bald top in pretend anger. "This here was real."

John stopped for breath. "Old man, quit pulling my leg. Wild cats we got. A few bears and deer. Sometime a wolf. But elephants, me eye!" Once more his laughing rang through our cabin, his eyes beckoning me to join in.

Unc Harry puckered his mouth. Big evil-tusked ones they were. And why not? America was big enough for all kinds. Wasn't an animal that growed that did not find its way to our hills. As for elephants, Clyde would bear him out. "Did me and your Pa encounter elephants in these hills or no?"

"And sure." Clyde was barely holding back his grin. "Many a time I heard Dad tell about it, eh Dol? Long trunks they had and hides tougher than any bull."

John glanced from the men to me. I felt my cheeks

aburn. "Miss Dolly, come over by us?" When I clung by the stove he turned back to Unc Harry. "Shoot! It better be good."

The old man appeared hurt. "Not till you make a wager. When I'm done, either I told you true and you owe me a match or whatsoever I choose to ask. Or I told a galloping whopper and you call the tune?" John termed it a bargain and Unc, mollified, started on with relish. "I only wish Jim was here to tell it. For he was first to spy that pack and making right for us! And us with no guns and barely able to keep on our feet as it was." Unc Harry stopped to fill his pipe. "I know what you're athinking, John Cooper, but you're dead wrong. True enough, Jim and I had been down the valley of a Saturday night having a kind of celebration with the lads. And maybe we had stopped short of a bottle too many and maybe we hadn't. But it had nothing to do with those elephants."

"And just didn't it now!"

The old man spat careful like on the coals. "Wait till I'm done," he said. "You'll see who'll be claiming the wager. Jim and I were footing it home, an arm on his mate's shoulder kind of steadying the other and feeling first rate. It was uphill the whole route and the moon— my, was she bright! Brighter even than with us a fortnight back."

"Couldn't be, old fellow. Moon don't come any brighter than that." At John Cooper's look the taffy I was lifting from the fire nearly spilled from my hands. "Maybe it's your eyes turned dim, compared to then."

Unc smiled to himself, saying be that as it may, it was full bright. They were treading it uphill slow like, Jim yodeling and me trying to follow and us cherishing the echo our hills gave back. When all at once there he come! Right over the brow of the hill straight ahead of us we saw him. Like a mountain of flesh he was moving down on us, his trunk up and bellowing like Kingdom Come. Jim stopped short, a yodel in midair. We stumbled over to the side of the road. The thing moved closer. For a time Jim and me lay there keeping an eye out. Not a word passed between us.

"Good old bottle!" John Cooper said.

"Bottle nothing." Unc emptied his lungs. This thing was real, he said. But tell you true, Jim and me doubted our own eyesight. Never such a critter in our hills. Outside a geography book. So we lay there ashaking, not risking a word. At last Jim turned his head next mine. "Harry," he says. "By the love of heaven, you see what I see?"

"You mean—?" My hands shaped the thing lumbering down on us. Jim grabbed my arm. "What's it got? A long trumpet in front?" I closed my eyes. "And legs like tree trunks!"

Jim rubbed his sleeve across his eyes. "The Saints be praised! You see the same. And I was thinking—" He had no need for saying, I was thinking the same, maybe it was evil moonshine we got in Shamrock. Maybe the Lord was apunishing us for our sins.

"And—" John Cooper sucked his lips.

Wait. I'm not done, Unc said. Just when Jim and me got feeling a bit easier in our minds the critter got abreast of us. It shot past. Then another. Was he heading for us? We dropped low in the brush. But he kept on down the road bellowing like all hell turned loose. And onto its tail swung—when Jim and I saw that we rolled flat on our bellies trembling afresh. How could we believe what we saw. We lay, not daring to speak or move. Woods were dark and quiet around us, the moon like day on the empty road.

Jim edged his mouth next my ear. "You see what I see?"
"I—You mean?" I was swallowing fast. "Holding onto the tail?"
"Go on. What was it?"
"I couldn't rightly tell."
"You're alying, Harry."

The old man crouched by our fire was chuckling too hard to go on. John was impatient, with Unc turning the moment over like a nice tidbit on his tongue.

"You're alying, Harry." Unc settled back, his solemn storytelling mien once more in place. And so I was. And again I wasn't, he said. How was I believing my own eyes or admitting to Jim the queersome thing I spied? Flying through midair like human kite from that tail! I was never one for holding with witchcraft or old woman's magic. Jim nuther, though plenty in our hills did—and still do for that matter. Yet to bear witness to what I had seen was beyond all normal believing.

So Jim and I lay there sparring who was to own up, let himself in for being called bewitched or a plain goldern fool. The ground was damp and it getting toward morning. And our missus waiting up to give us whatfor. By which let me tell you, and due respect for the departed, any nightmare was a mild displeasure. So Jim being the pal he was, we got it out. And what Jim thought he was seeing was the same as myself. From that monster's tail swung a man or shedevil with painted body and chalk face. Its arms stretched like rubber double length and

flapping up and down with the galloping beast, the critter was ahollering, "Whoa, Jumbo! Whoa!"

When we had done laughing, John, wiping the wet
from his eyes asked, "And now for proof?"

Unc settled his plug like a fruit pit in his cheek. "Don't
rush me." For sometime after this night coming home from
Shamrock we lay off the bottle. The missus' were full
pleasured at such model spouse. But at that bewildered.
Jim and I made it up between us not to tell anybody
what happened to us on the road. Nobody was calling us
whiskey-crazy or bewitched. We knew they would be
ragging our pants off us down the mine hole. Yet, there
it was. What we saw, we saw. It as preying on Jim's mind.
Nor could I sleep easy of a night for dreaming of an elephant getting his tail twisted. The missus even hinted I
was easier to lie by when I had my regular nip. "Own up,
Harry, what's preying on your mind?" I was not breaking
my word to Jim. All the same I could be sending out feel-
ers, sort of offhand like. "Wife, you been hearing of any
strange animals in our hills?" She turned on me with a
poker. "Harry Boone, I knowed it! You been drinking bad
moonshine." I stood my ground. "You know I ain't touched
a drop this fortnight." She stopped half way then all at
once began to crow and rock. "Strange animal, eh? Like
an elephant maybe?" She was agiggle till I had to shake
the truth from her. Then I got into my pants and ran to
rouse Jim. But first I routed up the old bottle.

"In the name of the Saints!" Jim rubbed sleep from his
eyes. "And what's bringing you here middle of the night?"

"Here, Jim, take a swig fast. We got to celebrate!"

"Not me. I'm on the wagon."

"Lad, you can end your fast." Seemed a circus playing

out from Nashville had worked to a town eighteen miles other side the valley from Shamrock. They had set camp that night by the river, waiting for morning and a barge to ferry tents and animals over. Their king elephant had broken loose and gone galavanting uphill and down. A workhand who doubled as clown was clinging onto his tail, still in his suit and paint. . . . "And do I win the wager or not?"

John Cooper admitted he had, and over-readily I thought. "Name your price, Unc. What'll it be?"

There was a wicked scheming in the old man's eyes. "Lemme think. Shall I choose—no! I choose you pay off by bringing your music box and yarns to our place every rainy night this week."

"Why, I never!" I covered my face grown flaming hot. John leaned over to tap the old man on the knee. "That's no proper forfeit." He was grinning at Unc and they in cohoots. "It's downright pleasure, in fact one I had promised myself. If you won't be minding, Miss Dolly?"

What could I say? Unc was under his own roof.

"Sure, and Sis likes a good tune or tall tale same as the next." My brother came over to help me pour the taffy. While it was cooling on a platter by the hearth he was telling another prank they had worked on long-suffering Ike. I barely heard him. As we spun taffy John kept making his hand touch mine. I was trying to figure out what was happening, like I had fallen in a stream and aiming to go upriver and finding the current's pull too strong.

Never had I watched clouds over High Top with so calculating an eye. The day might start fair as a June

morning, by nightfall the rain had come and with it John
Cooper and his music box. With our fire and kettle humming and rain drubbing down on our pine logs, I found
myself welcoming stormy times again. I knew there must
be a reckoning time ahead but I kept putting it from me,
just living each day as it came.

Soon after John's knock, come nightfall, my brother
would josh around a bit then make excuse boy-fashion
and light out for Sal Campbell's place. Whatever might
have been waxing between her and John Cooper had
petered out fast. And maybe she wasn't altogether the
bad sort, yet Clyde was Hawkins enough to keep me
bothered.

Sitting around our fire the old man and John and I
would trade jokes and stories of what we did as young-
'uns, then John strum us a song and tell about Kentuck
and the fine horses and blue grass. Some yarns he told
almost measured up, Unc Harry declared, to getting his
forfeit back. Like the time he caught the forty-pound catfish, only to have it make off in his coat!

As the evening wore on John would plong the strings
and hum, on purpose making the old man drop off. When
I saw Unc drowsing I nudged him awake, not to be left
alone by our dying fire with John.

Skies cleared, with change of the moon, folk were gathering on Toewad green around dusk to make merry to John Cooper's strumming. I donned my blue dress he fancied and gave my hair a hundred strokes till it curled free of itself, fastened it back with a ribbon, and went out to watch.

I was standing in the shadow behind a clump of azaleas when John spied me out. He gave over his fiddling to another and came beside me in the bush.

"Miss Dolly," he asked, "how come you're not swinging a foot?"

Before I could so much as catch my breath he had me around the waist, kind of rough but gentle. Without so much as a "By your leave?" he swung us into line.

While we danced the moon came out on High Top, lighting John's face. He kept it turned to mine, now laughing, now searching as if there might be something I was having that by rights belonged to him. It sent me atremble.

"I could dance like this all night." John gave a laugh between his teeth. "Couldn't you?"

I wanted to break away, but even if I'd had the will, his grip was too strong. The moon came out in full, making the stars fade. Only along the border of the sky you could see them. And that's how I saw all the dancing figures and faces around me in the clearing, dim and blurred. Only John's stood out. Once seen, his was a face to carry with you your whole life through. His eyes were set deep and far apart, his nose arched straight and high from his forehead, and his mouth—I could hardly bring myself to look at it, full and ripe as a fruit in season.

The music kept on, and we dancing. I don't know what came over me, spring madness some call it, with others it goes by a deeper name. All the strength of our hills was in John's arms. Yet far down inside me something kept warning, *Break away, Dolly. Little fool, break away while there's time.* Was I forgetting the bitter truth I'd learned early, when most girls had barely given over playing with dolls? *Break away, Dolly!* Love was something I could put no faith in. Here today, tomorrow gone. I had no heart or mind to be learning it over. John Cooper was a bird of passage, he'd told me that himself. Some day before long he would take a notion to head on West, like he'd said. We would wake up at Toewad and find him gone. . . .

Toward midnight, the moon still high, brother Clyde came looking for me. John went back to his strumming and I to my room.

There was a full moon all week, but I did not go near

the clearing. Each dusk time the music beckoned. I scoured our cabin from stove to chimney, put by preserves, made a bed tic and gathered herbs and a mess of sassafras for a winter's store of tea. I worked like mad, aiming to get the spring madness out of my blood.

John Cooper came to our house asking for me, but I ran off.

After three days and nights, when he came no more, I crept out with evening to watch from behind a pine. John found me, my face streaked. This time he was all gentle.

"Miss Dolly," he said, "I can't be making you out. I'll not be urging you to dance, if you've no mind to," he said, "but can't you say why?"

I was too choked up for answering him. He stood fiddling with a pine cone, watching me with a queer teasing light in his eye. "Well then, I'll be telling you this," he said. "Straight out! You're a coward to be running away from me!"

With that he went back to his fiddling. I ran up the hill. Coward, was I! And little he knew of what he was saying. What could he know of what was past and gone, left me with dread in my heart.

I climbed until beyond hearing of the dancers and music. My anger burned in me. Nobody could call Jim Hawkins' girl a coward and let it pass.

I stayed up our hillside until the green was empty of dancers, and the moon behind clouds. Not wanting Clyde or Old Harry to be searching for me, I came down. I slept little. The next morning I packed their mine buckets, then as soon as the men started their tramp downhill to the diggings I made ready for my climb. This time I was going all the way up. It was five hours by fast climbing to the crest of High Top, and half again coming down, so I needed an early start.

As I headed toward the trail up the mountain I passed John Cooper aswinging his pick on way to the mine.

"Miss Dolly!" he waved his cap and started over. "I've been wanting to tell you—"

Picking up my long full skirts, I headed on a run up the hill. I didn't aim to see John Cooper again until I'd had it out with myself. I knew by the look on him what was brewing in him, the same as in me. Only for him it was easy-come, easy-go, or well it might be. For me, once set on a thing, there was no turning back. I was powerful like my Ma in this.

Once out of John's sight I climbed with a slow steady pull, not stopping as I did at other times to mind the ferns and sumac, and redbirds nesting. The trail worked straight up, though overgrown in places and washed out by spring gushets.

By the time I had come to the edge of the oak woods my blouse was clinging to my wet back, and I had my skirts wrapped around my waist. No danger of running on anybody unexpected, this high up. I took off my blouse and wound it around my head, for the mountain glare was full bad at this height and the clouds coming and going didn't help much.

Up here if you didn't watch it was easy to lose your way on the boulders, because of the mist. One minute you might be right on the path, and the next stepping over a precipice. No wonder Ma had forbidden us children to climb High Top. By now I knew the trail up full well though it wasn't often I could spare the time to make it clear to the end. By now I knew also that I could not see from High Top all my old Granny had promised me. Yet, in another way, I could.

The sun was hot on my face and shoulders, my thought still angry. I kept climbing, John Cooper's face and words beside me.

By high noon I had mounted the last boulder. From here I looked down across a forest of oak, hickory and gum and pine, a forest my Dad and his Dad before him had feasted their eyes on as young men. I looked down across the ridge back into our valley. Things took on a different shape and hue, from this distance.

I lay on the rock and let the sun and wind go through me. Like cloud drifting over me, to disappear down the valley, I felt my anger dying. It was for this I had come, for I must get beyond anger and hasty thought, and if I could, beyond fear.

I had to cling with both hands to the ledge for the wind was blowing high and mighty. High Top was breathing close under me. Here I might have it out with myself, be ready to put it to John straightforth, in the way I knew he would be putting it to me. From long back I had been one who took pride in being honest and forthright with herself. There was truth in what John Cooper had said, if only in jest. I had been running, fighting off and giving in at the same time. But no longer! I would not go down until I had my answer.

On the ridge below me, just above our patch, I was viewing the place where we had laid my Dad, and a few years later, Ma. If only they might speak to me now, out of their years of wisdom under the sod, tell me which turn of the road was mine.

The wind singing like a monstrous fiddle, I gathered my strength to go back over my years that lay between myself and John. Even to think on it stirred up things in me better to let lie, yet I had to look back before I could get a clear view ahead. My streaked face pressed close to the earth, I wrestled for the deepdown truth. For I had loved my Dad and all he stood for. I held to him beyond all men. What he had given me, bitter or right, was to remain with me so long as I lived. Whatever I was, what I hated and what I clung to with all that was in me, I could trace back to him. And to Ma. John had to reckon with this. . . . Dad was not one, his heart set on a thing, to stop half way. Nor Ma, once she had hold, one to let go. They were like our hills. And in this I was child of them both. How could I hope it might turn out better for me?

My eye traveled to the faroff hill by Chumley Hollow. In my thought I saw the slow line of chained men tramping down the pit, like in the 90's. And we young'uns crouched hidden in the brush to stone them. Those years also had shaped me to the girl John must reckon with. There was more in them than hate and confusion. This was before Parasidy's coming. I had known pride in my Dad, and the way our hills stood by him. There was danger well met, and meaning. Once more I would draw on them. . . .

. . . . *chapter 6* . . . .

Waiting in a clump of alderbush, our small band peered down at the line of penitents moving up the trail. "Get ready!" My brother Alec, chosen leader, signaled to us. Hugging my empty belly to drive off its ache, I stared down at the guilty ones. Five hundred we counted, white and black men Cap'n Chumley had got from the state pen to mine our Dads' coal.

"Dol?" Little Clyde was yanking my sleeve. "I'm ascairt!" I pushed him behind me. Ma forbid our coming to Chumley Hollow. No fitting sight for God nor man, she said, let alone a child. "What for your Dad fought with Lincoln? To see poor sinful critters adriven like slaves down a mine hole? And honest men left above ground to starve!"

In the stillness we heard irons clanking. Sunup was touching our pine wood and marking off stripes on their backs. Smell of laurel in full bloom was heavy around us.

"Hist!" Alec raised his arm. We raised ours, stones ready.

"We are bound. . . . ."

Penitents were moaning a dirge that stopped our arms in midair. An old prisoners' song it was, fit for a death watch.

> *We are bound. . . . .* (then, the echo)
> *For John Brown's. . . . .*
> *Co - al mine. . . . .*

Over and over it kept rising, these few words, each time in a higher key. And our hills echoing it back.

> *And it's Lordy me*
> *And it's Lordy my*
> *We are bound*
> *For John Brown's*
> *Co - al mine. . . . .*

I came to hear it in my sleep and their clanking tread on our quiet mountain. And men breathing heavy, not speaking except in the song, with guards over them ahollering and swinging their rawhide and guns.

"Lowdown cheats!" The line was abreast of us now. "Sneak thieves!" We let fly. Taking our bread they were. "Get outa our hills!" The Hollow rang with their yelps.

Guards started up the mountainside after us. We ran to a new hiding place and started in afresh. Penitents were moving faster down the mine hole. A clump of dirt my sister Hallie threw hit a powerful black man behind the ear. I saw his hand go up. He turned on us a look so sorrowful I dropped my clod.

Last penitent inside, Joe Barlett, head guard, double-barred the pit door. Seeing him climb up into his lookout tower, we shivered like with cold. Suppose a cavein started down the mine? Not till quitting time would Potato Face Joe come down from his lookout to unlock the pit door. Last week a gas pocket took fire. The chained men below were caught like rats. We had cause enough for hating them, but Potato Face more. Once beyond his guards' reach, we yelled up at him all the dirty names we knew. As for skinflint Chumley, he daren't walk alone in our hills of a clear night.

Before my brothers and I could make it home from Chumley Hollow, our Dad overtook us. Work being scant in free mines he was off idling and catching us a rabbit for supper.

"You Doll!" He made a grab for me. "Your Ma's gona whallop you proper." He emptied my apron of stones, then pulled me close to him. "Never you mind, lass," he whispered. "Leave it to your Dad."

Lying on my pallet in the far corner of our cabin, I saw him take down his shotgun. He began to polish and sight along her barrel. From outside came the low hoot of a night owl.

"Jim?" Ma came by him. "What you aiming for?"

"Just a foxhunt, woman." He slung his rifle over his shoulder, his words distinct like he meant us children to hear. "Don't wait up."

Through the wind I caught his low words to Ma—"Since Chumley won't so much as dicker with us, we'll see the Governor. Take him his penitents!"

With a quick hug for Ma he was gone.

I ran to the door. "Dad!" The dark was empty. In the distance I could hear tramping—not one, but many. They were heading for Chumley Hollow.

"Dol, you bad girl!" Ma hustled me inside.

My Dad did not come all that night, nor with day. Nor evening. Our valley was emptied of clumping mine boots. Womenfolk stood around in knots or went about their work tight-lipped.

My brother and I made it over to Chumley Hollow. The penitents were gone! But our Dads, had the laws locked them up with those thieves? Not a word could we get out of Ma. "In good time your Pa'll be home," she said. "And God willing."

Only afterward we heard what had happened. Dad and his mates made it double-quick time over to the Hollow, then crept up on the chaingang stockade. In no time they overpowered the guards, and not a shot fired. Penitents, chained to their bunks or working nightshift below ground, were soon rounded up.

"Take it easy," my Dad told them, for they were ashivering. "Just do as you're told. We mean you no harm."

A few hotheads among our miners were aching to settle accounts. Dad and his Knights o'Labor kept a sharp eye out. "Men, we aim to do this peaceful."

"Where you ataking us?" a penitent asked.

"Back where you belong," Dad told him. "Out of our hills." He reckoned they had no cause to love prison mine camps. A few bad ones among them, I heard Dad telling Ma, but take a close look at them, they were a sorry lot. Most were in for little to nothing, taking a bottle too many or rounded up as cheap labor on a vagrancy charge. Their worst crime, he told his mates, was being born poor.

The long trek down the mountain started. Such food as miners had brought along they rationed out, a portion to each striped-back along with free men. On the trip down, Toewad was joined by other miners' columns with prisoners from Shamrock, Tracy, Inman, Piney Bend. Traveling by night and sleeping in the wood by day, they came to the wood just above the state capitol.

"Halt, men!" I could see my Dad, standing free and upright, in the lead. "There's the city. Down yonder, where you see the lights." By the moon it was not long after midnight. With good marching they would reach the Governor's place before sunup. That was how they had planned. Quiet and peaceful. Nobody wanted trouble.

"Oh, Lordy!" a shackled man cried out. "I'm a-feared." Others took up his muttering.

My Dad went over to them. "What you a-feared of? You penitents ain't to answer. It's us Cumberland miners. And so we'll tell the Governor."

His mates crowded around him. "We'll tell him all right!"

"Now keep your tempers, men." Jim Hawkins turned about. "Come on, form ranks. And see that you step quiet." They skirted the sleeping town, not to raise alarm, and came at last to the Governor's mansion. A big square house with white pillars, it stood in a grove of locust trees.

My Dad stepped up and rang the bell. Nobody answered. He kept on. The door flung open and a tousled man came out arubbing his eyes and pulling a funny coatlike thing over his night shirt.

"What's all this infernal ringing in the middle of the night?"

"The top of the morning to you, mister!" Jim Hawkins gave a bow. "And who might I have the honor of speaking to—the Governor himself?"

The little fellow drew himself up. "Of course not! I'm his Excellency's secretary. And who are you, you ill-mannered—why—what?" He stared out at the dark mass of men behind my Dad. "So many of you!"

My Dad grinned. "Please tell his Honor, the Cumberland miners are here."

"But what is this? I don't understand!" The little man wrung his hands. "It's the middle of the night."

"Sorry to disturb him," my Dad began, "but—"

"Call the Governor!" Miners were stepping from the wood. Dad signaled them to hush.

"So many of you!" The secretary turned to my Dad. "Listen, what can I do? The Governor's in bed!"

"Sorry. But we kinda thought—" my Dad leaned down, speaking each word slow-like so that the secretary would get it. "We kinda thought it might be quieter this way? Seeing what we come about."

"Rouse the Governor, blast it!" A miner called. "Quit the stalling!"

The secretary disappeared indoors. Pegleg, who somehow had managed the long march, stepped up. "That fellow—" Peg nodded after the Governor's man, "Kinda slow-witted like, ain't he? Plague if he ain't."

It proved some time before the secretary came back. "All right, gentlemen! It's most unusual. But the Governor will see you. Please send your delegation this way."

There were murmurs among the men.

"Er-r. Tell the Governor if he don't mind," my Dad voiced their thoughts, "we'd as soon see him right here? It's a long way we've come, two nights and two days, and our boots caked with mud. We wouldn't be wanting to track his fine house. Besides," Dad chuckled, "all the way down our mountains I've promised my mates a sight of the Governor. Up in the hills we've heard tell he's a just and true man?"

"That's right." The secretary was fidgeting, not knowing where to turn.

"And we heard more. That the Governor's folks born and brought up in our hills?" At the little man's nod, Jim Hawkins raised his voice. "Men, you hear that?" He turned back to the secretary. "Then tell his Honor, not a man of us could go home and face the missus, if he left here without laying eyes on the Governor himself!"

At the general friendly laughter, the Governor's man looked startled. "Well, that's fine of you. But there're too many to go inside."

"To be sure!" Dad clapped him on the shoulder, nigh about knocking him off balance. "So if you'll tell the Governor, with our respects?"

But the secretary was staring like at a ghost. "*Who's that in your midst?*" he demanded hoarsely. "*In convict stripes!*"

Jim Hawkins waited to let him have his fill of looking. "The ones we came to see the Governor about."

"Governor! Governor!" The secretary rushed off, our miners' laugh following him—and not a pleasant kind to hear. When you've gone hungry a good spell, you and your kids, and all through somebody else's doings, a body's laugh takes on a peculiar ring. Or so the man thought.

In no time he was back, the Governor with him.

"Good morning, gentlemen!" His Honor was a fine figure of a man, standing level with my Dad, his yellow hair a bit rumpled from sleep, his gaze steady.

"Top o' the morning to you, Governor!" Dad pulled off his cap and the woods cheered.

The Governor put up his hand for quiet. "Thank you. But no more of that, please. Unless you want my neighbors roused?"

"That we don't, Governor." Jim Hawkins stepped closer. "This is between you and us."

The Governor eyed him. "What brings you here?"

"Your Honor, we came—not to make trouble—but to settle a matter, man to man. Bring peace to our hills. You see us, five hundred miners from the Cumberlands. There's many thousand more like us, back home. We and our fathers before us have been digging coal out of our hills for three generations. You know that."

"Go on. Get to the point!"

My Dad held his eye. "I'll go on, right enough. Now they send penitents in on us!"

"Striped-back labor!" Angry miners broke in. "Labor straight outa the pen!" "Murderers!"

"Thieves!" Peg thumped his wooden leg. "Labor nobody pays a goddam cent for—how can free miners compete with that?"

"Quiet, men!" Jim Hawkins called. "One at a time. But, your Honor, I reckon they put the issue plain. It's come to the place in our hills, Governor, it's them or us."

The Governor was looking the ranks over. "What do you mean?"

"I mean who's gona mine Cumberland coal—slave labor

or free? We say, as God is our witness, it's gona be free labor—us!"

When the cheering died off he went on, "Well, you see how it is, Governor. So we brought your penitents back."

The Governor seized his arm. "*You what!*"

Jim Hawkins gave the signal, "Open ranks, men. Bring the penitents here." Miners pushed the chained men forward. "There ain't nothing to be a-feared of," my Dad told them. "I've explained to the Governor already, what's happened is the miners' doing, no more or less."

"Now see here!" The Governor stepped forward, not believing his eyes.

"Jim Hawkins' the name, sir."

"You realize what you've done, Jim? It's beyond the law."

"I reckon it is, as some figure. But we miners figure human law goes deeper. Governor, as a just man we put it to you. We miners can't stand by and watch our bairns starve?"

The Governor inclined his head, a bit more kindly. "Naturally not. But—"

Jim Hawkins' voice raised. "Governor, here's your penitents. All we ask, be so good as to keep them out of our hills."

Once more the men cheered and flung their caps in the air.

"Just a minute!" The cheering died. "Listen, men. I know how you feel." The Governor beckoned them closer. "But this—this thing has to be handled in a reasonable fair way."

"That's how we want it, Governor. Peaceful and democratic like. That's why we came direct to you. A just man."

His Honor nodded, they could see he was thinking fast. "Men, I want to help you. But the state of Tennessee has let contracts to Captain Chumley and other mining firms. It is beyond my power to set aside those contracts by a wave of my arm!"

An angry muttering went over the crowd.

"Now see here, Governor. I reckon you don't know how we feel."

Pegleg stepped forward. "Governor, it's thisaway. No striped-back labor's gona drive free labor outa our hills!"

Above the shouting the Governor said, "Believe me, miners, nobody wants that!"

"Oh yes they do, if you'll excuse my crossing words with you, Governor!" Pegleg hobbled to the step. "Coal's a heap cheaper thataway."

"Go on, Jim!" miners urged. "You tell him."

Once more my Dad took over. "Governor, we've marched a long way for this talk. We didn't aim to say what I'm going to, if we could help it. Governor, not so long back our Dads fought a war to rid our country of slave labor. Many of us took part. We stood with Lincoln in our hills."

The Governor's glance faltered. "What you getting at?"

"Hear him out!" Miners edged nearer the doorway.

"Governor—" My Dad looked him full in the eye. "We Cumberland folks figure, every last miner's son of us—if we have to, we can fight it over. America was built, sir, on free labor. By heaven, we're keeping her thataway!"

Before they left they had the Governor's promise to call a special meeting of lawmakers, pass a law forbidding convict labor in Tennessee mines. On the strength of his word, our miners marched back to the hills. And the penitents went back to Chumley, Shamrock and other camps to work out the contract.

The Governor kept his word. He was a hillman. When he called the lawmakers together my Dad was among those who went down to testify. How Ma readied him for the journey!

Chumley and his like blocked the law.

Our folk stood it long as they could, then come evening, Peg was knocking at our door. "Fox hunt, Jim!" And Dad was off, with Ma on her knees till daybreak or walking the floor. Watching her, my empty belly atwitch, I grew afraid. But deeper than fear ran my pride in Dad. These had been his glory years, before the witchwoman crossed his path. Though hard-pressed he had stood firm. He led our hills to victory.

My look moved from Chumley Hollow to the mountainside where he lay. I felt myself drawing on his courage. The wind blowing through me, I lay against High Top, feeling back over my childhood years. If Ma could have been different, my Dad would not have changed. . . .

. . . The wind ablowing was like my own Ma and Dad speaking, awhispering the long wisdom of the dead. The part of them that could never die. That lived on in me. In those yet to come.

Seize hold of life, Dol. It was Dad himself talking with me. *Don't be doubting. Stake all you have.* That was his way. Not to fear hurt nor danger. Nor, when it came, love. I knew what he would be telling his child. Face each as they come, and seize hold.

And Ma? Her answer lay on the hillside below me. At the last, she had charged us to put her under the earth by him. " 'Tis my place." I was hearing her through the wind. *If it means this much, daughter. Only God grant, for him it is the same.*

When I was nearing the time to let down my skirt and upbraid my hair, my Dad called me to him. Let any coal-digging stranger come to our Hollow, he said, before a girl of mine steps outside our doorway with him or gives him place by the fire, let him be judged by our Hollow. My hands deep in fern, I let my thought keep adigging. By what right was I doubting John? Because a silly flip by the name of Sally had flirted her skirts at him, raising the shadow of a Parasidy long gone? I remembered how he was with young Tobey, gentle as a woman.

Like a storm, I knew my fear was passing from me, and what I lost with my Dad's going, my joy in the rightness of things, acoming back. Lying with the cleanswept earth under me, I felt things deep down taking fresh root. What was I going to make of my life. And with whom, if not John? I saw now we must face this between us, search one another out.

Calmed, like I had passed from my girl-childhood and become a woman, I started down the mountain to prepare supper, then await John. Everything in me was rushing toward our hour of meeting, my feet not able to carry me down the trail fast enough.

Coming to a clearing above our Hollow, beneath me I saw women and old miners running toward the pit, and children after them. My knees buckled under me, then stiffened to a run. Mine afire! Those people by the shaft, roped in, waiting . . . John and Clyde had been working the same alleyway . . . In my haste I stumbled over a

loose rock and fell headlong. I leaned against a pinetrunk
to right my senses, race on.

When I came among the women, waiting in silence for
word of their men, I took hold of Gourd, the first miner
I could reach. What had happened? Gas pocket, he said.
Exploded an hour back. He put a steadying arm under
mine. The crowd around us pressed closer.

. . . . *chapter* 7 . . . .

Cageloads of diggers from alleyways not afire were coming up. Hank's small lad dodged under the rope to greet his cousin, then Mattie Foster her man. Pop Mc-Fever stepped above ground, his grey hair singed. I called to him.

"Dolly—" He put his blackened hands on my shoulder. There had been a cavein following the explosion. "Some made it to safety. I feel sure Clyde's among them."

The last cageload emptied. Women hurried off with their men. Those of us left waiting moved nearer. Pinned against the rope, I watched the rescue crew disappear into the earth. And God alone knew if they could dig through in time.

Toward evening a slow drizzle set in. Women lifted aprons over their heads or wrapped them about a child they were holding, scarce knowing what they did. We stood without talking, body to body, eyes fastened on the shaft where they must come above ground. Near me Tobey was burrowing his head against his mother's hip, not able to stifle his crying. Only yesterday Tobey and I had gathered hickory nuts in the wood.

From a lunch pail Hank had passed among us I took a biscuit for Tobey. Eat, he would feel better. It was long past our supper hour.

"Dol, I want my Pops."

"Eat, Tobey child." I stooped down, whispering. "Your Pops will come. You eat now, be a brave lad." Remember how that time he had cut his leg, how it bled and he'd not cried out?

The boy's fists knotted. "It ain't the same."

I hugged him to me. "Tobey, I know . . . But to help your Pops. And Clyde. And—and the rest."

I saw his lips moving. Such a mite he was. Another five years and he would be down the mine.

In the gathering dark the flares lit up, casting dread figures in the gloom. Women kept their eyes turned from one another, their faces white, withdrawn, yet drawing together as one in our need. I was numb with effort of holding in. *God, don't let it happen. Don't let it be him.* I could feel every woman praying the same . . . all the memories and questions racing through me. John by our fire . . . John and me dancing . . . John the first day he came up our hill . . . my brother's face the night word came of our Dad going. . . . Had John, Clyde and the others had time to make a safety pocket? Or had it come without warning, snuffed them out like rats down the hole. . . . I pushed with others against the rope. Would the waiting never end?

The slow rain had wet us through. Hardly speaking,

we stood with ears straining for any sound. Tobey had tight hold of my hand. Some of the littler children, tired out, had fallen asleep against their mothers' shoulders. Back of me Maisie Turner's baby started whimpering. Maisie did not seem to hear, for the cry kept on, till Pop could stand it no longer. "For Kingdom Come, woman. Feed your brat!" Maisie fumbled like somebody in her sleep, undoing her blouse. She thrust the child against her breast, and the cry turned to a quick sucking gurgle. Then silence, heavy with promised rescue sounds.

Through the mist and gloom High Top looked down on us, brooding over her stricken children. *John! Clyde! What is happening to you.* In the quiet all I heard was labored breathing, growing harsher. Why couldn't they stop? Or was it my own?

The cage was coming up! From below ground came a faint rumbling. We surged against the ropes. I shoved and pushed my way through, nearer the exit.

Bill Swanson, leader of the rescue crew, stepped above ground. "We found them. Eight alive." Bill dropped on a sawed-off stump. They had sent him up to bring word. Eight had made the safety pocket. They had located them by their knocks and were digging through fast.

"Won't be long now," he said.

Eight alive! God be thanked! A sigh went through our ranks. *But eight . . . Eight out of twelve. Then four were gone! . . .* Every woman of us turned her face from her neighbor's, fearful of letting another read her grim prayer. *Oh dear God, somebody else—not him!*

Granny Morse brought the rescue miner hot rum tea and he went back below, an extra crew with him. "We gotta work fast!" I heard him telling them. "Not much air left." I knew what this meant. . . . Clyde and John lying on their faces, breathing slow and little as they could, trying to make the air last. . . .

"Dolly!" Old Harry had worked his way through to where I was standing. His voice was low, with a rasping edge I knew of old. "I been searching you all over." By his look I knew he was thinking why couldn't it have been him down there, instead of Clyde. I took his gnarled fingers between mine.

"I was wanting you," I said. He'd been one of us for long. . . . Unc had taught Clyde how to mine, after our Dad was brought low. Clyde, little as he was, had to start in. . . .

At my words the old man straightened. "Don't you worry, Dolly," he whispered. "Clyde's all right. If anybody got away he did."

"Sure." My throat was parched till the word barely came. "Clyde's quick as a flash," I said.

"And so's that Cooper lad," Harry patted my arm.

My lips were too stiff for answering.

We stood on, chilled through the bone, waiting. My lips kept moving, but I could not pray any more . . . just repeating the same words over. *Not him. Not him.* My thoughts were racing back and forth, without reason, over our past weeks since John had come. God forgive me, even beyond my brother, my own flesh and blood, my heart was hungering after John. Right or wrong, that's how it was. *For better or worse . . . in sickness or health . . . till death do us part.* . . . Something broke inside me. I was grieving over John, like already gone.

"Steady, Dolly," Unc Harry stiffened his hold around me. "They're acoming up." We heard the cage rising.

Word reached us, "They're bringing up the dead." In their digging they had come first on them.

Word ran through the crowd. Nobody moved. The cage reached the level. Bill and another miner stepped out. Between them they carried—I could not bring myself to look. Yet I had to.

I heard old Mrs. Hagan scream, saw her drop to her knees. "It's her boy, Charlie," they said. Bill Swanson and his mate put down their burden, hurried back to the cage.

"Oh son . . . son." The dead boy's mother crawled through the muck to where he lay. We stood like frozen. It might have been us. "My son. My boy." She stretched her arms across his charred body.

Somebody helped her to her feet, led her off. In silence the crowd parted to let them through. Here and there a hand reached out to touch her, say for us what no word could. . . .

The cage was rising again. We waited, not drawing breath. My head dropped.

"It's Pa Higgins," Unc whispered. I raised my head. They brought out Pa Higgins . . . then his oldest lad. This time there was no anguished cry. Only silence.

"God help Myrtle Higgins!" Dropping her chin on her sunken bosom, Granny Morse kept crossing herself, like one bewildered. Myrtle, lying abed with her youngest. God help her and God help the tiny soul Granny had delivered into her arms only last night.

We bowed our heads, suffering for Myrtle Higgins and her brood like for our own. *Why couldn't it have been somebody else besides Pa Higgins? Somebody without six mouths to feed.* Myrtle still had two boys down the mine.

Boys little bigger than my brothers Tim and Caleb, when our Dad went.

Slowly hands went into pockets, silver clinked into Old Harry's cap as he moved among us. For Myrtle and the young'uns. Harry emptied his cap into Granny Morse's palm. Slowly she turned off, head down, dragging her feet toward Myrtle's door. On the stoop she braced herself, then went inside.

The cage had descended once more into the earth. We heard it clanking upward, bringing, God willing, the last of our dead.

Old Harry stepped back to his place beside me. I leaned against him. *One more.* I could not breathe. *One more. Was it John they were bringing up?* . . . *Or Clyde?*

I covered my eyes.

"Harry," I whispered. "You tell me."

Bill Swanson stepped from the cage.

"That's all," he said.

All! I uncovered my eyes. A shouting went up. People threw their arms around one another. *All!* That meant the rest were safe.

As sudden as it had come, the shouting died off. Only eight had made it to safety. *One was missing.* That was it. Missing. Lying down there somewhere. *They had not found him yet.*

Bill Swanson stepped back into the cage. "Any minute now," he said. Any minute they'd be digging through to the men still alive.

"Bill, take me with you!" Little Tobey dodged through the crowd and under the ropes. "I want my Pop!"

"Get back there!" Bill caught the boy by his overall

straps, shoved him under the rope. *"Goddamit, every minute counts!"*

The cage disappeared.

They passed the lad down the line to his mother. Tobey was sobbing. His Dad had been working next to old man Higgins.

"Stop it, Tobey!" his Ma told him, dry-eyed. "That ain't what your Pa'd want." She was one like my Ma, never to give way till the cup drained empty.

"They're coming! They're acoming!" Joyous word ran through our ranks. We surged forward, jammed in a solid mass against the ropes. Tobey had wriggled his way through the packed mass of legs and bodies, up front near us.

The cage reached level, tight with men. Men come back to us from the tomb. A cry went up. The ropes holding us in snapped.

"Stand back! For God's sake!" Bill Swanson commanded hoarsely. "Give 'em air!" He and others formed a cordon. We stood back, God knows how, craning in our tracks and trying not to shove like wild animals for a sight of our own.

It was that dark I could see nothing clear.

The first miner came out, too weak to walk alone. Supported under the arms by a crew member, he passed near a flare. Tobey darted forward. "Pop! Pop!" The boy's face was like none other. Next came Seth . . . then the Bryan lads. *Oh Father in heaven, where were mine?*

Rescued men and their families were making off. "Get 'em to bed!" the crew leader called after them. "Hot drinks down 'em." And women holding back since morning were letting go as they ran to make ready a welcome.

Tobey's Ma had her shoulder under her man's and was half acarrying him toward their shack, tears of thankfulness running down her flat cheeks. They passed near us, Tobey's face ashine.

"Dolly, there he is!" Unc Harry swung me up by the waist, high over the crowd. "There's Clyde!"

They let us through to him. And my arms were around my brother, hugging his great tired body to me . . . even while the question was burning my throat.

Unc asked it for me. "Where's John?"

"John?" Clyde passed his hand over his eyes. "Sis—"

The darkness closed over me. Then John Cooper was grinning down at me, that queer light in his soot-grimed eyes. Was I going out of my head? . . . I held onto my brother. John was gone.

"Miss Dolly!"

I opened my eyes. His face was still there. It moved nearer. I felt his breath on my cheek. I put out my hand.

"John?" My fingers met thin air. "John!"

He gripped my fingers. "Here I am."

I swayed against him. With my free hand I made certain, feeling his arm, his shoulder. *John was alive.* I touched his cheek, then grew shamed before my neighbors. I stepped back, but he kept fast hold of my hand.

"Dolly," John was whispering. "Know what I was thinking down there? How everybody had a woman up here, praying for them. Bringing luck. And so had I." He put his mouth close to my ear. "God bless you, honey. I could feel it, plain as I hear you now."

I did not trust myself for speaking. Folk around us were crying and laughing for happiness at having their own back, and I among them. From far off I heard someone saying, "Was Old Barth missing. For once a lone man." Another answering, "Poor devil. Nobody'll lie awake nights agrieving him."

Sal Campbell came tearing through the crowd to throw her arms around Clyde, then John. As everyone moved toward home, people jostled me against John. I was walking between him and Clyde, Unc Harry holding my brother's far arm. "Holy Moses, how we'll celebrate this night!"

"Not tonight you won't." Bill Swanson, coming along behind us, had overheard. "Harry, you help these men to bed fast. With luck they'll be fit to go back down the shaft tomorrow."

At sunup the boys went down the mine. We waved them off smiling tight-lipped, downing the fear still heavy on us. The day was clear as a bell, not a cloud or puff of wind, only the clean-washed smells of the good earth to fill our lungs, make us want to shout hallelujah for being alive. High Top was leaning nearer, proud and friendly like she knew my secret and what time of the world this day was going to prove for me.

Cleaning, cooking, singing, pressing, I tugged that dragging sun along the sky. Come nightfall, I hurried my boys through their supper, then chased them outside so I could make ready for the church gathering over at Marked Oak. And John. All Toewad was going. With eager fingers atremble, I donned the blue dress John fancied, and with the help of a piece of broken mirror, curled and tied my hair. John, I kept thinking, must be busy too making ready, scrubbing to get the coal soot off him and into his good clothes.

I slipped out the back way and headed down the trail to Marked Oak, laughing to think how put out John'd feel when he called at our place and found me gone ahead. Woman-like, I wanted our coming together to start in our little Rock Church.

It was a magic woods I passed through: the same I'd known since barely able to crawl along its pine-needle sweet-giving floor, yet every branch bewitched, touched by a kindly all-seeing hand. All the little voices of night-fall ran singing through my veins. *Dolly*, I told myself, *it's your time of the world*. And High Top nodded back.

The singing in our Cumberland church sounded powerful sweet. The lamp on the parson's stand was flickering, nigh driven out by a rising wind. Behind me in the corner shadows I could feel John Cooper, his eyes on me, his voice sounding clear through the rest.

> *By Greenland's icy mountains*
> *By India's coral strand.....*

I had always placed a store by this song, traveling to far parts. Parson Beechum was waving his arm, marking the beat as the little church kept filling up and mine boots shuffling down the aisle. We had come to mourn our dead, give thanks for the living. We sang Ma's favorite, *Whomsoever will*, and other tunes more rollicksome, everybody aswaying and keeping time, and I thought how Ma used to pleasure in it. I felt her close, watching over her daughter, and my Dad too—though it was not often you'd catch him inside a church.

Through an open window I could see the hillside where my Ma and Dad lay sleeping. At the last she had charged us to put her under the earth alongside him.

" 'Tis my place," she'd said. And we had decorated with bits of crockery and shells and planted honeysuckle vines, our mountain way of making pretty their last resting place. And I fell to wondering—maybe it was a queer thought and solemn for a young girl on her promise night, but to me it was like our hills going on forever—I fell to wondering if someday John Cooper and I might be taking our long rest together next High Top. With all that was in me, that's how I hoped it would be. For John's wanting, the same as my own . . . I could feel his eyes burning through me, his voice ringing above the chorus, and my restless fever for us to be off kept growing in me, as in him. . . .

The service done, John Cooper made his way over to my side. We stood in the flickering light, our gaze locked. Folk around us were talking glib nothings off the end of their tongues. We said not a word. John's eyes put the question plain enough.

"You ready?"

"Yes," I answered him, "I'm ready, John."

He was standing high over the crowd, his cap turning about in his hands. The half light was throwing shadows on his forehead and eyes as he looked down at me, a man in need.

"Miss Dolly, could I be seeing you home over the mountain?"

Now anybody in our hills knew what this meant. Walking home together over the mountain was same as being promised right out. I had no way of telling whether John, somewhat a stranger to our parts, knew it. I walked outside. High Top stood clear and bare, her head resting against the stars.

John Cooper came to stand close beside me. I could feel the tremble in his body. He took my arm. "Come, Dolly."

His arm was urging me, but I held back. Like a storm down our valley it was coming down on us, fierce and sudden.

"Before we go," I told him, steady as I could, "there's one thing I need to be asking you."

He looked down at me, an agony in his face. "What's holding you, Dolly? Don't you trust me?"

That wasn't it. Still, I had to find out.

"Dolly, honey," he whispered. "Trust me. Don't be a-feared."

I looked up at him. "I'm not a-feared, John." At least, not deep down I wasn't.

We drifted to the edge of our pine wood, out of sight or hearing of the rest.

From far off I heard folk around the church doorway gadding and joshing. Like in a dream I let John head us for the trail. A few meandering through the churchyard must be seeing us. I did not care. The trembling in his arm locked through mine had seized us both.

When full in the wood he pulled me against him. A blinding light went through me—cleft me like our gum tree by lightning, then made me whole. His heart was pounding under my head, his mouth like draining the blood from my veins, then giving it back twofold, along with his own. "Dolly . . . Dolly." He kept saying my name over, like a prayer, and I calling to him, my face hidden against his chest.

"Dolly?"

I lifted my head. He leaned down, once more finding

my mouth. When the storm passed we rested together on the hillock. "You're the prettiest thing I ever laid eye to." John was fondling my hair. Soft as corn tassel, he said. Eyes blue as the morning. "Look how you fit in the crook of my arm. You'll not be getting angry at me this time for saying it?"

He took my hands between his own. "Dolly it's not much I can be offering you. Just a miner's lot."

"What I've always known." I was smiling at him.

He held me off, then drew me back. "I'll never again be looking at another woman." Was he guessing what I most needed to hear, like his want of the hidden things I was bringing him? Searching, we found one another out, and were content.

Before the leaves had turned for autumn John and I stood up together in the old Rock Church. Then we started up the mountain. On a Saturday high noon we set out, a roll of blankets strapped on John's shoulder and a good-sized basket of food I'd packed on his arm, for we aimed to spend our first night and day together up High Top. A fancy of mine it was that John took over, right off. His free arm around me, I was carrying his music box. High Top out of a clear golden sky was smiling down at us and beckoning us on. Still we took our own time climbing up. Look like with all John and I had said and shared together, we'd hardly begun. Each turn of the trail held a cove or memory I'd be having to share, and we'd rest our packs and ourselves on the good-smelling pine needle carpet . . . and forget where we were and our climb ahead.

Like stages on a pilgrimage, John said it was, and us leaving a kiss to mark each stopping off place. "You're a blaspheming idiot!" I told him and dodged on ahead, in and out among the trees and him chasing me, till he was all befuddled with trying to catch up. Soon as I showed myself in one spot and he reached it I'd dart on to another, just giving him a glimpse of my blue dress from behind a far pine trunk to tease him on . . . till at last he was begging for mercy and I out of breath with laughing, and pitying him a bit, loaded down with our packs.

"Dolly, you vixen!" He caught me to him. "You'll pay double for this."

Around us the woods grew still.

When at last we started on, the sun was lowering, throwing long purple shadows along our hills, and birds beginning their evening call. We took up our packs to start on, for we wanted to make High Top before sundown. John gave a remembering look around.

A gentle wind was breathing against our faces as we climbed. A few evening clouds gathered behind our mountain had turned all the heartening colors of the rainbow. Smell of pine was thick in our lungs, John's body moving steady and eager beside me toward the ridge.

On our way we passed near my Dad and Ma. We stood for a time by their resting place, hands clasped, not needing to speak. John knew all of it. I'd told him, our first time together over the hill. And John understood. Leastways, he came as near it as anybody as different in makeup as he was. And I blessed him for it, both ways.

Dad and Ma, down inside me I was whispering, *here he is. Here's John.* And I knew they'd be telling their

Dolly that between John Cooper and me all was as it should be. And learn from us, daughter. Keep it that way, clear to the end. . . . John's clasp told me his thought was like my own.

We started on, climbing faster now, wanting all powerful to come to the ridge.

Of a sudden John's step faltered. "Dolly, hearken!" he whispered.

In the sumac bushes bordering our path a cardinal was raising his low sobbing cry, signaling his mate. From a distance came her timid answering note. Again he called, this time closer. Then again, again. And in the stillness came her answer. John's fingers, locked between mine, tightened. So quietly that not a twig broke, we followed the calling bird along his path. We could see the red flash of his wings overhead. His calls came faster, deeper, the answering note just ahead. Then a quick flash of scarlet toward another in the woods, the notes blurred together and a quick fluttering silence in the brush. . . . John turned to smile down at me, his dark eyes moist. We started on up the trail together. And I knew I had chosen well.

Harlequin Romance

Listening for the distant tramp of men homing from the pit, I looked out to find John making it up the path ahead of the rest. I started down to meet him. Granny's chuckling nod to me from her stoop put me in mind of women's friendly jibes down at the creek these past mornings. I turned back to wait him inside.

"Dol, rig out your finest!" Bounding in, John swung me clear of the floor. "We're aheading for town!" And a proper way to celebrate our first Saturday since we'd stood up in church. Mert Bedlow, his workmate, had promise of a hitch from his Uncle Silas, a farmer driving his wagonload down to market. "We'll ride in style! Atop a cartload of cabbage heads!"

"Let me down, you loon!" John was whirling us around the kitchen.

"Dol, I'll buy you some of this newfangled sody!" John was bumping chairs, hardly missing the stove.

"And dress goods you never find the likes of in our Pluckme."

Marketday in Clancy! A thing to go on remembering, since the time my Dad and his friends had hired a farm wagon and taken the boistering lot of us there on a hayride. Pesky mules had gone fractious and nigh dumped us in a gulley, but once Dad got them in hand, we rode in handsome and got us an eyeful—and like as not gave a few as well! Would it be the same, I wondered, farmers' carts lining Main Street, hawkers singsonging their wares? "Pep'mint sticks! All day licks!" "Bal-loons! Red ones. Blue ones. Only a penny!" Dad got a fistful, enough to go round, then let me pet a black wooly lamb somebody had fetched to market. And Ma laughing and frisking her balloon like a young'un.

"Clancy?" I nipped John's ear. "If we only could!" We'd choose a present for starting our homemaking right, he said, and maybe beads to match my eyes.

"John, put me down!" I heard Clyde and Unc Harry joshing on the path outside. Let them find me in midair and my face coalmarked, I'd never be quit of their sly ribbing.

Laughing at me, working to get free, John kept on waltzing. "Who says a man can't swing his old 'oman?" With a final turn and Clyde's step on our doorway, he let me go. At my brother's grin I ran to tidy my hair, then emptied a kettle of water in his iron tub, the same my Dad used. "Clancy can wait till next Saturday!" I said. "Now we got something not to be put off!"

John stripped to the waist and was dousing his chest. He lathered his arms. "And what might it be?"

I was scrubbing coal from his back. "Wheedling a

three-room place from Nate Brown!" Just this noon I heard Mark Wilson's family was vacating their house. Laid off with miner's asthmy, Mark was going on his cousin Emmet's farm, Mark's girls being handy to pick Emmet's cotton. "And if we hurry we'll be first to get our bid in with Nate." He was the super that Cap'n Chumley trusted with parceling out houses.

"Not so hard, honey! You're taking me skin off!" John slipped a wet arm around me, his eyes aspark. We had scant place to ourselves in this two-room box.

"Nate? That tightfist!" My brother leaned on his elbows against the tub, his tongue darting like a gartersnake between the gap in his front teeth. "Sooner try getting 'lasses from a turnip!"

"But we rate an extra room, now we have two diggers under our roof!"

"Nate's that tight—" Unc Harry, edging over by Clyde, dropped his voice to a confiding whisper, "I hear tell his ole 'oman figures he don't need two legs in his pants, one'll do him."

When their laughing simmered down, John asked me if Wilson's was the place by the big sycamore?

"That tumbledown wreck!" Unc emptied his lungs in a rumbling snort. Steps all whichaway! Roof aleaking.

"And who more handy than you, Unc, with a saw?"

"And why in gumption, Dol, you awanting such!"

"Three rooms!" John was reaching for me before my brother. I stepped by him out of the kitchen so they might get their scrubbing done and into fresh things. "There's ample space for a garden. And a fine view down the valley from Wilson's stoop." And if only they hurried, we would catch Nate at Pluckme before he finished his books. Nate's other job was managing Chumley's store.

Uncle was grumbling. "What's Dol up to? Means more rent." Three good round silvers a month, in place of two.

"I figure the extra's on us," John said. Clyde's part would stand at one.

"Unc, there'll be no end of nail and hammering to do!" I broke in, for we never talked money before Unc Harry, put it to keep a few coppers by him. His chew of baccy and tin of snuff I got with our staples from Pluckme and slipped of a night in his jeans. "Unc, I'll have you sawing and hacking clear to Christmas!"

"Reckon you will, at that." Harry trailed back to the kitchen, his face creased up with trying to hide his pleasure. He turned his whittling knife between his thumb and forefinger, feeling its good edge, then its curved bone handle, made he said of pure elkhorn. The storming night Dad had fetched him from his cave at the diggings, Unc Harry had searched his ragged jacket over for his knife. Many a yarn he told us young'uns about it, a straight hand-me-down from his Great-Grandpappy, Daniel Boone. This blade had tasted wildcat blood and bear's meat, clipped off a rattler's head. Boone had marked off the trail for first-comers through the Great Smokies, using this knife. With it he had carved his name on a greatoak near our Hollow, we had seen and felt the letters with our own hands. "Now it's housebroke," the old man concluded. "Content like our dog, Spot, to serve household needs." He had carved Ma a nut bowl out of wild cherry and three-legged stools enough to go round, and shaped a gourd dipper.

Some day not long off now, he said, he hoped to be called on for turning a cradle.

John came in, his hair shining wet and brushed flat to his head, and high cheekbones aglow from his scrub. He had on his good suit bought in town for standing up, and for a minute the look of him took my breath. "I'll step down to Mert's," he said, "ask him to save us a place for next week."

"Don't bother!" Clyde stopped his splashing to call. "I'll take your place." I turned to give our kettle of stew an extra hard stirring. Clyde, with a loud jig, began singing, "Make way, Clancy! Here I come."

I took up my brother's Bobtail envelope he had left for me and emptied it on the kitchen table. Braggety Sal might be getting my trip to Clancy but she was not running through Clyde's hard-come dollars all of an evening. Once spent, she gave him a cold shoulder for any gander with a jingle in his pocket. And my brother flat broke and fit to be tied, with next payday a fortnight off.

"Dol, don't you think—?" John stood by, hunting words. "Clyde's nigh twenty!"

I stopped my counting, my cheeks aburn at his interfering. "He is still my kid brother." I spoke too low for Clyde's hearing. "And the promise I gave Ma, not yet done with." When my brother had him a woman of his own to manage for him, good. And the Lord grant him a girl up to it.

John slipped an arm around me. "Don't you worry. Though it's fair to warn you, she won't be your match. And now ole 'oman—" I saw a teasing flicker pulling at his mouth—"Come on, own up. You're awondering where your own man's pay is!"

I was not giving in to him. "And why should I? Or maybe you lost it, awading the creek?"

John laughed outright. "Dol, you make a poor liar." From his shirt front he drew out his Bobtail envelope and handed it to me, its flap still unbroken. "Here you are, girl. And stretch it six ways to Sunday."

My face still aburn, I handed it back. Best he was opening it himself, dividing it between our household needs and his own.

John whistled. "So! Young Dol Hawkins's got her dander up!" His glance warned me. "From last Sunday on, you are Dolly Cooper. And don't be forgetting it. As for this—" He put the envelope in my hand. "It's yours— and welcome! You think I'm begrudging it?" Once more his look was smiling. "It's downright relief, honey. The goldernest thing, how a single goof lets his pay slip through his fingers!" I put the company account slip and few bills in a blue handleless cup I kept hidden on a top shelf behind my sugar crock. With our errand to Nate done, we would sit down and work it out together. And little enough figuring we might need to be doing, for after Graball checked off the carbide and explosive a miner had to take on account, groceries and such, there was not much left but a neat row of ciphers on a bob-tail check.

"Sis!" My brother walked in sniffing at my rabbit stew. "I'm that hungry, I could—"

"I know. You'd relish a weasel." I heaped his plate, then John's and Harry's. Most nights we lingered at table, seasoning our food with good talk, Unc with bits he garnered around the diggings, John and Clyde with tales on blunderbust Ike adriving his pitblind mules.

Tonight we had scant time for doing my fresh blue-
berry cobbler justice, even foregoing a second cup of
tea. I slipped on my go-to-meeting frock and gave my
hair twenty licks and a promise. Before we left I handed
John a parcel to tuck in his back pocket.

"And what might this be?" John shook it next his ear.
Through the paper came, like a spring freshet, its quick
pleasuring gurgle.

"For Nate's rheumatiz," I said. Unc snorted.

We walked at a brisk pace, two of my steps to match
one of John's, my head bobbing level with his shoulders,
us tossing back friendly "Howdy!"s and "Ev'en!"s to folk
coming out on their stoops and pipes lighting up like
fireflies along the path.

"Stop, rest a minute?" Granny Morse hailed us. "You
all make a sight for sore eyes!"

"And where in thunderation you going so lickety-split!"
Pop McFever stepped in our path. We dodged past
him, then Big Seth Campbell. "If we told, you'd be there
afore us!"

Pluckme stood on a rise of ground not far from the
old workings. We found it crowded, and not waiting our
turn to give in our order, made our way past the coun-
ters to a door in the rear marked "Private." At John's
knock a raspy voice we knew for Nate's called, "Go
away! I'm busy." And no doubt he was, ascratching
down items in his Doomsday book. John knocked again.

"It's Dolly Hawkins!" I called through the panel.

Nate swung open the door. "And why didn't you say
so!" Everybody knew the old rascal had an eye out for
the girls. In his younger days Nate had been a pal of
my Dad's, that was before he'd done—as some put it—

right well by himself, tied the knot with Mistress Wiley
Matt, second cousin once removed of Cap'n Chumley's
wife. Nate shifted his lodging off the patch down to the
bossmen's Hollow.

"It won't take a minute," I said. Nate beckoned us in
and shut the door. His office, if you might call it such,
was piled high with papers and junk and that close-
smelling with stale baccy, I had to hold myself not to
throw open a window. I nudged John to slip me my
parcel and I laid it on top of Nate's Doomsday book.

"Now I call that downright friendly of you, Dolly."
Nate's small eyes glistened. He took off the wrappings
and held my cordial up to the light. "My rheumatiz has
been troubling me extra of late." He eased his bulk into
his swivel chair and gestured me toward a straightback,
leaving John to stand. "You make as pretty a bride, Dol,
as our Hollow ever laid eyes on."

You old fox! I was thinking, not daring risk a glance
at John.

"Sorry I couldn't get to the wedding supper, get my
turn at kissing the bride." His laugh died off in a wheeze.
And good you didn't, I thought, you'd still be laid up!
I could see John's fists going open and closed, restless
like.

I took my shopping list from my skirt pocket. "I de-
clare, if we didn't forget to give in our order!" An extra
big one this week, seeing we had a new boarder!

Nate eyed the order, then handed it back looking
pleased with himself, for nothing he fancied like gathering in other folks' silver. His little eyes moved about the
room. "Now what you reckon I got around here," he

ruminated, "make a proper wedding gift for Jim Hawkins' girl?"

"A first-rate one!" I took up his hint. Let my husband sign up for Wilson's house?

Nate pursed his lips, the color of dried apples. "Now I dunno about that. I'd like mighty to oblige you, Dol. But that's a three room house." And two diggers in our family now, I reminded him, able to outmatch twice their number in the coal cars they filled.

"I dunno." Nate wagged his head.

The place stands in bad need of repair, John said. Leaky roof. Front stoop gone. "I figured, you spare us a few boards you got lying around here, we can put it in shape. And no cost to you."

"Well—" Nate was fondling his bottle of cordial. "Let me reckon on it." We knew free repairs had swung it, Nate would go boasting to his second cousin by marriage, Hardflint Chumley, what a close manager he was. "We got a long waiting list. But—" Nate slapped his hand down on the Book. "For Jim Hawkins' daughter, I'll do it!" He went to get the papers to sign. John hardly bothered to read them through, we knew ahead what the printed form said, a miner had to promise away his shirttail to get a roof over his head, but who cared for wordings no company in our hills was daring put to a test!

John, toting home our order, gave little heed to my eager talk about our new place. "That old coot! I should have biffed him." He gave his load an angry hoist. "Who he thinks he is? Apawing you with his eyes. As if he had some right. Like a king, and you a serving girl or something."

I rested my hand on John's arm. A sliver of moon

was mounting the ridge, cool air rising full of fresh
mountain smell. Supposing we went past Wilsons, by
lantern light we'd not be seeing much? John's mouth flickered. "Can't sleep on it, can you now. Can't wait till good daylight!" But his stride quickened.

Unc's pipe was aglow on our stoop. "So you got it!"

"Who said?" John slid his load to the step and flexed
his cramped arm.

"What Dol goes after, she gets. Powerful like her
Dad." With a last draw, Unc pushed to his feet. Reckon
he had to beat Pop McFever at checkers. I hooked my
arm through his, knowing him anxious to be coaxed into
coming with us for a look at our new place. John with
the lantern and me a broom, we started for Wilson's at
the far upper edge of the patch.

"And look at her!" Unc rocked on his heels. Even a
dull moon was not hiding its roof askew and hanging
blinds. Window cracks were stuffed with bits of sacking.
"What a bargain! Give a good blow, John lad, and over
she'll topple!" I was regretting we had brought Unc
along, till I saw he was aglorying his sore pride, relishing how the place cried out for his fixing. John went to
look over his gardening space. A few branches cleared
back from the big oaks to give more sun, he said, and
young saplings uprooted and we were ready for planting.
Maybe a bit late, but time for a crop.

"Bust my buttons, if that ain't sound of water hitting
stone!" Unc wandered off to find the gushet, and we
turned back toward the house. John handed me the key,
the door swung wide and before I knew it, he had lifted
me over the sill and given me a quick one, for luck. He

held up the lantern and I measured off the kitchen, four paces longer from east to west window than our old one. A room to pleasure in, John said, with fireplace facing center and a door each side the chimney opening on two small rooms in back. John stepped outside and made as if to enter. "There's a sight of logs burning and you, Dol, in your blue dress and a ribbon in your hair. And smell of fresh rabbit stew!"

Laughing, I ran to throw open windows, for the place cried out for my good lye soap and bucketloads of hot water. If only I had good daylight now, or tomorrow wasn't Sunday. John was poking around the fireplace. Good deep one, he said, ought to draw well. Wilson's girl, Maud, had told me it was the one decent thing about the place. But with a fine hearth to start on, we could build any shack over like new, replank floors, put fresh newsprint on walls, whitewash sills. In our mind's eye it was already done, and red curtains at window.

"Which room'll be ours?" John beckoned me over. At first glance they were alike, big enough for bed and pinechest and a shelf with hooks John was putting for our clothes. We chose the room with window facing east, toward High Top.

I ran my finger along a ledge and blew off the dust. "Reckon I'd better knock over a lamp," I said, "muster out your fire brigade." Let a cookstove blow up or a blaze start, his band of volunteers formed a human chain from creek to burning house and passed water buckets hand over hand. But for daily needs, us womenfolk had each to haul her own.

"If there was some way now to store water—" John was looking around as Harry came in. "A tank like,

maybe?" Down at the diggings he'd spied a coupla iron
barrels arusting their bottoms off, Unc said. As for asking
Nate or somebody for them, not even the old tightwad
was begrudging such. John clapped the old man's shoulder. "And we're only aborrowing, in case he asks!"

I was through my dishes and checking our groceries
when John came back, rubbing rusty stains off his pants
and hands. "You'll have your water, girl. And now for a
turn up the mountain?" He took down his music box
and we climbed to a favorite rock that jutted out for a
good looksee over our valley. This spot I once used for
a hideout from Ma. With a bit of moon rhine traveling
up behind us, John and I looked down on our new house.
"Lonesome old thing, reckon nobody ever gave her any
mind?" He tuned up his music box. "We'll give her a real
welcoming!"

A mockingbird perched in a wild cherry near us began
singing his guts out, like they will for a waxing moon.
John gave over his strumming to listen. Stretched flat, he
began answering. The mocker would wait, then make his
trill climb, John's after. And I, not able to sound a note,
felt something inside me start a whistling climb, till the
bird's notes reached beyond hearing. John had a way of
rousing strange notions in folk, making you hear and do
things where before you couldn't.

We stayed till the sky was lightening, then overslept,
waking to hear church bells ringing along our valley.
There was no rousing Clyde. Unc Harry had disappeared, his fishing tackle along. "Don't be hard on the
old fellow?" John said, smiling to himself as we joined
the trek of families down the hill to our Cumberland

Rock church. All through preaching my thought kept awandering to our new house. Sal Campbell was in her place, preening herself in a new slazy blouse like as not my brother got her in Clancy. During hymn singing she was cutting her glance around at John, and his voice rising clear through the rest.

When we started home, John pinched my arm. "Think you fooling me there in church? Looking so innocent, sun making a halo out of your red top, and all the while the parson was talking you off playing hookey, same as Harry!"

"Sinner yourself." Him sidling his knee against mine during service, and Amanthy or my cousin Fay sure to notice.

Unc Harry was waiting by our doorway, looking for all his grey hair like a small boy up to mischief and sneaking proud of himself. Lying astride our table was a fresh caught trout.

"So that's where you were. And church bells aringing!"

John gave a whistle and hoisted the fish by its tail. What a whopper! All of four pound?

"Four and eight ounces." Lowering his eyes to hide their sparkle, Unc edged over by me. "Dol, it ain't I'm expecting you to take it kindly, my missing service and breaking sabbath. But downright truth, honey—" His voice dropped to a mourning singsong. It's bare light when he woke and knowing we aimed to sleep a bit longer being Sunday, he thought to fix him some gruel and begin the Lord's day by wandering through his tabernacle in the wood.

"And not forgetting to carry your fishing rod to worship?"

First thing Unc knowed he was over by the fish pond, cooling his heels. Pole resting between his knees. And it must have slipped like— "And next thing to come, but I felt a nibbling!" His voice in spite of him was creeping up. "Then a monstrous pull on my rod. For a time it was a tussle and a tossup which way it'd go, me into the pond or this trout out of it." Unc darted a look around at me. When I had conquered him I sat on the bank awiping off sweat, he said, legs astraddle my fish. I was kind of praying out loud, awrastling with my sin.

"Lord, Dol ain't gona like this." I reached my fish toward the water. "It's sure a big one. Happen I better be throwing it back?" Then plain as you hear me I heard Him saying, "Harry Boone, don't be wasting the food I sent you." "Dol's sure gone be mad at me, Lord." "You tell her I forgive you. She can too. Tell her you had scant luck all week, those timbering fool ascaring off fish from biting and her no proper meat for Sunday dinner. So take it along, and sin no more." Unc drew in his breath. "It'll go nice with tater cakes and simlins?"

Smell of Unc's broiling fish roused Clyde where church-bells couldn't. When all left of the trout was backbone and head and Unc nodding in his chair and my brother once more asleep, John forewent his Sunday nap to thumb with me through a mail-order catalogue borrowed from Mert's Uncle, a heavysize book crammed with pictures—good for much else John said than hanging on a nail in an outhouse! Going through it was like taking the peep my Granny told of faroff things. Stoves that ran without wood. Farm wagon without mule to pull it. Pearly white tubs and citified men's clothes and women's of plaids and silk and hats with do-dads to marvel over.

Shiny stuff to brighten your kitchen floor. Such patterns might addle the brain and sure as not fade under my lye soap. John was admiring a thing they called a spigot. "I sure fancy getting you water by turn of the wrist!"

"First get the company laying a pipeline to a handle pump."

We spelled out an order, not minding that Nate had fired a family off our patch for trading beyond Pluckme: a half gallon of green paint for window trims, steps and roof, a dime's worth of red to brighten my cans of geranium, coveralls for John, and for me a shiny cabinet with mirror to stand on our pine chest. Medicine cabinet the book called it, John was smiling to think of hill folk squandering their bright keepall on such. Sassafras tea in springtime was all we had need of, for purifying the blood, snake root and a dose of castor oil. When loosened rock felled a man down the pit, what thing could his woman be reaching down from a medicine shelf to be mending him whole? Hot water to wash in, hot toddy to ease him till we found a medic willing to come up our mountain. More often we took our injured down in Uncle Silas' cart. . . . Looking at the shiny thing in the picture, I felt a quiver go through me, like cloud over the sun.

"Eve'n, folks!" Limpy, mine cap aslant his nodding head, was toting a melon fresh from his garden patch and cooled in the spring. We were splitting it when Granny walked in with her dead son's girl, Flossie Belle, then Tobey and his parents to offer a hand with our moving. "This row of houses won't seem right without you all next door." Pop McFever brought over his family, and Limpy fetched another melon.

Nate won't be letting a chance slip to be getting even, Limpy warned. John looked up from his strumming. "Let him try it."

My brother slipped off around sundown, making he said for evening service. "Good excuse as any!" Old Gourd called after him. We heard Sal's high laugh and Clyde joining in, then faint echo of hymns rising on mist from the valley. I rested my glance on Pop McFever's seventeen-old Mary. A likely girl, smart and winsome though quiet like a mouse. If only I might be switching my brother's fancy. . . .

I mentioned it to John as we made ready for bed. I folded back the covers and he lifted me in by him. "Folks ain't a pair of socks, Dol, to be matching up."

After he was asleep, I lay awake listening for my brother and thinking.

.... *chapter 10* ....

Damp sourgrass tugging my skirts, I hastened toward
Turtleback Creek, empty pails ajiggle at my sides. The
fresh early air was promising a good workday.

"Lazybones!" My cousin Fay called up to me. Buckets
dipped full, she made way for Manathy, next woman in
line. "Whatever's been keeping you?"

"And what keeps all brides alaying late!" Sal Campbell tossed her head, enjoying the round of laugh she
got. I let it pass, turning aside to thank Granny for the
extra rags she had sent over by Flossie Mae, I'd be using
up plenty this week areadying our new place.

Granny nodded. "I heard steps, spied your man toting
water buckets afore light. Reckon he nigh filled your
borrowed tank?"

Sal's laugh went ringing along the wood. "Dol's starting in on her Big Handsome same as her brother. Getting him housebroke!"

Granny shifted her heavy bulk toward her. "If I was you, child, I'd not let envy be arattling my tongue."

"Envy! Why, if I'd wanted—" At my look Sal's words trailed off.

"Empty kettle makes biggest clatter!" Tobey's Ma pursed her lips, clear as day thinking with Granny the usual talk in our patch: too bad Sal's Ma had to pass on early, leave her raising to Big Seth, as kind and easy-going a critter as the Lord ever breathed on, but no match for a spirited colt like Sal.

Humming to myself, I waited behind my brother's girl for a turn at the spring. In her thick black curls she had sprinkled some of the wispy store smell I'd heard her bragging Clyde had got her in Clancy. Yet it wasn't my brother, I knew, on Sal's mind. . . . The creek was running smooth and deep, its mossy rocks covered by over-flow from our midsummer rains. Restless to be done with my wash and afreshening our new home, I must have pushed against Sal for she flipped around with a quick, "Wobbly on your pins, eh? Bet your Handsome ain't let you get a decent sleep all week!"

Swooping down with my bucket to the overflow from the creek, I let Sal have it over her head and shoulders. "Reckon your mind's needing a scrub!"

Sal made a leap for me, but the laughing women circled her in. "You had it coming!" Sal was crying from rage, Fay on the bank over us dancing happy. Nobody better tangle with a Hawkins!

The dripping girl grabbed her pails and started on a run up the path. "If I know John Cooper!" she called back. "He'll tire of you and your quincy ways soon enough!"

My buckets filled, I sloshed my arms deep in the stream, let it cool my face. A fig with her, giddy dunce. And Dol, you're another, letting her sass get under your skin. Now all Toewad and Shamrock would be relishing the story and shooting their mouths off about green-eyed cats. And the worst of it, my brother mad as hops. All the while I was sudsing my clothes and getting them into the breeze, High Top stood ablaze in the sun, heat vapors rising from our valley toward her. Limpy, on a run with his cars up the tipple, waved his arm at me. I saw in memory two carrot tops poking over side of Peg's car, and I knew I'd be finding it in me to right things with Clyde.

I was ahumming my three-note song *duddle-dum-dum, duddle-dum-dee* as I started ripping old newsprint from walls of the room that was going to be John's and mine. Unc Harry kept up his drubbing, like a woodpecker on our roof, nailing down fresh tar paper we took on credit from Nate's Grab-all. "From looks of this leak," Harry slid a couple of nails from mouth to hand, "Wilson and his old 'oman musta woke many a night to find it apuddling down into their bed!" And what kind of a ditty was I atankering with, he said, no start and no finish, like a silly pup achasing its tail! If I'd raise a good hymn now. . . . His nail dribbing drowned out the rest.

Old newspaper off and piled outside to burn, I was going down walls and over floor with my lye soap biting off dirt, when I heard a kind of cracked yodelling travel up our hill. "Dol-ly!" For a second I got a crazy feeling it was Ma. "Dol-ly!" Granny Morse was standing at the foot of the rise, abeckoning. I squinted up, true enough the sun was far beyond noon.

Over a batch of pancakes and lasses, Granny gave Unc her juicy version of how I sloshed Sal. Unc cut short his chortling to fix me with a look. "Reckon you know what devil's mess you've stirred up? Go fix it, man to man like, before Clyde home from the diggings."

Granny took my part. Go down to Sal's in the temper she was in? There might be more than water flying. But she would take word. Tell Sal I'm sorry for wetting her, I said, and if she's wanting, I'd come over and say it in person. But let her keep her dirty tongue off me, or I'd toss her hindfirst to the minnows.

"Now, Dol—!"

"No worry, Harry." Granny's deep bosom was heaving, merry tears running down her wrinkled cheeks. "Go on back to your hammering and scrubbing, trust me with knowing what to leave unsaid."

But one look at Clyde's dead eyes and I was down at the creek with sunup, waiting my chance to tell Sal howdy and ask her folks over for supper, come Friday. Though I was not one for holding with good luck and bad, I wanted to start in our new home with no shadow of begrudgings across our doorway, nor my brother coming to table with the angry face of a stranger.

John was lifting our pinewood bed, a four-poster that
had been Ma's, through the doorway. Unc pushed by him
inside, his stooped body hunched up like with cold. "Dol,
what you up to? Dividing us, asleeping under two roofs!
Bad luck. And don't make sense."

My brother reached over to duck Unc'd head in the
feather ticking I piled in his arms. "And who's asking
honeymooners to make sense! It's a waxing moon, Unc,
that makes sense. And shame on your old bones for forgetting."

Unc was moving around touching sills and mantel,
like saying goodbye. I followed him outside, all at once
feeling with him that going from here meant leaving
something of ourselves behind. I slipped my arm through
his. "In no time our new place will seem home. We'll
make it that frolicksome!"

The old man was digging his heels into the clay earth

near our stoop. From this cabin Ma had bidden us bury her by Dad, then given him charge while Hallie, Clyde and I finished our growing up.

"Make way!" John and Clyde hoisted our bed sideways through the door, then righted it for use as a carry-all. I piled it high with pallets and flourbag sheets, and for want of a store mattress a pad made from layers of sacking and stuffed with cotton off nearby farms. Each picking season, Ma had opened an end to add a mite. Grown a trifle knotty, it was a sight better to lay on than pallet quilts on hard board, though Granny held that sacking filled with new mown hay made for happier sleeping.

Our procession started up the path, John and Clyde moving careful-like not to spill their load, Harry walking behind, a plump bantam with his feather tick, his eyes barely peering out, and me carrying our Family Bible and picture album and John's music box. "Where's the circus?" Folks ran out on their stoops to whoop and call after us. "Save me a ticket!" Clyde, whopping back at them, was cutting monkeyshines with his feet, Old Harry off somewhere in his thoughts.

"John, do it proper, lad!" Limpy clumped his wooden leg and cupped his hands like shouting from his donkey train down the valley. "Set your bride atop your litter!" John never slacked his pace. "You old hoot owl! Quit your screeching and come lend a shoulder!"

I moved ahead to swing open our doorway. "And wherever'd you get such finery!" John asked. Merry red curtains for our kitchen I had made from best-quality sugarbags bleached white and hemstitched, then dipped in sumac juice. I chose for our bedrooms the blue that pressed gooseberries give. John afingering them declared they pure matched my eyes. "Give you a wooden crate, Dol, you'd make it homey."

John fetched up our chest, I put on the whiff of scarf dyed to match our curtains and set out the little standup mirror John had got me. "Every morning to be seeing a pretty witch in. And a happy one! This I promise." On the mantel I placed his music box and our cross-stitch piece, our Bible and album on the small table Ma kept for their use. Seeing them was like her blessing.

When we started gathering brushwood for a fire Clyde said, "Dol, you gone looney? And weather hot as blazes!" Reckon Clyde don't know what it means, Unc said, kindling your first blaze in your own grate.

After they had gone John and I knelt by the hearth. Balling up paper to fit under the twigs, I blew on it slowlike while John lit the match. In the small glow his face was sternlike, with a kind of shining he must have had as a boy.

The sky was turning the color of churned butter when Harry's rapid drub on our window had me up and down the path in a flash, John fast on my heels. "We are clear done with breakfast!" Harry grumbled. "Dol, you'll send him on an empty belly down the pit?" John was bolting warmed-over porridge as I packed his dinner pail. He made it tailend of the miners heading for the pit, with Mert and Seth tossing their jabs at him and John laughing and throwing them back, and me wondering why I couldn't meet Sal's quips with so easy a tongue.

By nightfall we had things ready for Harry and Clyde to move in. Mert, Limpy and Big Seth came by to help finish off the jug of applejack my brother told them I was hoarding against this day. Spying my cousin, Fay, in our kitchen, Mert fired up like a sumac bush in Spring. Fay slipped off to our bedroom. Granny Morse swung her broad hips after her. "Skittery as rabbits! And however you two'll ever hook up, I'm asking. Needing me to butt your heads together?"

Fay grew overbusy admiring my curtains. "Gives me a notion myself."

"You—saving sugarbags for your hope box!" Granny pinched Fay's hip. "Afore Mert gets up nerve, your pretties'll go yellow with age!"

"Hush, Granny; he'll hear you." At the burst of laughter from the kitchen, Fay blushed to the roots of her brown hair, in a little while she slipped off through the back way to her folks' cabin. Since my Dad's trouble, she was the only Hawkins who came near us. Her father, Timothy Hawkins, was still digging coal and nursing his grudge against Ma, even to the second generation.

Our jug was soon emptied and friends saying goodnight, for it was up and down with the sun in our patch. Long after John was asleep and Harry's labored snore trailing Clyde's hearty one through the partition, I lay awake enjoying our new home.

By Saturday I hustled through the last of our settling in, and was waiting for John, things ready for an early start on our trip to Clancy when Unc Harry came in, doubled over and moaning with his back. I got him abed, a hot brick wrapped in cloth between his shoulders and a draught of strong tea down him. "Don't you be astudying about me," he kept moaning. "Go right ahead with your plans." Bending over the old man, I half-fancied a slow twinkle in his eye, before he turned his knotted face to the wall.

John brought news that Mert's uncle had some mixup, and there'd be no room for us in his wagon till next week. "Can't make it out. Mert had the grins. Don't reckon Fay and him getting hitched?"

Something told me to get into my good dress. Down at the creek this morning there had been bits of whisperings and shushing when I came by. I was tying a bow on my hair when we heard a scuffling and low murmurings outside our stoop, like after church service, then folk laughing and singing out, "Surprise! Surprise!"

John flung open our door to find our stoop crowded and folk still acoming up the trail, arms loaded with goodies and housewarming gifts.

"Catched you this time!" Granny called. Old Harry leaped out of bed, taking care to keep the jollying crowd between him and me— "Howdy folks! Sure fooled Doll!"

"Come in! Set anywhere!" John kept saying when it was plain before the last crowded in, they'd be on the ceiling. As the night was fair and moon rising, we hoisted table and benches outside. Younger folk lolled on the good dry earth while Limpy and Mac, gardening partners, carved up the pig they had slaughtered, in our Hollow a rare treat.

Feasting over, they blindfolded John and me and lead us inside. Uncovering our eyes, we saw by our hearth a fresh grass mat Amanthy had woven, another from Bess McFever by the door, and a new brush broom Tobey had gathered. Everybody had thought up something to turn their hands to, Granny table mats, Big Seth a drinking gourd, Uncle Billy one of his famous cane-bottom chairs. Fay beckoned me into our room. On our bed was a counterpane to match our curtains. "A present," Fay said, "like from all of us." A hundred and eight sugarbags they had pieced together, nigh every family in our patch giving a few. Looking around, from Fay's and Mary's fresh moon faces to Granny's and Manthy's lined smiles, I felt my throat gone tight. I walked over to rest my hand on the spread. "It's uncommon beautiful."

Unc Harry brought out a small-size rocker he had been making in secret and put it by the hearth. "Just in case!"

Granny nodded. A wee dodger'd sure relish drawing that by the fire! In the laughing and cider and good luck toasts going round, everybody grew noisy. "Outside now!" Pop McFever clapped his hands. "Pair up for play-party games."

When done with *chum-chum-a-loo* and *Step forth and claim your lover,* they called for John to fiddle, and began squaring up to dance. Young Seth, Sal's brother, came for me as partner. I was making excuse when John urged, "Go ahead! They're needing another couple to round it out."

As we swung figures, Seth grew overzealous in his grasp. "Must say, Dol, amarrying ain't hurt your looks!" There was smell of corn whiskey about him, I'd seen him going behind the house with Slim Treat, a smart-alec lowlander visiting Mert's folks. Slim was shining up to Sal, with my brother glowering from the sidelines, biding his chance. I was uneasy for the set to be over, for Seth was staring down at me, his look the same as when he'd come acourting, long before our valley saw John. I looked at John, but he tossed me a grin, bent on whittling his nails down on his strings, and Pop calling turns till our heads whirled quicker than our feet.

The set finally ended, John gave over fiddling to Uncle Billy to swing me a turn. Seth disappeared with Slim behind the house, and Clyde had his turn at Sal. Dancing the next set with Pop, my Dad's friend, I found myself in the grapevine twist once more facing Seth. He reached for me like a beartrap. "Dol?" he leaned near to whisper, "It ain't John but me should be putting his shoes under your bed."

Pretending to trip, I gave his shin a smart blow. With a whelp he turned me loose, calling back over his shoulder as I swung on to the next in line, "Same old bite! Woman, ain't John tamed you yet!"

Pop called time out and dancers leaned against trees or rested on the ground, catching their breath. Wanting a cool drink and to enjoy our new counterpane, I had gone inside our room when I heard steps in our kitchen and a woman's soft laughing. "Hello, Handsome!"

I stepped back, for it was Sal Campbell who had followed John in, she leaning over his shoulder as he bent down for a dipperful from our drinking water. Straightening, John brushed her upright. "Sal—" His words came slow and careful-like, "Happens you got your faces mixed?"

I knew now I'd best let him handle her alone.

"Pity your Dol ain't so partic-lar!" she blurted. "John Cooper, are you pure blind? She's got my poor brother dancing circles around her. Everybody here's seeing it but you!"

By her gasp, I knew John had taken her hard by the arm. "Another word out of you, you dirty-minded filly!

And so help me, I'll give you a dump in the creek. Seems Dol didn't finish her job!"

Sal ran outside and I heard Slim calling, "Here you are, beautiful! Come, do me a favor—"

"Anything you want, Slim." Her laugh was shrill. As they started behind the house, his arm around her, I saw her face, the prowling taking look of a witchwoman. Parasidy LaRue in her way had loved my Dad, but Sal loved no-one, and I knew my resolve well-taken, to save Clyde from her if I could.

The moon, climbed high over the Ridge, was fading into a lightening sky before our neighbors took leave of us. John and I stood in the doorway, hearkening to their echoing "Sweet dreams, ladies—" roll down the valley.

. . . . . *chapter 12* . . . .

I was setting out young tomato plants Limpy had
given me, when a man's shadow moved between me and
the sun. Looking up I saw John, his glance tight. I
sprang to my feet. "Quick! Is Clyde—?"

"Not bad hurt." John put his arm around me. Racing
in muck up to his knees, my brother had slipped and
wrenched his shoulder.

"Brace up, Dol. Might have been worse!" Right then
I had no liking for his joke, but I managed a smile for
greeting Clyde, when we fetched him up from Granny's,
where John had left him while he brought me word.

Granny, the nearest thing to a doc or nurse our Hollow
had, put one of her hot poultices on him and John half
carrying him, Clyde made it up the hill. We got him to
bed and a stiff drink down him, and soon, propped on
pillows, he dozed off.

"He'll be fine now, a few days in bed." John came into

the kitchen for a pot of tea. As I passed his cup, I saw his hand was not steady. Had more happened than he let on?

He shrugged my question aside. "Lucky stiff! Home all week with you."

"He can ill afford it," I said. Nobody got paid for laying off hurt or sick.

John doffed his boots and shirt and walked barefoot outside. No sense going back this late to the pit, he said, might as well hoe the garden. I went inside to Clyde. Lying hunched up, he seemed little more than the boy he was when we roamed carefree over these hills. Looking down into his face, I felt a slow eating bitterness. What kind of life was it, stretching out ahead for him, for John, all of us? This time he had come off light, but next? For every miner like Pop who lived out his prime, our Hollow had enough widows and half-orphans to name off nine of your ten fingers, and not counting maimed like Limpy and our Harry.

"Dol!" John called. "You acoming?" He was standing with his legs straddling a young corn row, his big shoulders and chest bare to the sun, his mane of chestnut waving over his merry eyes. "Come on, thou sluggard! Help me squince off 'tater bugs!"

I made a flying leap around his waist. In time, bending over the rows, the sun warmed me and drove off my fear, like rain clouds driven by fresh searching wind. John was real and everlasting as our hills.

"Boy, you sure had luck!" Mert came over after supper with Ike and was visiting with Clyde. "A smart thing you hurt your left arm, not your good right."

"Luck? Ain't the word for it!" Ike's voice was a roar. I

stopped my work to listen. "Clyde, you fell right on the track. And that load of cars bearing down on you. I thought you were a goner. But for John's grab and jump clear, you'd both be mincemeat! Fit for a pie!"

"When John slung me," Clyde said, "he nigh cracked my skull!"

Above their rough laugh I heard John saying, "Drop it! Dol might hear."

I leaned against our table, but it refused to hold me. John helped me outside into the night air. "Ike and his Big Mouth!" Patting my shoulder as you might a child's, he began humming:

> *When first I saw my darlin'*
> *Ahangin' out her linen clothes. . . .*

Propped against him, I breathed in smell of honeysuckle, thinking my sister Hallie had been the clever one and I must find some way, as she had, to get us free of the pit. *Once a miner, always a miner.* A by-word as old as our hills, rounding us in.

"John, think we might save up, get us a two-bit farm?"

He dropped his humming. "Hon, there's something I want you to get straight. I've been digging coal since thirteen, and never more than a lamed arm."

Shivering, I leaned against him. High Top had a swarm of lights over her.

"See that one, above the crest?" John said. "She's my lucky one." He pulled a rabbit foot from his pocket that his Unc David had given him, before he passed on. "Always bring you luck, son, he told me. And Clyde now, ain't it his first slip? These bitty ones don't count." Finding me silent, John went on, "My Dad used to tell me about Civil War days. Some have luck, some don't. If a bullet had your name on it, nothing you might do. Same with the mine. But for one that gets it, Dol, remember this. Another eight come through."

I fingered the rabbit foot. A slight thing, blown along by a wind. Yet how much more was my John's keen eye and strong body to match against a half ton of slate pelting down.

"Dol, there's a big mail-order package for you down at Pluckme." Tobey ran up to our stoop. "And Ma says tell you Graball Nate's fit to be tied." To spend our earnings outside Pluckme was a sin rarely overlooked.

Our cabin looked perked up as a field daisy with her fresh trim of whitewash and green paint, but John came home from the diggings with his cheeks burning angry beneath the soot. "Carson's put me on Widowers' Watch." This was our men's name for the hated night shift. "It's that pinhead Nate's doings!" John was for going down to have it out. "What if he fires me? Plenty more hellholes wanting diggers!"

"Leave the Hollow?" I took his arm. Do it the proper way, let Pop McFever and the pit committee handle it? And before the week was spent, Pop had John back on his regular shift.

Clyde by then was up and about, his arm in a sling and off with his fishing pole and Unc Harry to the Mill Pond. They came home with good sun in their cheeks and a nice catch, enough to share with Granny and Pop's folks. Then the mine had to lay off for a few days to repair the main shaft, and Ike tied up his mules in their underground stall and came to tell Clyde he would be over with sunrise to join their fishing trip. They were making off without him, set for a rare day along the stream, when Ike hailed them, "Hey, mates! I'm acoming!"

Around dark Clyde and Unc were home, glumfaced, buckets empty. "Plague take the goon!" Old Harry lifted my stove lid to shoot baccy juice at the coals. "Dol, we explained time over. 'Ike, you gotta learn, you can't handle fish same as a mule. You can't holler and whoa and giddap fish on your hook!' "

Gently Clyde flexed his sore arm. "Sis, Ike flips his hook and line like a pair of reins. And all the time his tongue wagging and boots kicking up scruff."

Unc began rewinding his line. "Ike's scared off our fish once too often." Before their next trip over, Ike would be thankful to get back to his mules.

In high mood Unc and Clyde set off next day, Ike tagging along. They stayed overnight and came back with no fish and no Ike, but mighty pleased with themselves. I could get no sense out of them, only Unc Harry mumbling, "Knock twice, Brother Turnbull!" and my brother doubled over with laughing.

On Sunday Ike appeared in church, and with him Addie, his 'Ole 'Oman. Ike had been living separate from her for many a winter.

"This your doing?" I asked Unc Harry.

He gave my brother a solemn bow. "Just maybe we have been lending the good Lord a hand?"

The tale being too rollicksome to keep, Clyde motioned for more tea to keep his throat easy, then began:

The more Ike blustered and scared off fish, the harder we racked our brains for a plan. Down the mine Ike was jumpy about omens. With dark and rain coming on and Toewad a good six miles off, we figured to stop overnight in an empty cabin. We asked farmer Simpson, "How about letting us stop over in the shack on your land?" and him tipped off by Unc to answer, "And sure! If you are not minding it's haunted?"

"Oh sure, we don't mind! We ain't ones for taking stock in ghosts. Are we, Ike?" He gulped and shook his head.

"Well, and that's right lucky." Ted Simpson dropped his voice. "They do tell of some funny goings on in this place."

Ike edged nearer. What kind of things? The farmer shook his head, declaring he was having enough trouble as it was, trying to sell the place. "Looks like, since old man Turnbull got strangled here, nobody wants to sleep in the place. They claim Turnbull's spirit prowls about, moaning and groaning, seeking vengeance."

Ike turned green. It was a lie out of the whole cloth, old Turnbull had died quiet as a lamb in his own bed, but how was Ike to know?

"Course, I take no stock in it," Simpson added.

"Me nuther," Unc said. "Let's go inside."

Ike hung back. We still had time to find a place closer home?

"Drop my britches! We ain't letting a crazy story about haunts drive us out in this rain." Unc turned to Simpson. "Open her up!"

We went inside, Ike bringing up the rear. Boy, was it a damp smelly place. Cobwebs and mould everywhere, rats darting from corners. Rotting boards gave way underfoot. By now we had Ike going proper.

"Fireplace still draws well." Ted Simpson told us.

"Watch out for the leak yonder in the roof." He started toward the door. "One of you come along, get a bucket of drinking water from my well." This too we had agreed on, to get Ike out of the way while we rigged up a contraption in the attic. We took a loose board and balanced it over an old table, tied one end to a rope that dropped down to the corner where Harry spread his blanket. In the dead of night Harry was to yank on the rope and the board knock against the table, making raps like a haunt tapping out messages from the uneasy dead. We tested it out, then stacked a mess of old bottles and dishes high on the table for a final downclatter. We found a pile of gunny sacks with dark rusty spots from where the rain had leaked along the stovepipe. These rusty spots might easily be mistook for something else, so we lugged them down by the fire. Ike came back with the water. We made a small blaze in the grate and sat around eating the snack you packed for us, Dol. We couldn't get Ike to touch a thing. We started telling about dead men of our Cumberlands who had come back, seeking justice.

"Wonder what for somebody took a notion to strangle old man Turnbull?" Unc asked. "He was a good man, did nobody harm."

"Maybe they were after his gold," I bit down on my lip. "Tell me he had some hidden away, under the floor here, or fireplace. Maybe that's why he comes back?"

Unc made as if to shake off the cold. "Maybe if he comes—'course now, I don't believe in such—but if there is more than talk in it, I calculate he is looking for the man who choked the life out of him. Right here in this room."

Ike jumped to his feet. "Can't you fellows ever quit talking!"

"Why, Ike—" Unc Harry opened his eyes. "I figure you always like to talk plenty, come fishing time. You got an uncommon loud way with fish. And mules."

I went for the gunny sacks. "Here is something I found for us to sleep on. Some bags of old Turnbull's from the attic." I held them out to Ike, the rusty spots glowing a mean dark color. His eyes bugged out.

"Throw them away. You fool!" Unc called to me. "They're soaked with blood!" He grabbed them from me and threw them to a far corner. "Poor old Turnbull, may he rest in peace."

We turned in, Harry in his corner with the drawstring, and me alongside Ike, and him tossing and turning in his place. We waited till along midnight, then Unc Harry called hoarselike, "What's that!"

"What's what?" Ike raised to his knees.

"There it is again!" Unc whispered. Like somebody moving about overhead, and groaning. Ike's eyes were frogging out. "Funny, I don't hear nothing. Now I do!" He grabbed my arm. "You hear that?!"

The wind was beginning to howl and sob till hard to make out whether wind or human. It kept up, regular as a man's breathing, rising and petering off.

"Let's get out of here!" Ike whispered to me. "Ain't healthy in this place."

"I hear somebody moving about." Unc said. Overhead, rats were scurrying. As the wailing rose again, Unc called softly, "Who's there? That you, brother Turnbull?" No answer, except the wind's low moan.

"Don't, Harry!" Ike begged. "For the love of heaven, man, don't be calling up spirits of the dead."

"I gotta know!" Unc whispered back. "I can't sleep in this place and not be knowing." He raised his voice, putting a quaver in it. "Is that you, Bill Turnbull?"

Now came the knocks, slow and solemn. I kept fast hold of Ike, for I tell you, even though I knew it Unc's doings, I felt my skin creep. Ike groaned like a man in pain and slipped once more to his knees.

"Who you wanting to speak with?" Unc called. "If it's me, Brother Turnbull, knock three times." Silence. Then a moan.

"If it's Clyde here, a true sinner, knock three times." Again silence. I had to stuff my shirt in my mouth to keep from hollering right out.

"If it is Ike you are wanting," Unc said, "knock three times." Silence. Then came the knocks. In the dark I could just make out poor Ike crossing himself. From then on the goof took over, like a man in a trance.

"What you wanting to tell me?" he asked. "What for you coming back from the dead? That man that murdered you, I don't know him!" he kept saying. "I didn't have nothing to do with such. It can't be that!" The wind's moaning had waxed higher. When it died off, Ike was still talking to the haunt. "You come back to tell me I did wrong to leave my wife, Addie? If you did, knock three times."

Now this we hadn't expected. Unc was twisting around in his corner, in something of a fix.

"Speak out, Brother Turnbull," Ike pleaded. "All these winters I been aworrying, and no place warmed by me to ease my cold feet. Did I do right?" Still, no knocks.

"She was a powerful nag," Ike whispered. "Still, I broke my vows. This what you come to tell me?" Now came the knocks. I near about choked with the gag in my mouth, for Ike fell on his face. "Dear Lord, you sent me warning. I'll get Addie back."

(John leaned over to tap Unc's knee. "You sure got a whopper on your conscience, harnessing poor Ike again with his scarecrow." The old man shook his head. Like as not Ike would have fetched her back, sooner or later. But hear the story out!) About the time Ike put his heart-searching question, something went amiss with the rope pull. Harry gave an extra hard yank. Such a down-clatter overhead! The rope jammed. "There's nothing in the attic," Harry said. "I'm going up for a look."

"Don't, Uncle!" Ike swung onto me with both hands. "It's worth your life!"

"Fiddlesticks!" Making for the stairs, Harry tripped on the rope. The board fell cluttering down on his head. With this, the bottles stacked for a grand finale started tumbling. A racket and confusion to raise the dead! And Ike amoaning. As I ran up the stairs, a dark gray thing darted out of the attic at us, snarling and whining. We flattened against the wall and it shot past us, and headed for Ike. He let out a shriek and ran for the door, the gray thing after him!

When we quieted down a little, Unc said, "Must have been a stray mountain cat, nigh crazy with hunger. Ike never stopped running till he reached Toewad!" And never again was he apestering them, tagging along on a fishing trip.

"Clyde?" I looked across at my brother, his face and

arms browned from these past days in the sun. His lame shoulder was almost good as ever, with only a twinge to remind him. John too had browned from our days, since the layoff, in the garden and woods. And I fell to wondering if there might be a living for my men to be made above ground, hunting fish and game and making things grow, out in the open like God intended, not burrowing like moles in the dark earth. This forenoon the whistle had blown for work tomorrow.

. . . . *chapter 13* . . . .

With morning dew still on our corn, I was dusting lime over their young tassels to ward off pests, when I found hills and sky turning on me. Resting on the ground to let things steady, I knew it time I made a call on Granny.

"Come right in, honey." She motioned me to a chair by her, put on the kettle. We were finishing our cup of her special brew of herbs and I still hunting words, when Granny leaned over to place a firm hand on my knee. "Well? I take it this no ordinary visit."

Her faded eyes twinkling at me, I said, "I am not right sure. Ma wasn't one for much talk with her girls."

Granny nodded. "Could be. Lemme see, coupla months ain't it, since John took you to wife? Nearer three? Hm-m. Miss your last turn of the moon? Thought so." Her hands, respected in our Hollow, softly felt my side. Turning my head toward the light, she studied my eye-balls. "Hm-m. Could be. Honey, it's nothing to be

ascared of, borning a child. Natural as breathing. Just
you do as I say."

Reclimbing our path, it seemed to me like when a
child and the whole earth mounting with me toward
High Top and the sky. And John, far under our mountain, not guessing the word I had for him.

Supper over and too dark for working longer in his
garden, John fetched a bit of lumber he was saving to
make me a knotty maple rocker. He was crouched on
his knees near my chair, ready to measure off, when I
said, "These are extra fine boards. Maybe we should be
saving them?"

He glanced up. "Whatever for?" I held out a booty I
was making.

"A young'un?" John was saying it over like scarce believing. And don't you go spreading it! I told him. Not
till I felt life, could we make sure.

My waist spanned till John no longer might circle it
with his arm. And still there was no quickening in me.
Granny laughed aside my doubts. Any time now, she
said.

Ours proved full days. John and I waked to find High
Top outside our window apruning herself with fresh
clouds. Our room faced east and on a clear day, John's
head next mine on the pillow, we watched light break
over the hills—till I heard Unc fussing about the stove
to get my fire going and I must bound from bed and
scurry to make breakfast and my men's lunchtins ready
before the whistle.

All the day through I was hustling the hours along
with my broom. When our poplar moved its shadow
across our doorway, I knew it time to meet John on his

way home aswinging his pick and a tune on his breath
like when I first spied him. And I had him above ground
and to myself for the night—before I must be seeing him
off, giving back sass to down the fear a mine woman
lives with. Since a child I had known its stillness. Ma's
face gone stiff in midafternoon. Not even the smallest
of us dared let out his breath, waiting for the mine to
shout its message. A short friendly blast and Ma turned
back to her ironing and we children to our play, knowing our Dad had work tomorrow. Risking his neck and
us thankful. For there came weeks when the monster's
screech failed us and our bellies grew big with hunger
gas. Ma might grow worn out, praying for the whistle to
find its voice. Finding it, scarce a fortnight passed but
somebody's Dad was hurt down the mine. And with us
now it was the same. Mishaps that cost a man his arm
or leg the whistle passed over, being all in the day's
work. Let a pocket of gas explode and the blast gave
forth its yell of doom. Often I had seen Ma drop her
work and run with other women for the pit, we young'uns
after them. In time the whistle mingled in my child
thoughts with the Voice of God, coming from beyond
High Top to herald life or death. Sometime now in my
sleep I heard it. Waking with cramp in my side, I was
confronted by John's even breathing. . . . Since Clyde's
fall I had known little peace. Even in my happiness,
fear was skulking overhead like mountain cat in a high
oak, ready to spring on me. And birds not far off singing.

John had Unc Harry guide him evenings in making
cradle spools and rockers to fit on the hull. I sat by him,
fashioning wrap-arounds, bellybands and things John
declared not size for a skeeter. Work done, we went out-

side for a rest on our stoop. Music box on his knee and head cocked, listening, John tuned her, then made up songs for the little fellow. There was one his Ma used to sing him:

> *Sleep, baby sleep*
> *Thy father's minding the sheep*

Listening, my eyes sought the Big and Little Dipper, then at a offshoot the North Star. My Dad had shown us, if lost in the wood after dark, how to keep our bearing by this star. Something to give your mind to, John said, how men from all over, on high seas or desert, might be doing the same.

In the night I woke, startled to think someone had knocked against our bed. Moonlight streaming in proved our room empty, John asleep on his side. I lay for a time with a feeling unlike any I had known. Then I roused John. "Feel how he kicks!" I pressed his hand against my side. "Now go abragging all you like to your mates!"

Frost came and our forest turned like on fire with reds and gold, our pine holding steady to its everlasting green. In the midst of our preparing, Unc Harry was brought low with misery in his chest. He hid it from us, till coughing and fever got the better of him, and we forced him to bed. Miners' lungs, some call it. Granny told us the most we might hope was for Unc to last out the winter. Times when the fever left him and he was clearheaded, he kept restless, wanting Clyde, John and me by him and calling up one story or song after another, like storing up a larder for his long journey ahead.

"Tell about the time that catfish flung you!" he'd say,

and John adding new bits with each telling, or relaying
the yarn about his magic gun with bewitched ramrod
that sprang from its owner's hand to go on a tare in the
wood, bringing down bear, wildcat and all living game,
then diving down to serve as fishpole and corral all the
trout in the stream. And Unc would laugh till a fit of
coughing shook him. Over a cup of hot broth he asked
for my Indian Granny's story about Old Joe, a wee critter with coat of rainbow that she'd found as a girl in the
Great Smokies.

I was cooling my hands in the Everlasting Spring,
she'd say, making ready to draw my bucket of drinking
water when a critter not like any living thing I ever
put eye on came idling to the surface. His coat of scales
was of many colors, like Joseph's in Egypt of long ago.
He swam into my bucket, and rolled his eyes, saying like,
"Take me with you?" He was too pretty to be athrowing
him back. I hid him in an old crock filled with rain
water near the barn. Little by little I got him landbroke.
Each sunup I gave him a bit longer to flop on the ground,
breathing in air till he grew used to it as you or me.
Wherever I went, Joey followed. He learned to tilt upright on his tail and do tricks. When Pop sent me picking cotton rows, I heard a pitter-patter behind me and
when I turned quick, there was Joey.

"Go on back to your pail," I told him. "You'll choke
to death, this long out of water."

Joey would turn back and I start on, till I heard him
flipflopping down the cotton row. He made it right
frolicsome while I picked. He could leapfrog over cotton plants and toss bolls on his fins.

I was crossing a log over Snake Creek and Joey flip-flopping behind me, when he tried one high flip too many. He slipped and I heard him cry out. He fell in the creek. I tried to save him but the current bore him downstream. My pet drowned like any mortal. I found him near shore and buried him in his bright coat of many colors by a giant spruce. And to this day you will find in the Smokies, close by our Everlasting Spring, our rainbows after a storm anchor one end where Joey lies.

Uncle Harry, hearing me end, would sigh and fondle his Daniel Boone knife. "It's for your lad, Dol," he said.

After mule-driving Ike's visit, Unc and Clyde were reliving the time they had robbed him of his wits, conjuring up spooks. "Clyde, lad—" Unc Harry rested a hand on his knee. "A fine thing if we could have another fishing trip, come spring."

"And sure we will!" Clyde started planning it, while I brought over hot tea and John stirred up the fire. Harry's eyes took on a fevered shine. "Just us two?"

Their trip was not to be. Yet Harry got his deeper wish, to see our child.

When my hour came, Granny ordered John off to the mountain. "With me and the Lord tending her, your Dol's in good hands. Off with you, lad! Go pray—anything! Just stay from under my feet."

John was soon back, and when the pain grew hard I swung onto his grip, and Granny let us be. I felt our child fighting and tearing his way to life and there was joy in it that outdid my terror, for I was fighting with him and to do as Granny ordered, giving him what aid I could. . . . After it seemed there might be no end, I felt the earth cleave and my body give forth. From far off I heard his first, delivering cry. Out of the tumult and valley of the shadow, I had come of a sudden on the mountain, and it was like the Good Book had it, all light and peace. And I felt the weak happy tears on my face.

"Quick!" My voice is like one in a dream. "Quick! Bring me our child." I try to raise up, but can't. Then Granny lays John's child in my arms, and I feel the rush of strength of ten thousand men—before I slip off into a blessed rest. And over us ahovering John's shining face.

They took son into Unc, and I heard him crooning to him like an old woman. After Granny left, John took over tending son and me, I never knew a woman more gentle and careful with her hands.

"Anything wrong?" I woke to find John nearby, his gaze going from son to me, then back. Anyway, he has your stubborn chin, John might say, or note the shape of his head or fingers square-tipped like mine. Our boy was pure copy of his Dad, with such power in him, legs and arms flying when John bathed him, till John was put to it not to have him spring clear of his grip.

By the fourth day I was up and we took our boy to the Cumberland Rock church. James Harry Cooper, we christened him for Unc and my Dad, knowing it bad luck to be naming a man's firstborn for him. We thought to forego a christening party, with Harry ill, but Unc demanded, "Make it a humdinger!" A spell of coughing cut short his words. And in the night, after our friends gone and son sleeping quiet in his cradle, our Harry started on his last journey. We did what we could to make the going easy, then laid him on the ridge, not far from Fightin' Jim Hawkins, his friend. Others who had come to take leave of Harry turned back down the ridge. Clyde and I stood on by the new earth turned over him, thinking. Harry had been a father to us, in the long years since our Dad's going. His had been the miner's lot, more doing without than rewarding, and thrown off, once the mine took his health, like slag dumped on the tipple. Harry Boone was a true hillman. Whatever his hope lost, he had kept his own counsel. And he had found his place by Jim Hawkins' fireside.

Unc's whittling knife I wrapped in a soft cloth and put away to be giving our lad when he came of age.

With first sign of thaw, my brother grew restless. How much it was Sal Campbell's trifling, how much the letter brother Tim, always a braggart, sent from Alabama. I was not sure. "Let the boy go, Dol," John told me. "You can't hold him. I'm not one for speaking against any woman, but if he stays here?"

I went to help Clyde pack his things.

"Till now I didn't feel it right, making off." He rested a heavy arm on my shoulder. "Now, you've a good man, and Unc Harry gone—"

I could not answer. Clyde's going was like all the days of our childhood going. Since nothing I might say would hold him, we asked in neighbors and saw him off with a will. He was barely over the ridge when Nate sent word he was needing our house for a two-digger family. To keep our home, we took in a roving miner, a thing we fancied hardly less than moving to a smaller place.

With war in Europe and our mines working day and night, the big T.S.I. had bought up Cap'n Chumley's

holdings and begun sending outsiders into our Hollow.
Among them was a six foot colored man, Elijah Turner,
and his wife Sarah. When my eye rested on this quiet
woman and her lean brown fingers binding my little
boy's hurt finger, I knew hers a gift like to Granny's and
our Hollow in rare luck. Some reckoned otherwise.

"A black man's coming means one thing—Trouble."
Not since penitent days had we seen any in our Hollow.

"Way I figure it," Big Seth dropped by with Limpy to
talk it over with John, "Down the pit, black man same
onery luck as a woman. Anybody fool enough to let a
skirt below ground, sure as hellfire a gas pocket flares!"

John stopped bouncing Coppy on his knees. "Look
at his carrot top! Pure Hawkins." Our lad's hair was
darker than mine, like shining metal, earning him before
able to walk his nickname, Coppy. He had John's dark
eyes and my Dad's swagger, altogether a blend of
Cooper and Hawkins that lead us to wondering talk.

"True as gospel, since this black Jonah starts in,"
Limpy pushed his fist into his cap. "Looks like we can't
finish a day without somebody hurt."

"Ain't you mixing things a bit? Not that I'm wanting
to differ with you, mates." John gave Coppy over to me.
"But it's this rushup fever that's taken hold, them wanting coal for war. Can't hardly blame Elijah for that!" He
turned to my brother, who feeling our hills acalling him,
had come back on the flood of lowlanders to our Hollow.
"Clyde, how is it down in Birmingham? More black than
white, I hear, adigging coal?"

Clyde nodded. "Two to one. Reckon I know how Seth
feels. Tim laughed it out of me. Down the mine hole, he
says, with soot, dark and all, who knows the·golden color

of your skin? Or gives a hoot! And that's how I come to figure—so long as a man does his part."

John opened his arms and Coppy made a run for him. "Elijah does his." Everybody had to admit him a quiet, hardworking man. I knew John had taken to Elijah for his voice. Like a bass drum, sometime the two of them raised a song below ground, John said, their voices bounding off the coal face in time with their picks.

"All the same, I don't like it." Seth was taking his grievance to others. We had little time for minding, taken up with welcoming Coppy's new sister. I lay on my side, watching Coppy trying to make friends. He dragged the hobby horse John had made him over by the cradle vacated for her. When he found Lucinda Sue (named for John's Ma and mine) could not ride or even talk, his small face puckered. "Take her back. Her no good!" He poked a curious finger in her middle, she gave a true Hawkins yelp and Coppy ran for the door. Granny Morse limped past him, wiping laugh tears from her wrinkled cheeks. "And sure, Coppy's met up with a banshee!"

Sitting by me while I nursed the baby, she fell silent, then eased out a sigh. "Dol, who will take over for me, welcoming babies to our Hollow?"

I shifted my daughter to the other breast. "Go on with you, Granny. You'll live forever." More easy to think of looking out and find High Top gone.

Granny took a fresh draw on her corncob pipe, pursuing her thought. Amanthy now was willing, but uncommon awkward with her hand. Gert McFever, bad with her heart. Who then? Patty Gill, a lazy nocount.

"Any baby worth its salt gets here afore her!" Granny rocked her body. "Anyhow, I fancy a younger woman." What about Sarah? Granny shook her head. "Fay? Able enough, but skittery as a kitten! Goes faint at sight of blood." She hobbled stiff-kneed over by our hearth and spat her disgust into the grate. With her bright eyes fastened on me, Granny drew her rocker nearer the bed. "I been praying the good Lord to direct my vision." She spoke from under her breathing. "And now for true I am knowing the one for my mantel to fall on." Before I could speak she pressed on. "Oh, I know you got young'uns aborning fast. But I figure the Lord akeeping His eye on our Hollow, asparing me till your wee ones get a size to manage a bit on their own."

Granny straightened up as if things settled. "Once you're about, I'd like you coming along to help born Mirandy's child, kind of get in your hand?"

I looked down at my girl's tiny fingers on my breast, not daring to let on I shared Fay's weakness and risk Granny's scorn.

When Mirandy's hour came I went with Granny, and afterward spilt my supper in the wood back of our cabin. And I prayed before the next borning the Lord open Granny's eyes to her true helper.

Cindy, a sunny-hearted towhead with Ma's dark eyes, in no time was toddling after her brother to play rescue.

With young Coppy strapped to his shoulder and Cindy to mine, John followed me Sundays on the trail for High Top. Digging on his knees and bad air down the pit did not faze him, like it did many. Come evening or free day he had life enough for hoeing his garden or loving, and fiddling tunes while the patch beat time to Ocean

Wave and Figures Eight. John outmatched my climbing and spying out eagle's roost. Perhaps there was more he was outmatching me in, but it was full give and take between us and neither stopping to wonder over things that seem to vex a lot of folks.

Coming home, we passed Elijah and his wife Sarah. They returned our nod, going half way to be friendly and no further. Seth's grumbling against Elijah had spread to others. I noticed young ones drawn to Sarah, not alone by her cookies but for her whimsy tales of God's critters.

With accidents still on the up, Big Seth went to Pop McFever. "This black Jonah! Ain't it time we took steps!" John talked Pop into holding off. Worst feared was the deadly white damp, a gas with scant odor that did men in without their knowing.

Now spring was on us, we planted a monster garden, no more for greens than our common hankering to make things grow. Nothing sweeter than corn or salad green you raised yourself, John said, or tomato lying round and smooth in your palm and red like the sun. "Love apple" some call it. Our crop proved ample for ourselves and neighbors, with enough to put by for winter. Near our stoop I planted rainbow zinnias and sweet william. Coppy helped me drop a row of sunflower seeds near the trellis of wild rose John placed to shield the outhouse.

We looked up to find a group of miners homing early from the pit. Ahead of the others walked Elijah. From Big Seth we learned what had happened. Deadly white damp. Elijah had sniffed it in time and lead them to safety, then walked off before they had time to thank him.

Seth and Limpy lead the men after supper over to Elijah's place. They had come to be swallowing their wrong talk in this jug of applejack Limpy was carrying. "Would you be asking us in?" And Elijah swung wide the door.

. . . . *chapter 14* . . . .

"Your son is below school age, Mrs. Cooper. I am
sorry." This slip by the teacher's desk was none of our
parts. Her curly brown hair was cut short like a boy's,
her clothes city folk, like her manner of speaking. Not
a day over twenty, I judged her, with a way of holding
herself to look taller than she rightly was. Her eyes were
blue-green, kind of pretty.

With a firm grip on Coppy's hand I stepped farther
into the schoolroom. "I aim to begin him young." Coppy
was going on six.

"Seven is the beginning age!" Mary Laird blocked my
path. I guessed her a bit scared and this her first school.
"You can see for yourself how crowded we are!" Five
grades in one room and not a seat empty.

Coppy was sniffling, the children making faces. I
pressed his hand. None of that! Show teacher he could
spell his name and count to fifty.

Mary Laird looked from Coppy to me. "You want to start him early? Why?"

I had no words for telling her. John and I had plans for the boy. He was not working his days out down a coal mine.

"He's got a long ways to travel. Might as well get on with it." I caught an answering spark in her eyes.

"James—" She leaned down to take his hand.

"I'm Coppy, ma'am." "Coppy, then. Come, help me. There is a small bench near the stove. We'll place it here, near my desk." She straigthtened up. "I'll give him a try. But I have to warn you, Mrs. Cooper, if he can't keep up—" Then she smiled and held out her hand. "But he will! I'll see to it."

For me it proved beginning school over. Coppy's questions as to where thunder came from and why the wind blew, and what drove the new cable hauling Limpy's donkey cars up the tipple, not even John could rightly answer, so I went down to Mary Laird and school out, she hunted through books to find pictures explaining electricity.

When we were making to leave, she asked me, "Send your son on ahead?" I saw the color mounting her cheeks. "Mrs. Cooper, I have to talk with someone." She kept her hands tight in her lap. Could it be this girl, lonely for her kin, felt out of place in our hills?

"Mrs. Cooper, tell me what have I done wrong? Why don't people like me?"

"My name is Dolly." I took a seat by her, knowing from now on we were friends. "Mary Laird, it is you they are thinking standoffish."

When my brother heard I was bringing the new

teacher home for Sunday dinner, he darted his tongue between his teeth. "Count me out!" He was going down to Mert's or Sal Campbell's, no pert knowitall was spoiling his appetite, looking down her nose at him from across table!

Wait till you see her, I told him. "She is not like you think."

Coppy stopped galloping his broomstick about the kitchen. "She's purty." Clyde tousled the boy's head and left for the Campbell's. Not content to let her fancy settle on one man, Sal was flipping her skirts once more my brother's way, making ready as John put it to heat over stale biscuits.

Since I asked it of him, Clyde remained through Sunday dinner but refused to lift his eyes from his plate or share our talk. Leaving early, he gave Mary a sharp going-over that deepened the flush in her cheeks. Mary was wearing a filmsy yellow dress when next she came and had fluffed out her brown hair, and Clyde proved slower to make off. Mary soon was coming regularly to our house and I could draw my breath in content, watching her girl-fashion drawing my brother out, and Clyde for the first time measuring his full growth.

At square-dances, Sal Campbell was openly flinging herself in Clyde's arms and breathing up in his face, then leading him outside, making time, but I knew deep-down my brother was not caring, only waiting for Mary's return from her spring vacation in Chattanooga with her people.

In April word reached us our country was at war. Limpy's coal train added more cars. With early May and our hills abloom with wild lilac and daisies, Toewad,

Shamrock and all camps in our Hollow packed lunches and climbed our ridge, for it was spring and time for remembering our Dad's march on Penitents' Hollow. Big Seth and Limpy made certain that Elijah and his wife, Sarah, came along. "Reckon a man good enough for risking your neck by, good enough to break bread with." Seth hearkened back to another saying in our hills: God made all critters and breathed in life, and when all said and done, human is human.

With John riding Cindy on his shoulder and Coppy between us atugging my hand, we climbed the trail, Mary and Clyde ahead of us. The look between them made me think of the spring John came.

No girl at the picnic was in demand like Mary Laird, all the young diggers wanting to swing the pretty teacher, and Sal eating her eyes out, hardly able to wait her turn with Clyde. Toward nightfall I noticed Sal leading my brother aside.

Full dark came, people started homeward. My brother did not return, nor Sal. I sent John looking for them. When he rejoined us and still no word of Clyde, Mary, her eyes angry, let Jeremy Brood, a middle-aged farmer, see her home.

Even with dawn my brother had not come. Big Seth, his lined face more drawn than ever, stopped by on his way from the pit. Rumor had it that his daughter and Clyde had gone off the mountain toward Clancy.

Toward nightfall it began storming. I could not sleep. Waiting up for Clyde brought back the nights we children had watched Ma keeping her vigil for Dad, and we knowing where he was, and none daring say.

Around first cock's crowing, I heard my brother's step

adrag on our path. Slipping from our bed, I looked out to make certain he was alone, then opened the door.

"Where in the name of all the saints—!" Seeing him drenched through and the wretched stoop to his body, I pulled him inside. *What strange evil had Sal wrought on my brother?*

"Sis, I—" He looked around the empty kitchen, his eyes gone dead.

I pushed a chair under him, brought the waiting kettle. "Remember how Dad used to say it, Clyde? Naught so bad, a nip of tea can't ease it."

He drank it down in big gulps, not looking at me. "You might as well know it," he said, "Sal and I got married yesterday."

My cup slipped from my hands. "It's not true! Say it's not true?"

John came in, still half asleep.

"You fool!" I was crying and beating my fists on Clyde's shoulder. "She's ruined you. And what for!"

My brother sat like a man dazed, not lifting his head. Gently John lead me aside. Come, give over, let Clyde tell us.

After a time my brother looked up at me, Sal had told him she was carrying his child.

"She tricked you!" I went over to him. What about Mary?

His mouth trembled. He lowered his head. "God knows I never meant—"

I was keening over Mary like my own sister.

My brother straightened. "Mary will know. I did the right thing. My child is needing a father."

"And for Mother?" I was beside myself. "Sal lied to

you, Clyde. How can she be knowing it yours, the cheap lowdown—" John put his hand over my mouth. Wasn't it enough, without us turning on each other?

Cindy had wakened and was crying.

Slowly my brother got to his feet. Sal was waiting for him, he said, down at Granny's. "Seeing how you take it—" He stood on, his need fighting down pride. "Reckon no place for us here?"

"Reckon not, Clyde." John's answer was firm. Tear-blind, I went in to Cindy, thankful not to be witnessing my brother's face, for he must know what lay behind John's words.

Later, my anger softening at thought of the child, and realizing with Clyde gone we had once more to take in a boarder, I felt myself ready to give in. John would have none of it. Rather a stranger under our roof, he said, than this devil. Clyde made his bed, let him lie in it.

When I could bring myself to go to Mary Laird, she found ways to avoid me. With school out, Mary left our hills with only a goodbye sent me through Coppy.

Big Seth, openly grateful to have Clyde taking over with Sal, gave a big wedding supper. I made excuse that Cindy was ailing. Better go, John urged, nothing gained this way but hard feeling.

I lifted Cindy to my shoulder. "You would have me go? It it's two-faced pretend you are wanting, then go yourself."

Clyde left soon for the war. I learned it from my children. "Look what Unc gave us!" They came running in with pennies balled in their muddy fists. When I asked had Unc given them a goodbye for me, Coppy, shaking his head, tossed his pennies to the ceiling then scrambled with Cindy to gather them up.

Hearing Clyde had landed overseas and Sal, Granny said, grown big with child, I tried to bring myself to be doing as Granny urged, prove a sister to Clyde's wife who had no woman kin of her own.

Before I could find it in me, Sal's child was stillborn. At Granny's word I hurried over, my feel of real sorrow shamed by an unwilling relief—for what claim now did she hold over my brother?

Sal did not bid me enter. Propped up in bed, she stared through me. "I know you hate me," she said, "and I give it back. But for you, Clyde'd never gone off."

I had nothing to do with his going, I said.

"Don't give me that!" She tossed her head, as of old. "But for you—" Her voice slid higher. "You and that flat-chested, skinnylegged Mary—!"

"Don't you speak her name!" I turned to leave.

"Wait!" Sal's glance was a whetstone. "You are glad my baby died."

I could not look at her.

"Go on back to your man and young'uns," she said. "I ain't needing you." And she turned her face from me.

I tramped the hills, then home to write Clyde. The paper, for all my desiring, stayed empty. And soon the woman bearing Clyde's name was flinging her skirts and her eyes at the boys, as always, her laugh a bit more shrill. In late fall Mert's cousin, Slim Goodwin, drove up in a shiny Ford and took her to Memphis. Big Seth told people his girl had a place waiting table.

In the night I woke to find John's hand on my shoulder, for I had been crying out in my sleep, thinking Clyde lying hurt and gunfire blasting over him like some mine whistle.

"War can't last much longer." John took my hand and I fell asleep.

John brought home Jake Valitsky, a gentle-faced Pole who worked near him, to take Clyde's room, for Nate was hinting about us having empty space and everybody else war-crowded. The old man's cheeks had deep furrows and his clothes many tears for my caring, and it seemed we had Unc Harry back at our fireside. Jake's pidgin English and tales of the Old Country delighted our children, and his talk of Pennsylvania mining opened up new territory for John and me.

"Trouble with us," I told him, "we are cut off. Kept ignorant."

Same in all mine towns, Jake said.

Shut up back in our hills, I said, and nobody outside knowing, or giving a hoot!

"Time will change things," Jake said. "And us."

With October, Mary Laird came back to our Hollow and Cindy took over Coppy's stool by her desk. In our valley more than one beside the farmer, Jeremy Brood, was asking to spark our teacher, but Mary held them off, only joining in at square-dancing time. And seeing her young face fired up, eyes aching, I would nigh hate my brother.

From our hillside John and I had watched the Good Book's words coming to pass, a cloud no bigger than a man's palm grown without warning to shut out the heavens. Since war had brought its rushup to our valley, it seemed I was carrying this mite of cloud in me. With each new mishap, the sky over our patch took on a foreboding hue. When the mine whistle sounded, Coppy would come by me. "Just ablowing for work tomorrow."

"Reckon I don't know!" Provoked that he had seen me start, I sent him outside to play. A lad shooting up tall for his nine years, he was near size of my brothers when they had followed Dad below ground. John and I planned otherwise for our son. When Ma bickered with Dad over each of her boys as their turn came for the pit, I had sided then in my heart against her. As I waited for John, I remembered how each nightfall her face lost its on-guard look. It was a strange thing, but I felt closer to her now than when she was alive.

"How it is?" I asked John, knowing this forenoon there had been another man hurt. He would tell me little, saying only, "Things should ease now a bit. Mac and our mates are working on it."

After he thought me asleep, he remained talking low with his workmate by the fire. I caught Jake's words, "Them prop reesky!" and John saying, "Hush! Dol might hear."

I knew what Jake meant, for I had ridden once on a kid's dare in Peg's cars down the mine. Even now I could feel the tons of earth and coal overhead, and all keeping them from crashing down to smother us the grace of God and wooden pine logs rotting from damp. Hewed from our woods, the logs stuck up like a ghost forest in the dark cave that twisted along the mountain's vein of coal. My ears drummed from scant air. Picks were whanging loose great chunks of coal, and shadow men breathing hard from heaving their loads. Dank choked my lungs. Scarce able to breathe, I started to run. I had seen this place in our Family Bible; "Gateway to Hell." A blind team of mules rushed by me. I tripped in the murk. A dark shadow whose voice was Old Mac's picked me up. He carried me to my Dad and brother Tim squatting at their work, for coal face and ceiling were that low not even a child my size could stand upright. "Blithering daylights!" Swearing under his breath, Dad pushed me in the first donkey trip above ground. "And see you never come back!" I had never wanted to.

Listening in on John and his mate reckoning how to handle rottening props, I knew the odds against them.

With gas, damp and weight bearing down, a pine log never lasted for long in the pit. Let a miner loose his foothold or bump against a prop, like as not it would give way and he have to run for it, before an earthslide started. Nate said miners were supposed to be checking on props each shift, replacing bad ones with new. Crouched on their buttocks against the coal face, with Big Boss driving pit boss and pit boss driving diggers for coal and more coal, a lot of time our men had for tending props! Most that John or Jake might do, when they heard a crack in the ceiling overhead, was to brace a sagging beam or replace a wobbly pole with a sound one.

"For why they give no men to feex?" Jake's voice rose. "Dirty *svollich!* Them prop fall. Cavein. Meester T.S.I. Big Boss, not him back broke. You, Johneey. Me. Eh?"

John banked the fire. "We'll go see Mac. But keep your voice down, Dol's got ears like a cat."

I turned in our bed till its aging frame shook. If need be, we women could take a hand in this.

Cindy was playing with empty spools on the kitchen floor by me, Coppy off to find lumps of coal on the slag pile for our stove, while I readied things for Sunday and all the while waiting inside me for John safe home. I knew him digging and acursing props, and racing same as I toward quitting time. He'd bound up the hill to greet his young'uns racing down, and me not far behind.

Digging away at the coal face, John nor his partner heard the first warning rumble. Elijah and Big Seth were working close by. The ceiling over them began to crack. Looking up, they saw a gap yawning out. Slate and earth poured down. They grabbed their shovels and made a break for it. All around them props were giving way, earth roaring.

"Make it other way!" Elijah yelled to John. "Turn back!" Too late. A cavein had sealed the passage, rock falling all around them. Before their eyes Big Seth was buried under coal. Elijah went next. The earthslide covered Jake to his hips. John, trying to reach him, felt a stab in his leg. When he came to, he found it pinned under a horseback.

For three hours (and me in my kitchen unbeknowing, Cindy playing alongside) Mert, Young Seth and others raced to dig through to them.

"Soon now, lads!" Mac kept calling, and Jake's answer growing weaker.

"Faster!" John called to them. "He's losing blood."

When they got a hole through, Mac told me they could see John, himself pinned down, doing what he could to save his friend. Before they could dig the opening big enough to crawl through to them, Jake was gone. And John too faint for knowing. A good thing, as they had another long stretch getting his leg free.

When the rescue crew brought John above ground and started with the stretcher up our hill, they sent Mac ahead to give me warning. "If we'd had a doctor handy, we might have saved John his leg."

I pushed him aside, ran down the path. My man lay with his eyes closed. On his forehead and cheeks blood was working through the coal grime. I saw his leg crushed, hanging useless.

"Thank God, John," I took his head between my hands, "You are alive."

. . . . *chapter 16* . . . .

John could not bear the sight of his children. The first days after it happened I had to send Coppy and Cindy to neighbors. He lay with eyes closed, not hearing or speaking.

"They're adigging through! Hear them?" John was calling to Jake, then crying under his breath, "For love of God, hurry. I can't stop him bleeding." We knew blood poison had set in. Pop McFever went to Super Benson. "We men talked it over. We dig no more coal till you get John Cooper proper aid." Benson sent Nate down to fetch a medic.

As John grew easier, he imagined cramps in his leg. Throwing off the covers he stared unbelieving to find it gone.

"John?" I ran to put back the sheet. He turned his face from me. I felt him wishing himself down there, under coal with his mates. Thrashing around, he would start his leg bleeding. I put on a fresh binding, then went outside for a look up our mountain. Never again would he race me up her, never walk free. Small wonder he longed to die. . . . My look fastened on High Top. Our hills seemed to give off strength.

Word of John's trouble spread through our Hollow and folk began traveling up to bring help, like once they came to join in our dancing. There was never a man for gathering folk around him the like of my John. As I had come to know him, like part of myself, I learned it plumbed from deep down, and his a heart rare and childlike. And now I must stand by and know it breaking.

With time his injured back mended and the stump healed, but not his spirit. When making him ready for sleep, I would hold his head against me. "Thank God," I'd say. He was like stone. My man, once so quick to give and take.

When I brought the children in to say goodnight, he kept his face to the wall, pretending sleep.

They grew afraid. "Ma," Coppy asked me, "Is Pop— Is he—?"

"He is sick, lad. Give him time."

With children abed, I would go outside for a look at High Top. No human could equal her waiting power. Often Granny, Pop McFever or Sarah came to sit by me. Not that we'd talk, but just to sit, a feeling human by you, brings comfort. Mary came, bringing the children oranges.

"Shall I send Clyde word?" Young Seth came to ask. I shook my head. What good burdening him with our grief, and 3,000 miles between us. Our miner folk kept us in food and medicine, after our savings were gone.

Nate had the company leave us alone on the rent. As for the rest, caveins were diggers' carelessness and the hand of the Lord. Miners' compensation was something Jake had told us about, but not yet known in our hills. John now was like Unc Harry, thrown to the slag pile.

With sundown Mert, Pop or some other of John's mates came by to ask after John, and visit with him awhile. How could I answer them. Let a man cross our sill in his miners' boots, John turned his twisted face to the wall, without a sign of greeting. John, who had been the first to hail his fellow, swap a yarn and wrestle or swing them a tune.

Mert would step over to his bedside, try to say something, then turn and make off, head bowed.

We had a late Indian summer, the moon of an evening was bright in our patch. Bright as last fall when John and I had danced. Nobody fiddled now or strummed a banjo in our part of the clearing or kept time with their feet. And nobody danced anywhere nearby, out of respect for John. Dance they did, as they should, but further off, taking care to stay beyond earshot at the far end of our clearing. There came an evening when the wind shifted. A snatch of music and hands marking time blew our way.

> *I'll climb the mountain top*
> *Plant me a patch of cane*
> *I'll make me a jug of 'lasses*
> *For to sweeten my Liza Jane*

Many a time John had swung this ballad. Swung me with him to its beat. I went over to him. He lay with eyes closed, the wet running over his cheek.

"John?" I threw my arms over him. "John, come back?"

He did not answer. Five weeks John had laid, more dead than alive, while his body mended. Was his mind gone, crushed beyond healing? Others were doubting and trying to hide it from me. I knew them wrong. Dolly Hawkins had been quick of tongue and no patience in her. Dolly Cooper I found another breed. When put to it a body can plumb things to draw on she never thought. And most of what I found I had from John.

Through the winter I'd gather my mending or knitting and come sit near him. Our children, in awe of this stranger, chose to play outside. When I moved off to get something, John turned his head, his eye following me. This gave me heart. As I sat by him, hands busy, I began telling him stories, pranks we did as young ones, memories of my old Granny, and Ma and Dad—snatching at anything that came to mind, struggling to touch a spring in him, make his laugh or anger—any part of the old John—well up.

It was a thing to ponder on, how it proved with a body when going back and forward over her life. Certain days, maybe even an hour or a look, stand out like mountain or deep gulley in the land. Others, whole years at a stretch, drop out as if they had never happened. Leastways that's how it had proven with me. All I could hold onto were times that cut deep, or took me high. "Like the morning, John, when you came." . . . I looked around at him. He lay more still than ever, his face like in death, though not so restful. Had he been so much as listening? What might be passing in him, I could only hazard. He had turned on the world, shut me out. I had seen others like this, coal-mangled, soured by their lot.

In the night I had a dream. My small brother and I were riding Peg's train up the tipple, and somehow John aboard. He was sitting with a gunny sack thrown over his lap, hiding the stump where his good strong leg had been. His face was pale and strained, but shining. It was a mixed-up dream, like most, yet clear as day, us riding like old times up the tipple straight toward High Top and the peep hole in the sky. In my sleep I could feel all the tugging and pulling back on our wagon, like Satan himself aiming to drag us downhill—set to break our car loose and send it cavorting like a lost boulder down the valley. The valley of the shadow—No! I feel myself swinging on for dear life to the cable, while many hands keep atug and pulling us on, from up ahead. Old Harry, Ma, Jake, my Dad, and Clyde. Granny halooing, "You—Dol-ly!" The sweat breaks out on me. Seems like everybody I know is aboard. Cindy, Coppy. Young Tobey. The whole world is mounting with us. Peg, his miner's cap at an angle, keeps right on driving, straight up to the place where High Top had poked a hole in the sky. . . . Our cars are slipping backward! Losing ground. I catch hold of the cable wire with my bare hands. "Come on, everybody!" I try to shout, but no words come. "Catch ahold! Pull! Pull! If all pull together, we got a fair chance to make it. . . ." Only a few hear me, then others. At last I feel John reach over to swing hold.

I woke to find the salty wet stinging my lids and mouth. I felt eased and could sleep. Come what might, I knew I would have John back.

"Ma, tell us a story?" Coppy begged like always when I was putting them to bed. About Penitent Hollow and the '90's when my Dad was leading the march to keep our hills free. *And so I will!* I thought, taking care to leave John's door open. He lay with eyes closed. If my Dad's long courage was speaking to him, like before, he gave no sign.

. . . . *chapter 17* . . . .

I was sitting near my Dad the night it happened, so close I could feel his arm quiver. His voice sounded dull and low.

"Sue?" He gave a quick glance from under his shaggy red brows toward my Ma. "Sue, if anybody strange comes to our door this night and asks for me—"

Ma turned sharp in her tracks. "Jim!" I saw her eyes widen, and her cheeks go white. Then the color flooded back, making her look for a minute fresh and pretty as a girl.

"Whoever'd be coming up the mountain?" she asked him. "On a night like this!" She looked at her Hawkins brood huddled about the fire, listening to the gale moaning through our hills like a bearcat who'd lost her cub.

"Whoever'd be coming—?" Ma sent her quick look at Unc Harry, then back to Dad. The words died in her throat. For days they had been up before dawn, going off somewhere before the mine whistle echoed along our valley. It was two winters since he lead the march with the penitents down to the Governor's mansion. Fearing trouble, they brought in National Guards, mere boys, and gave them guns. We children ran from them, but our Dads made friends, swapping baccy and yarns. When the night came for the big Fox Hunt, the soldier lads were looking the other way.

"Clear out of our hills!" Miners turning penitents loose were none too gentle. "Don't stop till you cross the state line." Penitents were trembling eager to be off.

"Head West. For the lumber camps." My Dad advised. "Try for a fresh start."

Ma's qualms over setting convicts free, Dad answered with a quick, "Reckon there's more guilty outside than in!" Chumley bribing lawmakers and same as burying men alive down his mine. And Easterners agrabbing public lands. Nobody heard of them getting locked up!

Shamrock, Coal Creek and a dozen camps set penitents galavanting down the hills. Over three thousand. The companies sent out posses. They spotted them in thickets by their stripes and up trees and they dragged them from mud caves and rivers and they brought them back. Friendly National Guards they replaced with State Troopers. There was talk of putting Dad and more leaders behind bars, but feeling ran too high.

Evenings now he gathered us around him by the fire, telling over his stories of the brave Hawkins clan. And we listened as never before, sensing something apressing on him beyond his words.

"Fox hunt, Jim!" Peg came to fetch him off. And Ma on her knees till daybreak. In the night I heard him creep in. And Ma, that quick of tongue, said not a word.

He crawled on the mattress by her. My empty belly pressed against the floor, I grew afraid.

We lived through the winter. In spring chain-gang stockades began emptying fast. Deeper than fear ran my pride in Dad. Who but him dressed a dead pig in convict stripes and left it by the mine shaft, a corncob in its mouth?

Unc Harry, stationed in a workedout runway hidden by a gunnysack, was giving men the signal as they passed down the mine, "Fox hunt tonight!" Word ran like brushfire through the hills. With morning, Inman, Piney Bend the same as Chumley Hollow found stockades empty. Miners at Tracy loaded a freightcar with penitents and guards and set it on the loose cavorting down the valley, headon for the state pen. And right thankful to get off with their skins whole!

Chumley, like the times before, had the penitents brought back. With our stomachs aswelling from hunger gas and Dad many months with scant work, we knew season for hunting fox once more was on us. Not the four-legged breed.

"By all the Saints!" She walked over by Dad's chair. "Get up! What's aholding you!" She nudged him, the sharpness we dreaded coming into her voice. "Water's getting that cold I'll have to be heating it over!"

He did not move. His full-blooded face was hidden under coal dust, only his eyes showing through. A body might tell a heap by Dad's eyes. A clear blue, most times they held a comeon dancing light. Not now. Something more than the overload of cornmeal gruel we had been living on through the winter was pushing hard against the pit of my stomach.

Dad stayed huddled by the fire, astaring at the coals. My brother and I had fetched them off the slag pile, good droppings thrown out with the bad—for how else was a miner's family to keep warm.

"Sue!" He called her from over his shoulder. "Send the young'uns to bed."

"Aw, Dad?" I moved closer.

"Off with you, Dolly!" He gave me a look that sent me moving fast.

"Sue—" From my pallet in the far corner it was hard hearing what he said. "If anybody knocks at our door tonight, don't put questions." He leaned closer. I strained my hearing. "If they ask for my clothes—"

I saw Ma drop into her chair.

"By all the Saints, woman! What's the good of turning 'em loose! Unless we give them clothes to shed their stripes? This time we ain't letting the posse spot them."

Sudden as a flash, Ma broke from Dad and ran over to grab his boots resting by the fire. She held them over the coals. "You shan't go!" Her eyes were like the time she had me spying on Parasidy. "I won't let you!"

Dad took a move toward her. "Sue Hawkins. Think what you doing." A move from her halted him dead in his tracks.

"Stand where you are! Hear me out—or—" She held his boots still nearer the fire. "So help me, I'll toss them in!"

Dad stood glaring at her, in his stocking feet. "Woman, you gone stark out of your mind?" I could see he was lashing back his temper. Once again he began to coax and reason. His only pair of boots. How'd he get to the mine tomorrow if she—

"How'll you get there?" Ma's voice caught, "if Chumley's gunmen shoot you down!"

Dad was looking full at her. "Sue Hawkins." He lowered his voice. "You make me shamed for you."

Ma dropped her eyes. But she kept her hands where they were, suspending his boots over the coals. I crept up to watch.

In an instant Dad had hold of her wrists, turning her about to get his boots free.

"You're hurting me!" Ma cried out.

I heard one boot drop, then the other.

With a laugh Dad pulled them on.

"Come on, honey." He put an arm around Ma. "No hard feeling. Give me a kiss for luck!"

She clung against him. "Oh Jim—they'll be the death of you!"

He raised his head. "Death?" Outside the wind was howling. "And what's this but death? Our kids going hungry, their eyes begging us for what we ain't got!" His whole frame shook. "What's this, Sue—but a coward's death?"

Ma wiped her eyes. "There's truth in you, Jim." But I knew what she was thinking—at least we had each other.

Dad braced his shoulders. "Sue, by tomorrow the hills will be ours again—free! Free as the good Lord made them!" He threw on his jacket, a high will in his face. Free and full of coal, he said, and something more about brotherhood.

As he took his gun, Ma broke down. "Jim, where you going?"

He gave her a hug, reached for the door. "It'll be like the sun coming out, Sue, after a long hard winter."

"Oh Jim—" She ran toward him.

But he was gone.

Ma stood for awhile, her lips moving. I lay in my corner watching her without her knowing, waiting my chance. After a time the wind grew less. Still praying, half moaning to herself, Ma set about fetching old things of Dad's and the boys, whatever she could find. Shirts she was intending to mend, with sleeves half gone or split across the back. A pair of overalls out at the knees. She stacked them up, took out her needle and sewed as rapidly as she could. I wondered where she found so much; Dad or somebody had been collecting against this night's call.

I was tossing about on my pallet, restless to be off. When Ma had her pile of clothes ready, she knelt down and folded her hands. Later she took her chair by the grate and sat waiting, listening for every footfall, her hands folded in her lap. The light from the fire played across her face.

There was no sound in our cabin, only the hushed wheeze of Hallie and my younger brother asleep. Caleb, Alec and Tim had already crept out. I slipped off my pallet and toward the back door.

Ma roused. "Who's there?" she called.

I stood without breathing. She peered out the front door, then went back to her place. I waited a good while before I dared ease the back door open and slip out. I put on my shoes outside and ran for the wood, heading for the spot I'd seen Old Harry disappear not long back. Keeping behind trees and out of sight, I ran till near the place, then crept up. I could make out the line of marching men. Like a whole forest they moved, stepping double time and close together. Each man toting his gun. Barrels shone like young silver birch under a moon. They had on their digging clothes, for the good reason whatever else they had was home on call, like my Dad's. Sneaking through the woods back of their ranks, I spied my brothers Caleb and Tim. Peg was stumping along in the rear. Wind had died down and moon rising over the valley. High Top seemed like dead.

Careful to make no sound, I ran along the woods edge trying to get level with my Dad. Pine needles made a soft foot bed. I spied him where I knew he would be, up front and swinging ahead fast. I wanted to step out into the clear and take him by the hand. I daren't, knowing they'd send me back.

The moon was climbing the hill fast, throwing light and shadow along our path. Marchers quickened their speed. Any minute now lookouts Chumley kept posted might spy us. In the trees over me a screech owl was hooting. I daren't stop long enough to throw a pine cone for hushing him.

Another half mile and the column took to cover.

"All right, men!" My Dad called a halt. We were in sight of Chumley Hollow.

There was a light in the lookout tower. Men shifted in their tracks, restless to be on. "What we waiting for?"

"For scouts sent ahead."

Miners leaned against pinetrunks or squatted on their haunches next the ground. Some moved back and forth till catbird set up a chatter. I clung tight behind a live oak, fearful one of the restless might happen on me.

At last a scout came running. "All clear!"

Dad grabbed him by his gallus strap. "You sure?"

"Sure as freedom!" he said.

We set out double time through the woods for the mine shaft.

"Halt!" The guard called down from his tower. He leveled his gun. "Who's there!"

Our miners kept on, I with them, as far as I dared. They reached the mine door. It was barred and locked fast.

"Joe Bartlett," Dad called up to the guard in his tower. "Throw down those keys! And don't make a move. We got you covered."

"Throw' em down!" Our miners closed in. "Throw 'em down before we come up and get 'em."

'Stand back!" Bartlett had his gun leveled at my Dad. "Let a man of you make a move, by God I'll blast your leader to hell!"

An angry muttering broke out. "Jim, give us the word? Let him have it!"

Dad signaled them quiet. "No hotheads here. You want they should fasten a murder charge on us!" He called up to the guard. "Now see here, Joe Bartlett. We're not wanting trouble. Just those keys. And damn fast!"

The company lowdown looking over the crowd, calculating. By now the night was clear, he could see to the last man.

"Stand back!" I knew him for a coward. Many a time we kids had jeered at him, perched up there in his box.

"Stand back!" Not a miner budged. His gun pointed straight at my Dad.

"Better stand back, Jim?" his mates cautioned. "He's a mean one."

My Dad stood his ground. "Throw down those keys! And be quick about it! Or we're acoming up!"

"Throw 'em down! We ain't got all night."

Barlett's gun barrel flickered, maybe his arm was wavering. "Make a move to come!" he shouted, "I'll fire."

My Dad laughed. "No go, Joe. You might get a couple of us. You can't get six hundred."

The guard didn't answer.

"Pull that trigger," Pegleg told him, "we'll get you along with the keys."

"All the same! I'll shoot!" His arm was wavering. "I'll shoot!"

"Then by all the Saints!" Dad said, "we're acoming up. We give you till ten." Slowly he began to count. "One—two—"

There was an angry shout. Two mine guards, roused from somewhere, had run up yanking their revolvers out of their halters. A squad of young miners pinned them fast. Their shots went wild.

My Dad had not moved from his place.

"Search 'em for keys!" he called back, his eye fastened on Joe Bartlett.

Our boys searched them. No keys on them.

"All right, Joe." Jim Hawkins warned the guard. "We're taking up the count. One—two—" The woods grew still. Not a miner moved. "Three—four—" Even the clouds on High Top stood still. "Five—six—seven—" Our ranks began to stir, ready, waiting. I wanted to run out into the open, throw my arms around my Dad, standing there so proud and certain, in the full line of fire.

"—eight—" he called.

"Throw the keys!" The miners yelled.

Jim Hawkins looked at the guard. "Your last chance Joe," he said. "Ready men? —Nine—"

With a curse, Potato Joe tossed down the keys.

Dad caught them in midair, ran to unlock the mine door. A crew of miners went down the shaft, guns primed. Others headed inside the stockade where the day shift was in bed. I heard a shot, then the sound of men running and shouts of "Hallelujah!" and "Praise the Lord!" I knew it the penitents, set free. They broke from the stockade and shaft and made for the woods. I knew it time I set out for home. All around me the forest was full of quick shuffling feet and low cries, and chains thrown off. Birds and woods animals were jumping about, startled out of sleep as if by a storm.

I ran straight as an arrow.

Before I reached Toewad I heard a sound that dropped me to my knees. The tramp of horses—heading for Penitent Hollow! Some sneak thief had got word to Chumley and the laws.

I started on the run to give our miners warning. But the horses and militia traveled faster than I could. They passed close by me, men in the lead cursing and urging their ranks on. . . . I kept on, my heart pounding my ribs. Oh dear God, let them be too late! Let Dad and our miners get a good start. And those penitents. Suppose it turned out as it had at Coal Creek? Our miners there had to barricade themselves inside the stockade. It had cost lives on both sides.

I ran till the ground burnt the soles of my feet. What if Dad or Caleb or Tim got hurt. What if they caught Peg—because he had to travel slow. This was what Ma had been a-fearing. . . .

I never knew how I made Chumley Hollow. Like a streak of lightning. Hard Flint and his troops had been too late. Penitents and miners had gone.

Troopers wasted time searching the mine and stockade. Then they set out on a man-hunt in the wood. Chumley's blood hounds, he had them trail convicts by last time, were snarling and pulling at their leash, ready to pick up the scent.

I ran home quicker than I had come. Outside our door stoop I hid for a moment in the shadow to catch my breath. I wasn't aiming to have Ma catch up with my running off.

While I was hiding, a shadow crept up to our back door. A penitent! In the dim light I made out stripes on his back.

He knocked. Twice long, once short.

Ma cracked the door. "Who's there?"

The man whispered something. My Ma shoved out a bundle.

"God bless you, missie." A hand reached out. "Where can I change?"

"Over there in the wood shed."

The shadow crept off.

Soon there was another, then another. All I might see was a hand, white or black, reaching out, and Ma handing bundles through the doorway.

I crouched in the darkness, shivering with chill, wondering when the laws would be quitting their man-hunt in the woods around Chumley and start making a house-to-house hunt in our patch, on the lookout for ringleaders. And my Dad not in his place.

At last I could stand it no longer. I went inside to Ma. "Dolly! You wicked child!" She gave me a rough shake. "Where have you been?"

But Ma had scant time to deal with me.

The knocks on our door kept on.

I dropped on my pallet. Hallie and near her my brother Clyde were lying on their backs, mouths open, fast asleep.

Toward morning I heard my Dad's low chuckle. He strired up the coals and called for a hot drink. Ma was crying with happiness. Our hills were free.

"And free we'll keep them." My Dad spoke like in church.

Peg's cars by mid-day were traveling up the tipple decked out like braggarts in convict stripes. Like sun dancing off our oaks and maple, penitents' shirts and pants flapped in the wind. Our Dads, called back to the pits, marched like to a picnic. And riding Peg's train, we carrot tops sang out to burst our lungs. Our Hollow never saw another pair of chained feet. The last echo of penitents' dirge faded from our hills. Ma made a kettle of dough-nuts and Dad fetched home cider and asked in the Hol-low for celebrating. We young'uns were allowed to stay up. Worn out with toasting and dancing the moon down the ridge, we gathered outside and my Dad raised a song from the Old Country:

> "Shoot me like an Irish soldier
> Do not hang me like a dog
> For I die for Ireland's freedom. . . ."

He sent the final word ringing along our Hollow. And the hills agiving it back. Long after, lying in the dark on my pallet, I thought I was still hearing the echo. Dad and Ma over in their bed were talking low, not to waken us children. Then all grew quiet. . . .

. . . . *chapter* 18 . . . .

As days passed, there proved no change in John. Not
until the sundown Mert came by to tell me our miners
were holding a gathering. "Pop thought you'd like knowing." He leaned against our doorstep, turning his mine
cap in hands still blackened with coal, for he had come
straight from the pit.

"A gathering?" Mert seemed waiting for me to speak up.

"Against rotten props." I glanced back over my shoulder, half fearful half hoping John might hear him. This
noon another brace of wooden beams had given way.
And a lucky thing for Tobey and Slim, for they had been
working that strip and just brought their lunchbuckets
over for a gab in Mert's alleyway. "We sat there, mouth
full of sandwiches, dropping open to hear the crash. The
whole ceiling! Then men started in acursing. 'We're a
pack of goldern fools!' And more, Dol, not bearing repeating. Timber's that rotten, Pop said, might as easy been
my alleyway. Or yours, Mert."

I was listening for some word from John.

"We reckon some laggards and weak-hearted among us. Pop was thinking you'd come, Dol? Tonguelash them into line."

Let me think it over, I said, knowing by the fury rising in me that I would go. Shades of our dead fathers routing penitents from our hills would rise and speak to us. And Seth's Dad and Elijah, and gentle-voiced Jake Valitsky, buried under coal.

Our miner's hall was already filled when I reached there, folk braced in windowsills. Men stepped aside to let me pass. It was hard making out faces, kerosene lamps give a fitful glow. Benches scraped as they rose in silence. Pop beckoned me to the platform. He stood by a long table hewn of our pine, the lamplight making his bristly grey hair sparkle and throwing his giant shadow across Old Glory behind him. When he took my hand in his strong one, giving me welcome, I remembered his long friendship with my Dad. And after the explosion his quieting arm as we waited in the downpour for word from the rescue crew. Till Clyde and then John came above ground.

Pop was smiling down at me, saying words I scarce took in. Thirty-seven years he had mined coal and never bad hurt—a record—then lost both sons down the pit. Looking up at him, I knew what I had to say was not alone for John but for Pop, and every breathing human in our patch. For who among us had not found the shadow of mine death across his doorsill.

I took firm hold of the table and turned to face them. Men like John, yet none so bonny. Searching, I found words from the Book. *Not death, but life!* Enough of dying and maiming. We must seize hold of more living. Not alone for ourselves and our children, but theirs after us. If only I could make them see it. And John. . . . From the Book other words came, or so it seemed. *From great evil, it is given man to wrest good.*

When I was done, the vote was quick taken. Miners came to press my hand, and their women who had grouped outside, and more than one not shamed to let me see their cheeks wet. And I felt among us new life aborning.

Pop McFever walked me home. "God has given you a rare way with words. Keep it by you, girl. Never abuse it."

I was anxious to get home. What good my gift of speaking out what all felt, unless John would hearken.

Granny met us on the doorstoop. "John has been like taken with fever. Ever since you went."

Through the night he kept saying words I could not make out, only my name.

"I am here, John." I knew I must not leave him again.

As he grew stronger, I undertook a bit of washing for bossmen's families, and single men brought me their clothes to mend. I stood my tubs out in the clearing, well beyond John's sight, fearing how he might take it. Not that I was not thankful, knowing it is not work that proves belittling, but how men view it.

My brother Tim, sending me what he could, wrote that Horace, his firstborn, had wandered down to the Gulf and shipped out on a steamer, the first Hawkins in four generations to let the sea win him back. I read Tim's letter over, thinking maybe young Horace right to get clear of the mine. When the sea took, it was quick and clean. I pushed the thought from me. Going over to John, I laid my hand on his shoulder, firm and hard. If cruel what I must do, he left me no choice.

"My Dad used to say, John. A true miner, so long as there is life in him, never gives in." I saw his fists grip the bed clothes, his face wrench as in pain.

"John, you are no quitter." I leaned down to brush the damp from his forehead, then closed the door after me, to let him have it out with himself.

When I came in, arms wet from suds, I found him lying with his sleeve across his eyes, his body shaking.

"Ma," Cindy whispered, "he caught on about the wash."

I sent Cindy outside.

"John?"

For the first time he put up his arms. "Dolly, Dolly, what's it come to!"

But I was crying more for joy. Me lying here, he said, and you slaving. "Dol, I've been a selfish beast."

"Hush, John." I held him against me. It might be a strange thing for another to make out. Burdened down as we were, I felt lifted up like on the mountain our first night. Maybe it takes sorrowing for a human to put true value where it belongs.

Coppy dumped firewood he had gathered for me on the hearth and stepped over to watch his father, propped up in bed, whittling a thick log. Cindy trailed after her brother. "What you making, Pops?"

My heart stood still.

"You blockhead!" Coppy whirled on his sister.

"Leave her be, son," John said quietly. He smiled at Cindy. "I am making a new leg. And high time, eh? And quit being the lazy-bones."

Cindy threw her arms about him as she used to, quick and free. "Now it'll be fun again—like before. And you can drive coal cars, same as Limpy."

Over her shoulder I saw John's face tighten. "Not so fast, bunny. More likely I'll be lending your Ma a hand at her tubs."

I came over by him. "Something will turn up soon at the mine." Nate had promised me.

"Nate!" John bit down on his pipe. We knew Nate's

breed. "Till hell's froze over there'll never be jobs enough
for the likes of us." He looked up, forcing a smile. "We'll
make out! That is, if you're not scorning my help?"

When Limpy had brought over the log and I found
what John was thinking to do, I had to step outside.
Proper wood it was, Limpy said, a midweight trunk of
good hard walnut that Pop helped him search out and
felled of a purpose, with girth a mite thicker than a man's
leg. John had fallen to work on it with a will, measuring
and shaping to size.

"Dol, how's for a drop of tea?" There was a bit of the
old John in his voice. Limpy was one of the few he felt
easy to have around. When tired from whittling, John
would turn on his side, our bed pulled near the window,
and stare up at High Top. Was she feeding him strength
too, I wondered. After awhile he would begin to fidget,
take up his boards and start to work, a grim set to his
mouth that I did not like, and again I did. Grey had come
out at his temples, and him not long past thirty. The
young hearty John Cooper free-swinging over our hills
with song and welcome for everybody, the John I had
first known and loved, was gone. In his place was a man
with puzzled stare and hard lines to his mouth, like a
man betrayed. But when his eyes fastened on mine, his
look was unchanged.

Before many days John had finished his work on the
pegleg and nailed on leather straps for fastening. As his
will gained, mine faltered. How was I to meet this for
him?

When young Tobey heard that all wanting was proper
handles, he traveled down to our County seat, and came
back with the fastenings, and a couple of new yarns about

the town. And Limpy came over to help John fit it into place.

After he left, John made me bolt the door. Sweat was coming out on his forehead. He swung himself out of bed on his powerful arms and lowered his good left leg to the floor. His grip around my shoulder, my arm around his waist, he took a step, grabbing hold of furniture or window sill, then another, that grim mocking set to his mouth. I tried not to watch him.

After a time I grew more used to seeing John hip-swinging around the room. And children have a way of making hard things easier.

John took to helping me, along with Coppy and Cindy after school was out, with cooking and wash. I hadn't the heart to cross him in it, for I knew him right. Man or woman, a body has got to feel of use. Take this from him, and he is better off dead. Give it back and there is nothing a person can't go through. If not by himself.

Nights, lying in the dark with John's arms around me, it was almost like before. Yet the thought nagged my sleep: maybe he still wished himself down there with Jake?

When Mert brought us word they had won a repair crew for props, John dismissed it with a gruff, "That's fine!" He kept his eye on the fire, fighting down the thought between us. For us, five months late. But for them—all our young folk in the camp—we were glad. Even little lads running about our patch were spared going through what John had. As for our boy, we were keeping him clear of the mine.

How high must we reckon in mangled bodies, I fell to wondering, for each step forward our miners had made?

Against powerful odds. And little the world beyond our hills knew or cared.

Hearing Mert or Tobey clumping home free and easy in their mine boots, the angry betrayed stare would fasten on John's face. I began to fear we must find us a life elsewhere. John refused to venture beyond our stoop. Of an evening he might come out by me to watch the day fade or moon rise. Sometime of a bright morning he took the sun behind our house. Nothing more. Not even my plans for a spring garden could presuade him, for there was scant digging or weed work he could manage as yet.

"John, swing us a tune?" neighbors asked. His features would knot up. "Give the thing away, Dol! I never want to touch it again."

I kept his music box hidden. Lucinda Cooper, John's Ma, had played it as a girl, handed on to her from her Grandpappy who had turned it himself. It had a rare winsome tone. In time folks knew better than coax John for music, but let neighbors come by, somebody must begin talking about the mine. With a glance at John their words trailed off. Yet what else is there to talk about in a mine camp? Borning and dying and the mine, who's sparking who and the mine, the cost of vittles and the mine. Wherever you might turn, this way or that, it was the dead coal face astaring at you. When you married you took its grit into bed, when you died, carry it with you below ground. Man or woman, it was the same. John and every digger in our Hollow carried its marks under his skin.

If John was to throw off his old life, start anew, we had to move on. Seeking and turning in my mind, I lay through the small dark hours before morning. Where might we

go—to my sister, Hallie? A crippled man was little use
on a farm. My brother Tim, mining. Clyde, off at war.
Where on God's green earth could we go?

"Dol, we come of pioneering stock. And see what it's
come to!" John was shaking his fists at our lines of wash.
We had finished a huge one and hung it back of our
cabin. "Scrubbing other men's dirty wash. It's a hell of a
way to be spending our lives!"

I dropped onto a bench, not knowing what to answer.
John was right. But where under God's heaven was there
a place for the likes of us? Who'd be wanting us?

I kept my eyes down so John might not be reading the
bitter thought in them.

"Dol, let's clear out of this hole!"

I glanced up at High Top. Leave our valley? . . .
Limpy's cars were rumbling up the tipple. The same I
hearkened to since a child. And the day John came.
Where'll we go, I asked myself. What can we do?

"Dolly!" John limped over by me. "Look at me." He
held up his arms, powerful still. His great fists knotted.
"From the knees up—" His words came from between his
teeth. "I am good a man as ever, ain't I?"

"That you are." I rose to face him. "Better." It was
God's truth.

He dropped his arms. "Then find me a man's work."

I walked the hills, his words staring at me from the
dark. A man's work. Where might we be finding it? What
place, not alone in a coal camp but anywhere, for a six-
foot coaldigger brought low by rotten props? However
was I wresting a job for my man?

John and I lay awake figuring, his head on my shoulder, like before. Nights it was like I had my young full-

hearted John back. Our love would go through us like up the mountain.

Whoever might be giving us a second look, John said, not of pity or a handout but justice and fair play? A man's work.

John's plan was to hie us out of Cumberland mine country, aiming on Oklahoma or land further west. Many from our hills had moved on, timbering and prospecting. John thought his half-uncle in Tulsa might find work in a lumbering camp, asawing up trees. Once settled in the wood, his powerful shoulders at one end of a two-hand saw and me with my extra strong-given grip at tother, John said we'd made a team to watch. Nobody need be making excuse for us. . . . Thought of leaving our Hollow was gnawing at my sleep. I hid it, not wanting to hold John back. He felt like a man freed from prison, he told me, and fresh adventuring ahead. "We'll raise our boy to a trade out in the open," he said, "like it was meant to be, under God's sun."

John sent Coppy down to watch for mail. No word came. At last our letters to John's Uncle drifted back, marked "Person Unknown." John tore them across and dropped them into the fire. He limped into our room and closed the door behind him. I put on my good dress and went down to see Nate.

He came around his desk, his bead eyes screwed up in welcome. "Why Dolly, it's a pleasure!"

I had small time for trifling. "What about your promise? Where's the job for my man?"

I saw him glance behind us, to make sure his door was shut. "Trust me, Dolly. These things take time." He made a quick reach for my hand. "Now if you—"

I flung off his grip, for the idiot was making to hug me. Smiling, he stepped closer. "Now, Dol, you're a pretty minx. Come, think a bit! We might do a lot for each other, eh?"

I let him have it hard on the cheek. "And make no mistake, John Cooper is still man enough to sock the daylights out of you!"

Of this I said nothing to John, but it gave me more reason for welcoming sister Hallie's letter urging us to come for the summer on her farm. "Besides hankering to see you," she wrote, "we got an extry big crop coming in and labor short. You and your young'uns be right handy picking and hoeing. And plenty for your man peeling fruit and greens for canning. We divy up what we fix, give you enuf to take you through the winter."

Mert offered to borrow his Uncle Silas' wagon to drive us over, and John agreed, knowing me set on making the trip.

Toewad gave us a send-off our Hollow was bound to remember. And John took out his music box and tuned her up. He sat on our stoop, our last night before setting off, a blanket across his knees, plucking the strings like old times while I called the turns.

> *Boys, git you gals*
> *Treat 'em right!*
> *We gona dance here*
> *Till broad daylight!*

Such cavorting, our men and girls outdid themselves, knowing they'd never be having another music-maker equal to John.

Pop, Mert, and other lads kept coming for me to take a turn, let somebody else call, but I liked it better where I was, with John fiddling like his life depended on it.

"Go on with you, Doll!" he said. "Go, turn a fling! Give the lads a treat." But Seth and others saw my mind made up, and they let us be.

I sat backways in the cart as we traveled down to my sister Hallie's, keeping an eye on old High Top, so long as she was there to see. John kept his hand over mine, guessing what was passing in me. "We'll be back, come fall," he said.

It proved good to feast my eyes on Hallie and get my fill of her noisy brood. Hawkins the lot of them, with carrot hair. But Tom Faulks, her man, was a squeeze-penny mole grumbling poor as the land he was ahoeing. Summer done and canning through, John was over-ready to be getting back to our Hollow. We bid goodbye to Hallie and her kin and started homeward, going into Forked Oak to wait for Mert to arrive in his cart.

We were footing it down Main Street toward the depot, John moving pretty nimble on his wooden prop, not minding strangers so much, Cindy and Coppy racing ahead to peek in store windows. I had a big canvas bag on my shoulder. Along the walk came a man dressed tall and fancy with pearl buttons on his vest. He stopped short when he saw us. I hoped John had not noticed. The man wore a tall silk hat, like I had seen in the papers on dudes of a Sunday. He stood there, atwirling his gold watch chain, his eye on John who had stopped to rest against a wall, hat turned upward in his hand while he mopped his forehead.

"Look-a-here, my good man!" The stranger came over to John. "You can't beg in my town!"

"Watch your tongue, mister. Ain't nobody begging in your ornery town!"

I could see John's fists aching.

"We don't allow it." The man fiddled his chain.

"And who's asking you!"

"We don't allow begging," he was talking to John, making out I wasn't there. "Here, my good man." He drew his hand out of his vest pocket. "Here's a quarter for you. But I'm sorry, you'll have to leave town."

"You lowdown blithering idiot!" John knocked his piece of silver on the ground.

"My man's no beggar!" I leaped for him. "He'd not ask a drink of water from the likes of you. For much I'd blast your puny soul to—" Well, Dolly Hawkins told him plenty.

"You'd better watch what you're saying, woman!" He turned on me then. "I am the mayor of this town. For much I'd clump you both into jail."

"Oh, so you're the mayor!" I had a firm hold on his vest. "It's you and your kind put my man in the fix he's in. You and your puking Midas breed! You kept decent laws off the books of this state to run the mines proper. What you care if there's rotten props! You dare talk of begging, you -* * *-!! You ——!!!"

John pulled my arm. "Come on. There's a smell of skunk around here."

"Skunk!" I spat on the ground. "Alongside this stink-weed, a polecat's fresh-smelling like a baby."

By now a crowd was gathering around us. Nobody would help the red-faced mayor. They faded out on him, except a law he hailed on the corner. They took us into a grocery store to wait while His Honor went off to hunt up his sheriff.

Looking about, I took note of a sign over the store: *Hanks Grocery.*

"This Mayor Hanks' grocery?" I asked the boy clerk.

"Sure is, ma'am."

I took another look around. He is getting the people both ways, I thought, coming and going. "And these here eggs? They're Mayor Hanks' too?"

"Sure are, ma'am."

I saw John's fists aching and eyes burned up. "Well then. I reckon you and me, John, we're needing us some eggs?" He nodded, a gleam in his eye.

We took a handful of eggs and we started knocking the shells against our foreheads and counter and tossing them down. Soon the place was reeking. Plenty of these eggs were not so fresh as Mayor Hanks made out.

When we started throwing eggs the guard started for us. With a whoop John let him have one square on the jaw. With a yelp and egg running off him, the guard made for the door. I gave him a farewell token on the seat of his pants. Arms thrown out he looked like a scarecrow running up the street.

"Come out, lad." The clerk had dodged behind the counter. We were not aiming any his way. He kept peeking at us tossing eggs, then dropped from sight. Coppy and Cindy ran in. "What you adoing, Ma?" They joined us aknocking eggs on first thing handy and letting them drop.

"There now, Dol. Reckon we had us enough chicken eggs!" We leaned back to laugh.

"What in thunderation!" Mayor Hanks came with his

laws and a crowd trailing them, laughing and holding
their noses over the stink and mess from walls to sawdust
floor. Mert drove up in his cart and hearing our story
they turned on the Mayor and he let us go and we started
home in Mert's wagon. John was laughing as I had not
heard him since his hurt.

News traveled on slow foot into our hills, it was late November when Mary came running up our path waving a letter from her Chattanooga kin. "The war is over!" We had a real Thanksgiving, knowing Clyde on his way home. I roasted a wild duck Tobey shot for us, opened a jar of candied .yams brought from Hallie's and Mary fetched cranberries from town.

With the New Year and Mary home for the holidays, my brother came. "Sis?" When I felt his arm about me, I knew things between us were like before his trouble. He tried not letting John see his shock at the change in him. When alone with me he said, "Dol, if only I had been here." He took over his old room and brought me his Bobtail, envelope unopened. When I spoke of taking out board and him keeping the rest he turned me aside, with a look toward Coppy and his sister playing on the hearth.

Eyeing their skinny bodies I knew him right, though John would not be relishing food he had no part in earning.

Of Sal, my brother and I spoke little. "She is gone. Reckon that settles it," he said, knowing it could not end with this.

Mary, held up by a rare snowstorm that blocked our roads, was unable to return on time for school. Our Hollow children made the most of it, sledding the day through in old crates and iron tubs down our white hills. My brother turned restless. "How about my borrowing Unc Silas' wagon and going down for Mary? If you think proper."

I took him by the shoulder. "You set tongues wagging about Mary, I'll bash your teeth in."

Clyde stood looking at me, then without speaking went outside to help Cindy and her brother make a snow hut. All Sunday he made figures in the snow, seemed he could not rest, filling our clearing with snow animals till even the children tired on him and went back to their sledding. He was still at it and dark gathering, when looking out I spied Mary by her bright red jacket working her way through the pine up our slope. With a whoop our children surged down on her. I saw Cindy point toward Clyde, and Mary look up, then quicken her pace. She gave him both hands in greeting, before hurrying on with Cindy to our place.

As our hearth fire flickered across my brother's eager face, then hers, I grew sore troubled. Mary's high color might be from the cold, but not the heady lilt in her glance that in spite of her kept going to Clyde's, then darting off.

"Mary, let me see you home?" Clyde asked.

As if she had not rightly heard him, Mary turned to our nine-year-old boy, her voice so low I scarce made out her words. "Coppy, walk me down the ridge?"

I kept my tug on Clyde's sleeve until they were gone. He moved off from me and went into his room, I following, not yet certain how war had changed him. He was putting things into a bag.

"Clyde, where you going!"

"To find Sal. End things between us."

We were seeing Clyde off when Limpy came by with word for John. "Witt is needing a helper, come Monday."

John pulled upright. "Dol, he means me!" Witt ran our Hollow blacksmith, where miners brought their picks to sharpen and farmers their harrows and plows.

"Don't pay much," Limpy said, a job in true for a learner. "Witt was doubting if he should be offering it to you. Told him I'd see."

John swung to his feet. "It's a job, ain't it!" They started off, Limpy swinging out his pegleg with long-accustomed speed, John still clumsy but with head up.

Soon I heard a restless drubbing on the sill and John stood there, something like his old grin lighting his face. "Ev'en, Ma'am. Got a horse needing a shoe? Maybe a dull shovel?" He doffed his cap and sent it whirling by me onto the table. "Dol, look me over, I'm a working man!"

At his shout Cindy and Coppy dropped their game to come running and John rubbed their heads together, smiling as he hadn't since his hurt. "From now on, look for your Pops under the spreading chestnut tree!" And it proved a sight worth the trip down to Witt's for seeing, John standing by the forge in his black apron, his big shoulders and arms swinging hammer down on anvil to make the woods ring, and sparks flying high as Coppy's bright head.

My brother, gone a fortnight, came back without glimpse nor trace of Sal. "I'd help you out if I could," her brother Seth told him. "Reckon Sal is rid of us for keeps."

Clyde grew more restless, and Mary's visits to us rare. "What's teacher mad at Unc for?" Cindy asked me. "Why, the minute he comes, she makes off!" Keep your silly tongue quiet, I told her, and quit making up things.

With the spring thaw and roads clear, Sal blew into our Hollow on the March wind, tossing her laugh and skirts, like always, and handing around chocolates for the young'uns. I was outside brushing our path when she came by and I asked her in, for there was no pretend in how anxious I was over seeing her. She was decked out in silk with a fur piece round her neck and hair stiff-curled, but her face was not happy.

I put on the kettle and pushed over a chair. "You came back. Why?"

She was looking at me sideways. "Maybe I got honing for the Hollow?" She glanced around my kitchen, then back at me. "Or maybe I got word from Clyde?"

I held onto my chair. "Sal, let's talk plain. What you wanting of him?"

She stood up and without answering me began moving about, picking up things and putting them down.

"You've come back to stay?"

She whirled, her eyes scornful. "In this dump!" Slim was waiting for her down the road in his car.

"Why'd he bring you? What's he thinking you are after?"

Sal's face quivered. "My share of things Pa left me." Her voice dropped. "Maybe something more."

I was beginning to tremble. Big Seth was a true man, I said. "And what more you wanting?"

Sal was looking directly at me. "You can't stop me." I knew she spoke true. I had not been able to hinder her taking Clyde then, how could I now, and she by law his wife.

The sun was edging down the ridge, my thought racing in circles. Soon Clyde would be home from the pit. Was it better he face her, here and now, or should I try sending her off. . . . Sal was pacing back and forth. "Slim can give me near about everything I want. He's asking me to marry him, legal." She stopped, her laugh rough. "And big fool I am, I have to wake in the night remembering Clyde's jolly laugh, his way of making love—"

"Stop it!" I pushed to my feet. "Clyde's changed."

"A lot you're knowing!"

"You are not wanting him," I said. "Not on the level. You deserted him a long ways back. Now Clyde's been searching you out. You know what for? To be rid of you."

She tossed her head, unbelieving. "Let Clyde tell me that!"

I saw my brother come in behind us, filling the doorway. "Sal?" He stared like at one long dead, his face beneath its coal soot a strange mixup of feelings.

She made a slow move toward him. "Hello, Clyde boy."

He remained by the sill, his eyes taking her in. I started to leave, but he motioned me not to go.

Sal walked over, her eyes flirting up at him. "Clyde, hon, say you glad to see me?"

His face was unyielding. "Dol told you true. I am wanting my freedom."

She rubbed against him, her smile abegging. "Come

on, big boy. Get this black off your face, then greet me proper."

Clyde's voice was rough. "Let's admit it, Sal. It was no good." He took her arm. "For us both, a mistake."

Sal reared her head, no longer smiling. "So you are wanting your freedom? Who is it, that skinny-legged, school-teaching—"

"You knew it all along," Clyde broke in on her. "I never kept it a secret." His grip was making her wince. She jerked her arm free and moved off, Clyde following. "We are no good for each other, Sal. Never were."

She whirled to stare at him, eyes narrowed. "I guess this does it. From now on, I'll see you like this. Grimy, blackfaced. A plain dirty clout!" She turned to leave.

"Not so fast!" Clyde took her by the wrist. "You and I got papers to sign." He walked her down the path to where Slim was waiting. As I watched him stride along, shoulders back and the minx by him nigh running to keep up, I knew that in my brother Mary Laird would be getting a man full grown.

Soon back, Clyde swung me to the ceiling, as John used to do. "Dol, nobody can be begrudging me a talk with Mary this night?"

Nobody human, I said. Let me send Coppy down to fetch her.

"A lot of women's foolishness! I'm going myself. What we got to be hiding?"

Maybe you can be flying in the face of Hollow opinion, I said. "You wanting the Board calling Mary up for a hearing? Then do it my way."

Sobered, Clyde went into his room to wash up. Before he was done, Coppy was back with Mary.

"Dol, what is it?" She hurried to me. "Is anything wrong?"

"Wrong!" I threw my arms around her. "It's not mine for the telling. Only that I'm happy."

My brother's door opened. "Mary?"

I could feel her trembling. He came by us on the hearth. "Mary, I am free."

As she turned, I saw the wondering joy in her face. I took Coppy and Cindy into our room and closed the door.

Our Hollow had taken on a silence heavy with sounds
wanting of men atramp to the pit, nor Limpy's cars rumbling up the tipple. Our mine whistle god had lost its
voice. When Coppy asked me why, I had only words
Dad had given me those times we had no coal for our
grate. "Reckon we've gone and dug too much coal," Dad
said.

The quiet in our Hollow leadened men's faces, made
even our young'uns fitful in their play. Miners wiped their
shovels clean and stood them with their picks, behind the
door. Home-fixing chores used up, they hung around
stoops or down at Pluckme, talking over bad times that
had crept like cornblight from the lowlands into our hills.
"If it ain't war," Pop McFever said, "then it's the scourge
that comes after."

John watched my brother stack his pick and shovel. He
lowered his glance to his hands, working open and shut,

his jaw set against knowing Witt soon must be closing his forge. I put on my sunbonnet and went in search of Mary.

"Hiya, Sis!" She hustled off the last of her scholars and came toward me. "What's up?" Since marrying Clyde, Mary had moved in with us, but only down here could we talk undisturbed.

"John is needing a job. Fast. Not alone the money." I told her of John's yen to go to Oklahoma, and work in the woods.

"Dol, you won't leave us?" She drew me over to a fallen log and sat facing me, her eyes more angry than pleading. "Now see here, I won't let you! Maybe I never told you, but all my life I've wanted a sister. Now I have, you think I am letting you run off! Besides, it doesn't make sense." With a sudden move down the log toward me, she took my hand. "Clyde and I have talked it over. We want to stay on together, you, John and the children, and ourselves."

Who had said anything about leaving? But word had come that men were felling trees on the other side of our mountain and sawing up logs into railway ties.

"Isn't it too far?" Mary asked. "How can John make it?"

"We will make it."

"We?" Mary's glance was sharp. "You know as well as I, on such jobs they don't take women."

"They are starting in tomorrow. Providing—?"

Mary was laughing now. "Sure, you don't need to be asking, I'll keep an eye on Cindy and Coppy." Arm under arm, we started home.

With sunup I was tramping over the ridge in search of lumbering posts. John, when I left, was readying a secondhand batch of saws we had given our last savings for.

The first bossman I asked to hire me, laughed in my face. "A woman hacking trees!" He guffawed till the timber rang. With scant time for relishing a good sass, I made for the next post. While the sun crept up, I trekked from one camp to the next. I took off my shoes, burning sore as my temper, and walked barefoot. I was not going home till I could tell John we had us a place. Nearing a camp I put on my shoes, smoothed my braids and walked in proper.

In myself I was acursing my feet and bosses and rotten props.

Around sunset I came on a crew working a buzz-saw and farther off, another chopping and felling trees. I asked for the chief, and a fellow shouted something and pointed over his shoulder up the trail. By the sun, it was near quitting time. I sat down on a log to wait. Ever see a pine wood burnished along its trunks by a sun going down fast? A sight to hearten the eye. I took it a good omen. The last log felled for the night, a great stillness came down on the forest. Two of the men started over to me.

"A pretty minx, eh?" The husky fellow nudged his companion.

"Drop it!" his mate said. "She ain't that kind." Pulling off his cap, the man said, "Lady, don't be getting the wrong idea of us." He pointed at my dusty shoes. "Looks like you traveled a right smart piece this day. What can you be wanting, ma'am? What can we do for you?"

I stood up and dusted off my jacket. "I am hunting a job. For me and my man."

They looked at one another, then off at the trees. "You know they ain't in the practice of hiring women?"

"I am uncommon strong." I proved it by lifting one of their logs, singlehanded. Loggers gathered around to whistle and clap their boots.

"And how come your man don't hunt for himself?"

Before I was done telling them, they sent a crewman to fetch the Chief. "Harry is the right kind," they said. He proved a leathery rawboned hulk of man with eyes pale and friendly like a child's. Backed against a tree, listening to me, he kept pulling his cap off and on with a worried flip.

"Don't make sense, woman lumbering!" He glanced around at his men who were urging, "Give them a week's tryout. What's to lose?"

Harry Law pulled his cap down toward his eyes. "All right, ma'am. A week's try. But ain't it a far piece for a lame man to travel?"

"We'll manage." As I turned for the road home, my sore feet took on new life. I ran through the wood, just looney enough to hug pine trunks as I passed by, saying, "John, we found it! A man's work!" Now I understood why I had been granted this extra power in my arms. Hadn't I helped lift a coal car as a child? Wrestled and thrown lads beyond my size, until the brag of Toewad camp? In those far-back days, my strength had seemed to no purpose in a girl, only Peg sensed it given for some reason.

When I reached our path, John hurried out to meet me, his face lighting up. "You had me bothered, coming late. Any news?"

I leaned up to kiss him. "Yes, John. Good news. Come inside."

After I had told them, and Mary, Clyde and the children gone to bed, John had me tell him over. "Kind of hard believing." He braced his shoulders. "How far did you say it was?" He leaned closer, studying my face, his grown doubting. "Dol, you're holding something back?"

I moved my chair nearer his, so we might talk low. "Remember the evening before we left for Hallie's?" We had gone part way up High Top, just the two of us, taking leave of our hills. Once at Hallie's, we had a notion we might not be coming back. John had not intended me to help him up the slope, but truth was he'd had to lean on me heavy. "Remember?" I said, "how easy it proved."

His grip on mine tightened. "Because you were set on it, I gave in to you." He let go my hand, his jaw firming. "Three miles? I'll make it." He pushed to his feet. "Woman, what you looking at me for? Reckon I'm getting handy enough on my new leg. Uphill or down."

"And sure you are, John." God help me quieten his pride. "We'll make it."

He lowered his head, bitter things pouring from him I'd thought done with long since. "Go off, Dolly!" he pushed aside my hands. "Find you a man that's some count." Seth, any man in the Hollow, would consider himself lucky.

I fastened my arms around his waist. Next my throat I could feel his heart pounding. "You had no call to say it, John." I made him rest on the bed by me, eased his forehead. "You know I love you."

In the darkness of our room I felt him quieten. "God knows I don't deserve it." A big lummox stumping along, bearing down on his woman. Folk astaring.

Hush, John. Deep in the wood nobody would see us. "Look at the strength in your arms. Can you be wasting it?"

He rose to stump back and forth, like a person distracted. "What about pride? Ain't I a shred left me?"

I waited, feeling after my words. Of the right kind, plenty. We had to place ours deeper than most. I went over by him. What of Coppy? We had vowed, come hell or high water, he would get his chance at learning, keep shet of the mine.

John left me and went into the kitchen. He stood looking down at our children asleep on their cots. He stood for a long time, then came back.

"Better pack our lunch. I'll get the saw ready."

Oaks and maples around our cabin were beginning to stir when we left, and the first light darting up behind the ridge. I put our wedge in my overalls pocket, hung broad ax and lunch box at my waist. John was carrying our two-handled saw, with one arm free to grip about my shoulder, as need came.

We crept by our children, still asleep, and stepped outside. Sparrows and robins were jumping about in the dew, on a worm hunt. Over High Top our Thunder Bird was circling. Every quarter of a mile John had us stop for a rest. Once in the forest and going uphill, he had to let me aid him. Woods were fresh, after a night rain, and sky streaked with primrose. As the light gained, a meadow lark began singing. The last part of our journey, I seemed to be wanting for breath. John poured me a drink from the jar of coffee we had brought along, then wet his handkerchief in the creek and ran it over my face and hands. "Dol, you see how it is. Won't you go back?" The wet was running down his forehead.

I downed the last of my coffee and took up our wedge and lunchbox. "John Cooper, you are daff! We are almost there."

We found the post empty, as I had planned, with a chance to settle in before others came. John rested against an oak, for his leg was hurting, I on the ground by him. We could hear the birds wakeful, moving above us in the branches.

"It is going to be a good life, John."

Harry Law and the boys gave us a hearty welcome. After the lads felled the trees, we were to saw them into railway ties. "Not enough buzz-saws in this goldern camp to go round," Harry said, "so yours will come handy. Though I reckon I warned you? Blasted company don't pay nothing for this work. A dime a tie."

John lifted our handsaw into place. "We will make out." And soon Harry was saying there was not another team to match us along the whole range. He never had reason to complain of us, or make excuse. Ring of axes on timber made a rousing song in our ears, like the crash and tearing of giants as they fell, and our handsaw abuzzing back and forth between us with a singsong atune to John's strumming.

Through summer and early winter John and I tramped to the wood, and in time I garnered strength in my arms to outequal a man's. With the sun glowing down through the leaves, our saw and earth humming, John grew more like himself. We felt things moving to plan: Coppy finishing next year as far as our Hollow went, and Mary writing her people in Chattanooga to see if he might be coming there, earn his keep tending furnace and neighbors' yards and so make it through high school. Our Coppy was a quiet lad with a knack for figures. We aimed to get him training in mechanics. For this he must leave the Hollow, for Cap'n Chumley and his friends on the School Board said what's the use of fancy courses for boys going down the pit? Their own lads went off to boarding school. And next we heard Chumley's boy, Chick, was tearing down the mountain in his opentop car, roaring drunk. Anything beyond fourth grade in our Hollow was nonsense, according to the Board, but we had been pushing it higher as every few seasons our miners added a bit to their pay and so not needing their boys to leave off their lessons to dig coal. In Cindy's time we might hoist it to eighth, and our girl end up with a rural teaching license, like Mary. So I was dreaming, like as not sassing fate, for with spring the thing John and I had been guarding against had happened. I was with child.

When Mary, her face aglow, brought me word of her coming child, I summoned such warmth as I had in me, my own bittering hidden.

"We timed it well, don't you think?" Her laugh had a new softness. She would finish out the school term, have her baby in late summer, go back to her desk in the fall. "With the mine running slow—you know how it is, Dol. Besides, I love my school."

Mary's joy forced my thought inward. Hers was the welcoming we had given our son and daughter, not the worrying twisted thing I was sheltering now. Like Jacob in the desert, I wrestled with my secret. What of drugs Granny or Sarah might brew me? Seeking a hidden way out, I kept my knowledge from John. If there was to be sin in this, let it rest on me alone.

Tramping with John to the wood, I found the pain in my side growing heavier. I felt my knees give and the ground rising to meet me.

"Dol, you did wrong." John was bending over me. "You did wrong, keeping this from me."

Stooped on the dull earth, we faced what until now had meant joy between us, in our throat a taste of gall. John was for turning homeward.

"You must go no more to the wood."

Then, I said, I could not answer for what might be happening.

He took me by the wrists. "I'll have none of that. You hear me? You might do harm to yourself."

Looking at him, I knew it beyond me, for this child not yet moving in me, he too was bone of our bone, part of our flesh. And was I God, to decide the giving or withholding of life?

"We can't stop from the wood now. What of Coppy?"

John's face was working. "I'll come to the wood alone."

I rested my head in the grass. Catbirds and warblers were jumping around in a maple overhead, squirrels dashing by us. Just a few more weeks, I said, thinking of the extra silver I might be dropping into the blue crock on our shelf, for Coppy a suit of city clothes. Let me come for another few weeks, it could do no harm. What was passing in me was not a sickness. My pioneer Granny, giving birth to thirteen children, had taken but a day each time off her feet.

He dropped his head. "Ours is heavy, demanding work. By rights, not for a woman."

"Once I feel life, John, I will keep my word, stop coming to the wood."

The time was soon on me and I had to watch John set out alone. How he made it, only his drawn face and dragging step at night told me.

"Harry gave me a new lad for pardner, Cort Jones."
John drank his tea in hasty gulps. "We made out fair.
Eighteen tire." John and I had done nearer thirty, but
with take-in wash I was angling for, we should even up
a fair part of the difference.

"Things picking up around the mine, Clyde says." I
brought the booties I was knitting by him near the grate.
"Like as not, Witt soon wanting you back."

John turned his glance from mine. "I know what you
are thinking, Dol. You are wrong! I'll manage to keep on
in the wood." He fashioned a cane from a hickory limb,
then a second, using them to swing a good part forward
by his shoulders, to ease some of the body weight off his
hurt leg. In the next weeks I saw his cheekbones growing sharper, his glance take on a fierce brightness. I
rubbed his aching chest and back with Granny's herb oil,
and though in me words were crying out, *Quit, John,
before too late!* I held them back, knowing them useless.

When the old scar below his hip turned an angry red
I could keep still no longer.

"Quit now?" John, laughing up at me, turned on his
side to still my hands. "Don't you see it, girl! Coppy will
get his schooling. Our young'un acoming. I am beginning
to feel once more a man." For John was hoping to give
our newcomer double measure, redeem our first begrudging. And Cindy shooting up spindly and winsome
for her ten years, had taken to seaming baby hubbards,
shy and rejoicing as if the baby might be her own. Coppy
kept funning at her, then toward the last got out his hobby
horse to spread on a fresh coat of paint. "For whichever
baby gets here first, Ma, yours or Aunt Mary's!"

"Like as not they'll be born to a minute. Twins like."

Granny Morse hobbled over to her place by our fire, pulling her shawl tighter across her sagging bosom, for midsummer chill had come on us early. "In such cases," Granny was looking at my brother, "Sarah and I'll have our hands overfull. So Clyde lad, hold yourself ready to be lending us a hand."

At his startled "Not me!" John threw back his head and let his laughing pour out, even Mary joining in, for it was rare chance we had to make my jokester brother's ears burn.

John's side grew worse from his forced walking, the old scar breaking open. He had to quit the woods. Just for awhile, he said.

"And sure, any time you wanting, job's awaiting!" Harry Law, his rawboned face redder than ever, put an awkward hand behind the jar on our mantel. "Something the boys asked me to leave you, ma'am. With their respects." He thrust a lump of bills on the mantel, yanked on his cap and vanished before I could thank him.

Our second boy we named for his father, as planned from the day Coppy was born. With his wee mouth burrowing against me and the children pressing around, eyes aglitter, I felt my bittering give way and something akin to our first child's welcoming. When John thought me asleep, he felt gently of little Jack's limbs, testing out their young strength. *He will never lose them down a coal mine.*

Harry and some of the crew walked over the ridge to gape and marvel at Jackie, like none had seen a human baby until now, only bearcubs and young of the forest. "Spot this mite of paw! What a grip!" While Jackie swung onto his thumbs, John lifted him level with his shoulders.

"Knock me down for a woodpecker!" Harry rubbed his knuckles in glee, not knowing all babies start off with this power, monkeylike, in their grip. "He'll toss giant oaks like broomstraws!"

After Mary's boy arrived, our place took on a fulsome noisy air.

"Dol, better have Limpy dump a coal car alongside our house!" Clyde was blustering proud-like about our jammed kitchen.

In Ma's time, I reminded him, we managed eight in one room! But seeing the longing in Mary's eyes, before she dropped them, I said, "Maybe you will be asking Nate now for a place of your own?"

Mary put her hand over mine. "Let's stay together."

Unable to bear weight on his leg for any stretch, John was grateful for occasional days in Witt's shop. In off hours he shaped useful things for our needs, or a neighbor's. With spring he would be ready, he said, for the woods.

March thaw gave way to April, things full greening, and John no better. "Likely by June," we said. Once more the cloud no bigger than a man's palm was troubling my sleep. John made the rounds to nearby farms, but for a lamed digger odd jobs proved scarcer than redbird in winter. Of an evening, when not coaxed into raising a dance tune or song by our fire, John whittled bits of wood life for our babies to play with: soon our mantel was overflowing with bobtail rabbits, bluejays and squirrels, winsome critters till I noted John had made all of them flying or racing, with overstrong wings or legs. One he worked longer on was a Thunder Bird making to leap skyward.

"I kind of fancy it, don't you, Ma?" Coppy and I were making our weekly trip to Pluckme, Coppy toting home taters, cereal and fatback while I strove to wangle a bit more credit from Nate.

"Hm-m, a big lad!" Nate stepped in Coppy's way. "Taller'n his Ma. Must be nigh fourteen?"

"Not till a year, come May." I moved nearer our boy for I knew Nate, sniffing like a hound dog at young blood for the mine.

"How things going for you, Dolly Cooper?" Nate kept his glance on Coppy.

"We manage."

"Hm-m." He edged closer to the boy. "Ready for a job soon?"

Coppy flushed. "Why, no sir."

"Our boy's going on with his schooling." I had firm hold of his arm now, pride in spite of me raising my voice.

"Mechanics!" Nate blew out his lungs. "I'm surprised at you, Dolly Cooper, I am for a fact. Putting crazy notions in the boy's head!" He turned aside. "High-falutin' notions you'll not be acarrying out."

I hurried Coppy out of Pluckme toward our path. "Pay no mind to him. Long-neck fool!" I walked the lad home fast, out loud wondering how much longer I'd be able to match my stride even with his. "And not a word of that old frog's prying chatter to your Pop."

With graduation moving each week nearer, and Coppy, the first Hawkins or Cooper to be stepping up for his diploma, I was determined on him not doing it in mended jeans.

"Cut down my blue serge to fit him," John offered.

"Wait a bit," Mary said. She had written her people, and soon came a package from her Aunt Sophie, enclosing a fine suit of broadcloth belonging to her dead husband, by careful cutting I managed enough over to get little Jackie his first pair of trousers.

While I basted and fitted his new jacket on him, then long pants, Coppy was darting looks at me over his shoulder. "Ma? I been meaning to tell you." He was trying to sound offhand. "I stopped off by the store yesterday. Saw Mr. Nate."

Quickly I emptied the basting pins from my mouth. "Whatever for?"

"Oh, I was thinking. With school soon over. About what he said, I mean. Using me this summer."

Carefully I broke off my thread and straightened up to face him. "Coppy, you'll not go down the mine."

"Just for the summer!" His young eyes darkening, he burst out, "How you reckon I feel! You sweating, going without! And Pop—"

"Hush, lad!" His father was in our room, as he often had to be now, sleeping.

Quietening, Coppy took hold of my sleeve. "How long, Ma, is it?" he asked, "since you had a new dress?"

I smoothed my faded blue cotton, thinking it not so long as my own Ma had managed. "Son, listen to me. You're staying in school—it's how I want it. And your Pop. More than all else."

He flung his arms around me, I could feel his young body quivering, then grow still. I sensed the dread waxing in him, the same as my own.

"You'd best go down to the city right off." I took up my sewing. Mary's folks would find him a summer job.

"I'll not leave sooner than need be." Coppy had a stubborn jaw like his father. He'd work out on a farm nearby, get home Sundays. With a nod he let me go, in the way of young ones his mood lifting fast. "I'll start in Saturdays, right off!" He buttoned his new jacket and strode about the kitchen, eyes twinkling at me. "Now you're getting me up fancy for the Big Day, what about yourself?"

"Reckon the standup dress I married your Pa in is fitten enough!"

With a cheery swoop toward our cat he went outside. I saw him whispering with Cindy, then later with his Aunt Mary. And sitting at my place at table, the Sunday after Coppy drew his first pay from Uncle Silas, I found a length of blue lawn flowered with daisies. "Surprise, Ma!" they shouted. Looking from the children to John, then my brother and Mary, I knew each had foregone something to have their part in it.

"You'll get it stitched in time?" Coppy was anxious.

"I'll start this night." Maybe with careful planning I'd manage Cindy a pinafore.

Mary smiled. "Knowing you, we allowed a bit extra."

I held the flimsy goods against me, eyes misting.

Coppy whistled. "Our Ma's gona be the handsomest lady of them all."

A good part of our Hollow footed it down to witness our boy get his graduating papers, for never before had a Toewad lad gone so far and taking first honors, at that. When Mr. Dozier, Board member presiding, called out, "James Hawkins Cooper!" our lad stepped out, tall and eager with his head atilt like I remembered his Dad in our first years. John's grip on mine tightened, and I had to stiffen to keep my gaze clear. Coppy had warned me, "Ma, if you dare bawl, I'll do a double handspring off the platform!" I held myself upright, feeling everyone's gaze on our son—and wondering if Coppy should note his Dad's quivering proud chin, would his warning hold as well for him!

Our Hollow folk held in till we reached the trail back up our hill, then let drawstrings and spirits burst out. And in the singing I could hear John's voice rising, like of old, above the rest.

We found Sarah, who had offered to mind Jack for me, watching by the window. Jack had a fever. I picked him up, his little body quivering hot to my touch. Yesterday, carrying my filled buckets from upstream, I had come on Jackie and other children playing in the dirtied part of the creek. Since early spring people had been coming down with sleeping sickness from bad water. Seepage from our patch had turned it rank. No matter how much we boiled it, it never tasted nor smelled right.

By morning more children had come down with the fever. Miners were keeling over at the face. Soon half our patch was down and everyone able to stand, John among them, nursing the sick and helping bury the dead.

In the night Jack's feeble cry roused me. He was burning with fever. Outside the rain was coming down in hard pelts. I closed out the night air and drew a chair by Son's cradle. After a time his breathing eased and I must have dropped off, for I was wakened by Son gagging, choked for breath.

John fumbled in his haste to fasten on his leg. "I'll go for Granny."

"We are needing a doctor." There was a glazed sink-ing look in Son's eyes. I eased him against my shoulder, forced my finger, as Granny did, down his throat to help him clear it.

I heard John traveling down toward Pluckme and our one phone station. Cindy had wakened and was crying. "My sweet little brother." I had her fetch me a wet cloth to cool his flesh. "Ma, is he going to die?"

"Hush it! Fetch me another cloth."

Not able to remain quiet, I walked up and down, Jack in my arms. Outside the wind was lashing the pines. Jack's breathing grew heavier. John at last was back. No doctor would come. The phone girl kept telling him it was no use, roads around Clancy were clogged with mud and drift, no doctor in his right mind would travel up our ridge this night. Wait till morning.

"Morning?" I slipped to a chair. "Get Granny if you can." I knew she was with Mattie Foster, in labor with her first child.

When Granny came, she took Jack from me. "Get him to a doctor." Her shoulders drooped. "He is needing help beyond my knowing." She stood up to go, numb quiet like those long used to bringing life and death. "I must hurry back, Mattie is pretty far along."

Mary came through the doorway, fully dressed. "I'll get word through to Doctor Walsh you are coming." Clyde had the cart waiting outside.

John's head dropped on his arms, his whole body shaking.

"Stop it!" I took him by the shoulder. "Get me blankets."

He moved about as one blind. I wrapped Jack in the cotton blankets I had stitched for him, his little body going hot and cold. Clyde had the cart waiting for us by the door.

"Let me go, Ma?" Cindy was getting in my path, holding onto my skirt. I left her with Mary. I gave Son to John, and walking by the mule's head, began coaxing her down the road. The poor animal balked and tugged, for the way was muddy and clogged with earthslide. The wagon lurched and all but turned over. Through the blanket we could barely make out Jack's little choked breathing, but I dared not stop nor slow down. There was no moon to guide us but the rain eased and stars came out, lighting the road.

"Hurry, Dolly!" John called.

I lashed harder. When the mule refused to go ahead, I pulled her by the mouth, then John tried. We coaxed and cursed her, using ways Ike had with his pit mules. Ahead of us we saw the lights of Clancy. Little by little they moved nearer, brighter.

Inside the blanket, Jack's breathing grew fainter. Maybe it was the cart creaking, I told myself, blotting out all other sounds. Whatever happened we dared not look inside the blanket, for the night air was a knife cutting your throat.

"Hurry, Dol! Hurry!"

I lashed the mule.

John was sobbing. "Dol, I can't hear."

"Hush, John. There's still time." I belabored the poor mule to go faster. Surely God had sent us enough to burden under, He would not take away our son. John was rocking the bundle in his arms.

We had come to Clancy. Our cart broke like thunder on the dead quiet. We turned the second corner as Mary had told us, and drew up to the curb. I jumped out and John handed me our child. In fear and trembling I lifted him. Why was the bundle so quiet in my arms? I ran toward the doctor's lights, John before me.

The old physician was waiting up for us, everything ready. Standing in the doorway, lamplight on his white hair, he was like God.

"Doctor, quick!" He hurried us inside. My fingers stiff with cold, I undid the blankets. Son's little face was purple.

Doctor Walsh performed a miracle, pulled our boy out of it, though Jack remained sickly and John for no reason was blaming himself. If I hadn't let you keep on working while acarrying him, he said.

"Nothing wrong with our Jack that good water and food can't remedy!" I headed our women down to call on Nate. We were needing that pipeline to our patch. "If you don't fancy us parking on your door-step till we get it, better send word to the Big House." We knew Nate daren't sneeze till first asking Super Dill.

"Now friends and neighbors. Let's reason together." Nate drew me aside. "You think the comp'ny will take it kindly, your stirring up this hornet's nest?" He rubbed his long beak, his little eyes peering down at me. "You ain't forgetting these many months we let you alone on the rent?"

"I am not forgetting." I looked him in the eye. "None of it." I pointed down the hill toward Cumberland Rock church, and fresh graves nearby. "It's those new mounds astirring 'em." Ask Mattie Foster, her little daughter was there and grass not yet greening on the earth over her.

Fay and Mac's Mary came over. "You'll be seeing to the pipe?"

Looking around at them and maybe remembering our Dads had marched as far as the Governor's, when need came, Nate said, "I'll see. You know it don't all depend on me?"

"And no shillyshallying," Fay said. "Else you find us women with our brooms astride every stoop. And not a man getting by us to the pit!"

Nate bristled. "You Hawkins women mighty big talkers. Not by any chance rattling empty?" Squinting at me, he fondled his long beak. "I told you, I'll see. What more you want?"

Just the pipeline, I said.

"And how is it with that big son of yours? Gone off yet to his high falutin learning?"

I straightened. "He is leaving next month."

Nate cleared his throat. "Is that so, now!" Something in the way he spoke made me think of Coppy's moody wandering about our place. Since his return from his summer farm job he had not been himself, and no way of hiding how poorly his Pop had been of late, or how empty the blue crock.

I moved faster up the path, hardly sharing in the women's elated talk. "Lawsy, I've been aching for this day!" Manthy swung her arms in front of her.

Fay laughed. "Dol, you yanked Nate off his high horse. I sure relished it!"

I saw Coppy waiting for me up the path.

"Swing your pardners!" Gourd was calling turns for summer hotelers whirling away the final dance of the season, John fiddling like besot, his body swaying out of time with the music. I moved nearer him. His face had gone still as when the pain caught him.

"Now doe-see-doe!" Without warning the music box slipped to the floor. John fell against me. Gourd ordered dancers crowding around to stand back, give him air. He helped me take John outside.

On the long trip homeward John kept saying "Just a dizzy spell. Don't let on to Coppy?" We must send the lad off tomorrow, a bit early start in the city won't do harm.

Coppy emptied what was left in the blue crock into my hands. "I'm aborrowing Unc Silas' cart. Fetch Pop down to the medic."

Dr. Blanton would tell us little. John's leg might prove

slow to heal. Keep him off it eight weeks. Give him this medicine, red meats and fruit, then return for a checkup.

"Doctor—?" I made excuse for seeing him alone. "How bad is it?"

He smiled in his quiet way, using long foreign words for putting me off.

"Doctor, the truth?"

He rested a hand on my shoulder. "It may not prove as bad as I fear."

Heavy with my knowledge I would not be sharing with anyone in fear of making it more real, I listened to John keeping up his light banter for Coppy as we rode home, knowing he was not deceiving the lad.

When we reached home and John resting in our room, Coppy beckoned me aside. "Ma, I'm not aleaving."

I went to the fireplace by him. "Son, your Pop is wanting you should." I was seeing our boy suddenly turn man. "Your Pop is wanting it powerful."

Coppy looked down at his hands, then straight at me. "I saw Mister Nate. I'm going down the pit."

I grasped the mantel, steadying my weight on its rough stone. "Never!" I closed the door to John's room. "I'll not have it. You hear me?" So young he looked, standing upright and grave, cheeks flushed, defying me. "God be thanked, you are still a minor!"

He jerked his head aside, boylike. "Ma, you heard the medic. Pop's needing special things."

"I'll manage." By heaven I'd put a stop to Nate's villainy, raise a stink clear to Memphis!

"You can't do it alone, Ma." Not even with Uncle Clyde's help.

"I told you, I'll manage!" Softly, not to rouse John, I

called him by me. "I can't let you, son. Don't you know
it?"

His shoulder stiffened under my hand. "It's no use,
Ma. You can't be sending me off."

He refused my glance, gave no heed to my words.
Since the day you first drew breath, I told him, John's
and my striving had aimed for this. "Get you schooling,
Coppy, get you shet of the mine."

He moved off, restless. "What's the use of talking.
Pop needs me."

"Coppy, he needs you to go. Can't you see it!" All our
striving, how could it end in nothing.

His eyes dropped before mine. Only till Pop's better,
he said. "Later I'll quit, Ma, go back to my schooling."

"You'll never!" I pressed back my angry despairing
words. "You'll never."

I went outside. Coppy followed me. "It's our one
chance to save Pop." He took my hand. "Ma—?"

Not the mine, I said. Go farm. Timber. Anything but
the mine!—knowing as I said it there was no farmwork
in winter and lumbering closed down.

We climbed toward High Top, Coppy still urging me.
Around us the sky was fading, the wood quiet with the
hush of late afternoon. Within me was none of it. We
came to our ledge and sat down for a rest. I let my gaze
travel from long habit to our roof aglittering up through
the leaves. Each spring John had given it a fresh coat.

"Coppy, your father—Try to understand?" Stretched
beside me, his hand tracing veins in the rock, Coppy
did not answer.

"If you stay, it will go hard with him, son." I turned
to look out over the endless dark pine, broken only by

fresher green of oak and maple. "Harder maybe than your going on."

When he made no answer, I kept prodding him.

"Stop it, Ma!" His hands were pulling at the rock. "Why you keep afighting me? Like I was wanting it this way. And you agin me!" He dropped his head in my lap, sobbing like the little boy he was when a rattler killed his pup, Sandy. I mothered him as I had then, remorseful that until now I had been feeling for John and myself, only in dim part for him.

"We had better go down, son." I looked aside while he wiped his face on his sleeve. As we came down the trail our Jackie and Mary's Stevie came running to greet us. I had Cindy take them to Granny's for a visit, then followed Coppy in to his father.

John had pulled up in bed. "Dol, I'm not believing this of you?" His eyes were two coals burning into me. "Speak, woman!" I had no words. He turned on Coppy. "Before I let you—" His fists lifted. "I'll strike you down with my own hands."

Coppy threw back his shoulders. "Mining's a good trade, Pop." His lips had gone white. "I'm not afraid."

I moved nearer him, knowing of a sudden his need beyond John's or my own.

" 'Once a miner, always a—!' " John's laugh was like a whip. "And what's it got us? Doing without. Crippling. Your Ma eating her heart thin. A filthy mess, the lot of it!"

"Don't, John." I ran over, trying to quiet him. Don't be denying the truth in him. Not to our firstborn.

"Woman, what's come over you?" He put aside my hands. "I curse the sun for rising tomorrow. Me alying

here rotting and you—!" He made a lunge for Coppy.
"Ain't it enough your Ma's got, without you setting her
crazy with fear?"

"Stop it, John!"

He motioned me away. "Coppy, listen to me. I am
doomed, lad."

Like one blind I groped for the window.

"You'll get well, Pop."

John lifted himself over the bedside. "Go on off, son.
Take your chance."

Coppy was shaking his head, tears running down his
cheeks. "You'll get well, Pop. You will."

John dropped back. "Dol, tell him." Only through our
son could his own life make sense.

I heard Mary come into our kitchen, our little boys
shouting and running around her. They headed for our
door. I hastened outside to stop them, closing the door
behind me.

When all were in bed for the night, I slipped into the
kitchen to ready some things I must have for Coppy before morning. With fingers slow to do my bidding I un-
packed John's mine things. They had a musty odor.
Memories flooded back. John. My Dad, brother Alec.
Was there meaning in it? Somewhere in me I had to find
it, something for Coppy to hold to. Like the spot of light
miners glimpsed far overhead when stepping from the
cage, and they looked up toward the earth's surface.
What guidance would my Dad be giving me? Words to
take the despairing from his young soul, rouse hope.
Without this, Coppy would be a body without living. I
had seen others.

Toward morning I wakened him for his breakfast, a bit early so we might speak together.

The lad ate in silence. I came around the table by him. There was something I had to be saying. "Coppy?" He did not look up. "Yesterday, when you told me, I was afeared. Since then, most of the night, I been thinking it over." I took him firm by the shoulders. "I want you to know, son. I am proud."

He pushed back his chair. "What we got to, we do." As he stood up I saw the naked dread in his glance, and his shame at feeling it.

"True, lad, we do what we have to. But this goes deeper." If only I might implant some hope in him. To uphold and guide him below ground like his miner's lamp. "Deep as the coal veins you'll be adigging. They took a million years to form. You were reading it to me. Remember?" I was talking fast, knowing soon the tramp of boots would start for the mine. "There is a meaning to it, son, I ain't fully worked out. One thing I know. This won't be the end."

He looked around at me, an answering flicker in his glance. "What do you mean?"

"You are young, Coppy. And things keep amoving." I nodded toward High Top. Look like the one thing astanding still was our hills.

His glance dropped.

"Son, I am going on forty. I've seen plenty of changes in my time."

"For the good, Ma?"

"That depends." I was listening to the distant tramp grow nearer. "All I know, it's a fight and a tussle. But **we move.**"

He came nearer me. "Ma, do you think Pop—?"

The light was topping the ridge. "He is bad hurt, son."

The tramping had reached our path. I heard Tobey call across to a workmate. I handed Coppy his father's pick and mine cap.

"Ma?" His eyes, fastened on mine were saying what his tongue couldn't.

My grip on his shoulders deepened. *Keep mad, son. Fighting mad. At the right things.*

The miners were level our door. I took him against me. Coppy put on his mine cap, lifted the pick to his shoulder and with a husky "See you tonight, Ma!" stepped outside to join Tobey and the others.

. . . . *chapter 24* . . . .

Not long after Coppy's going down the pit, I noticed a
further change in John. Pure fancy, I told myself, but
there were times when I could not help feeling his eyes
on me in a sorrowful knowing look.

"Anything you needing, John?" He would shake his
head. One thing alone seemed purposing in him, stirring
his will. Once our lad home and supper down him, John
had Coppy over his books. "So you won't be falling behind." We had Mary giving him lessons and Coppy, seeing how it pleasured his father, would fight down sleep
and weariness until I had to speak. "Reckon Coppy can
take it," John said. Lot of good folk got their start the
same. In Kentuck not far from the spot where he was
raised stood the cabin Logger Abe studied in by the
light of pine logs.

After others were sleeping I found Coppy hunched
over his books and papers spread on the kitchen table,

head fallen forward and eyes closed. Gently I roused him. "Past time for bed, son."

He started up and made a reach for his pencil.

"Enough for tonight, lad." I brought him an apple and folded back the covers on his cot while he munched it, then blew out the lamp.

Coppy soon was fetching his books in by his father. "Pop, it's all here. What Ma was asaying." They talked far into the night.

"That time I spoke hasty," John said. "You'll make it."

"Sure, Pop."

I had to step outside for a look at our hills.

John's thought began dwelling on Coppy below ground, astudying how to righten things a bit. He sent for Pop McFever and set forth his plan. A First Aid station is what's needing most, he said. Close by the pit mouth. Given help on the spot, many a digger might be saved his limb. "Mac, put it up to them. We diggers give our labor, fell logs and raise the hut. Let the company furnish the medic?" John began to fret, then sicken. He had me gather Fay and Manthy for a call on Nate.

"What's itching you women!" Nate peered up from his ledger. "Ain't we told you? Soon as the ground thaws we are laying the water pipe."

Nate flipped his ledger. "Times like they are, mine losing money and you wanting a medic! You people all alike, give an inch take a mile!" He returned to his figuring. "As it is, I can't make ends meet."

Pop told John, "We'll keep at them, wear them down like waterfall on rock. Things take time, man." John knew he had little left.

Phil Ballard tramped over from Shamrock to say the

men were asking for me. They'll listen to Jim Hawkins' daughter, he said. We never had anybody the likes of you. Not since Ma Jones, God rest her soul.

I was unready to leave John for long as it meant traveling back and forth, but to please him I went, then asked Pop to bring me no more requests. For I could put the knowledge from me no longer. My man was ailing from a sickness no doctor might reach. The sore on his leg had deepened. No doctor we found could help him.

"Soon it will be spring, John." I opened our door wide to let the morning breeze freshen our cabin. Just what he was needing, lungfulls of our spring air.

"Dolly? Come sit by me." John was smiling in the sad way he had when our baby crying for milk I did not have for him.

"We'll go outside to watch dogwood and laurel budding. And sumac fire up." I hid my face against him, not to see the knowing in his glance.

He comforted me, using words he had our first night up the mountain. How was I to grow used to not feeling his calloused gentle fingers, hearing his low voice. "Dolly, you know I'll stay by you long as I can."

There was much pain and wasting away toward the last. I felt wrong to be holding onto him. But his will held. These years since my trouble, he said, I've been thinking it over. The day will come when no man or boy must go risking his hide in the earth adigging coal.

"How, Pop?"

"I don't rightly know, son. Only a body can be thinking. It won't be in my time. Nor likely in yours. But if things keep achanging. Men inventing. Who can say where it'll end?"

The fire had burned low. After Coppy and we abed, John told me: When my time comes, bring me up the mountain to sleep. I want to watch the sun top the ridge and the eagle fly, and hear the donkey train going up the tipple. I aim to rest on the hilltop where I can peer down on the world and all that is taking place. Rest and watch for the time when a new earth shall rise on our sight. New because our human folk on it will be like newborn. No more of man misusing man. New the way you and I were, the morning Granny laid our firstborn in your arms.

Before light John asked me to pull our bed over by the window facing eastward. It was late fall, close to sixteen years since we had first viewed sunup together over High Top. We thought back over the years, John talking and me listening while the sky reddened. We spoke of our children. For Coppy we shared a hope that he might yet manage his training, not in the way we had planned but over the ridge at the Mount Eagle Folk School, then come back and in his own quiet way help our people. Cindy might go down to Mary's relatives, finish tenth grade for a country teaching license.

"Before many seasons Coppy will be chosing a mate." John stroked my head. "God grant he find one like you, Dol."

John lived through Christmas. It was his wish, and the children and our Hollow made it a happy one. On New Year neighbors gathered in our kitchen and John, propped in bed, called for drinks all round and bid them dance while he fiddled. Pop brought word that soon as the ground thawed our men were clearing ground for the hut. Not that the Big House had fully given its promise of a medic, but once we had the hut raised they would feel shamed to let it stand empty.

During the mid-January thaw I set out with my children and friends to take John up the mountain to rest. Folk from Shamrock and Chumley Hollow and even far off as Piney Grove and Mercy came up the hillside to do him honor. "Never was a truer man," they said.

After others had left I stayed on alone. My brother tried to keep me from it.

"Let her be." Mary, womanlike, understood. Cindy clung to me, wanting to stay. Coppy had my arm locked in his, young face stern with holding back his grief.

"Just for a little while, your Ma will be down soon." Gently Mary led them away. The sun was dropping behind our ridge as they went down the trail to our valley. From the ledge where I stood watching them I could spy the mine patch and incline where Peg once hauled his cars. I could still hear him calling, "Watch out below! Coal car acoming!" In my mind I made out the place with the stoved-in chimney where I had lived as a child. Not far off stood the cabin we had when John came awooing. . . . My thought was wandering, grasping out at whatever came to hand, looking back over my shoulder to keep from sight the bleak road ahead.

After a time I went down to my children. When sleep finally came to them, I climbed back up the hill. The sun long since had dropped behind our mountain and the swift darkness closed in. I climbed fast. As the stars came out, I fell to weeding the earth above my Dad and Ma, knowing it needful to keep my hands busy. I gathered shells to place on the earth over John. Once our Cumberlands were ocean bed, so Coppy had read me.

Long ages back, before the Indians made it their hunting ground.

The same moon by me that John and I had watched time over, I uprooted and planted ferns by him, then started my climb up High Top. I walked for hours, on fire like with need of something to do. I climbed till fagged out, nigh ready to travel on hands and knees up the ledge. I found no resting place.

Toward daybreak I went back to the place we had lain John. I put fresh greens around, then hastened down to see Coppy off to the mine and Cindy to her lessons. As I crossed the log over our creek I saw paper boats from yesterday riding on the polluted water. Seeing them was like hearing John speak. *Dol, our task is not finished.* Numb and burdened as I was with sorrow, I could not help seeing. Young miners' scarred bodies as they returned from the night shift. Women folk with their secret haunted look. Scrawny young ones. Grief sharpened my sight. I felt an angry will rising in me. With a final backward look up our mountain, I hurried in to my children.

.... *chapter 25* ....

Laurel was in full bloom and the sky freshwashed the day we made ready to lay the cornerstone for our Hut. Gourd's three-piece band of fiddle, mouth harp and drum was leading the way and our Hollow children prancing beside their Dads and atossing homemade kites. We gathered by the mound of Cumberland rock our miners had piled, waiting with logs felled for roof and siding. Young Jack was riding on Coppy's shoulder and flying a kite Cindy had colored with red berries.

"Friends and neighbors—" Pop McFever raised his hand, motioning us to silence. Women gathered their children by them. Things quietened until we could hear warblers twittering in a thicket. Clouds stopped moving on High Top. Our hills, seemed like, were listening. I thought how John might be relishing this day.

"We are aburying beneath the cornerstone this tin safety box." Pop held it up for all to view. In here we placed a record, he said, how this Hut came to be. Who knows, maybe our children's children might open to read and marvel on such times as ours.

Lowering the box, he looked around the circle of faces. "Our Local voted to match dollar by dollar what the company may figure on spending to equip our First Aid. And in the safety box are names we chose to honor for their part in it." Slowly he began reading them off, waiting after each name for people to nod assent. "John Ferris Cooper—" My children stepped nearer me. Other names followed, mine among them. When done, Pop had each of us spade a shovelful of dirt, then placed the safety box in the waiting earth. Cornerstone in place, we firmed the ground over it.

"Now, men!" Pop gestured toward the pile of granite. "Today being Saturday, we'd give the afternoon to raising her foundation. But first the womenfolk got something for us." Band playing, we followed the route of our new water line that ran downward from the upper hill to our patch.

In the center of our clearing, aglitter in the hot noonday stood our Pump. From its handle swung a red ribbon like for Christmas and a shiny bucket and dipper. To one side stood Nate and Super Carson with a crate of beer for celebrating. Must burn their fingers, Fay whispered to me, letting it go for free.

We formed a circle around the pump. Pop came over to me. "Dolly Cooper, you have been chosen to draw the first bucket." I laid my hand on its iron arm and began pumping. The circle edged in. Far up the pipe we heard the air sucking, then sound of quick-flowing water. As it gushed from the spigot a cry went up. Children leaped in the air. Grownups crowded around laughing and getting splattered, everybody wanting to wet their hands in the flow. And hearing them and the clear gurgling water, for the first time since John's going I felt laughter welling up in me.

"Stand back, everybody!" Carefully I filled the bucket and toted it over to Granny Morse. "Dip, Granny." I handed her the ladle. "You brought most of us into the world. It is proper you should have the first drink."

Her weathered cheeks flushed, she drank it off. "Pure tasting for a fact!" After Granny came our children beginning with the littlest, then our men and womenfolk and many wanting a second drink to wash down meat paddies and cherry dumplings my neighbors and I had been all week baking.

During log-raising Manthy and I were lending the men a hand when Pop brought a stranger up to me. "I've footed it from Marked Tree camp, Ma'am, to be asking you a favor." We have fallen on bad times, he said. Folk pulling two ways. The last cavein took seven of their men. "Our Hollow would take it kindly, Ma'am, if you'd be journeying back with me? We're needing somebody like you abringing the Word."

I was thinking how to put my refusing when Coppy touched my arm. "Go, Ma. Pop would want you to go."

With evening and our family asleep I prepared for my journey, then opened the pine chest in our room where I kept John's things. Near his fiddle was the cigar box where he put things he was atreasuring. Flowers we had picked together on High Top and pressed flat between leaves of a book. A small picture of his Ma taken when a girl. A lock of hair from each of our children. A fishing cork stained red with berry juice he had used as a lad in Kentuck, and a whistle made from a willow branch. A ribbon from my blue dress I wore his first evening in our cabin. More things like this. But from his years in the mine, nothing. It was like a man's lifetime hidden in this box. I put it away. Some later time to be showing the children.

On Coppy's next birthday, I would journey with him up the hillside. With him nearing mansize, there were things we had need to talk over.

Going into our kitchen to make sure the fire banked for the night, I found Coppy over his books. "Time you were in bed, son?"

He beckoned me to the bench by him. How like he was to his father. I could feel the coming strength in his arm. And in his glance.

He put aside his study papers and began talking of his plans for Jack.

"Wait." I placed by hand over his. Little Jack's turn would come. Now it was of him we must speak. "You are young, Coppy. Your life still ahead."

We spoke of him, then of my journey.

"You are young too, Ma." At my denying smile there came no answering glint, only the fierce eager look of eighteen. "Powerful young, Ma."

I was not full sure of his meaning. Nor ready for asking.

"Listen, Ma." He took up a book Mary had fetched him from the city. "It's all here, like you said. The world keeps amoving." As he read, the dying flare in the grate threw its glow over him. I felt a deep content rise in me and yearning. The strong will of the Hawkins and Coopers flowed in our son. He would dig deep and long, with others searching out as the Good Book told, the truth to set men free.

Afterword

I

Daughter of the Hills was first published in 1950, under the title *With Sun in Our Blood*. Myra Page, its author, began work on the novel in the late thirties.[1] In 1941 she published a radio play in which Dolly Hawkins narrates the story of "The March on Chumley Hollow."[2] The story dramatizes essentially the same events as those the novel's Dolly Hawkins recalls on High Top the day she decides to accept John Cooper's wooing. Page continued to work on the novel itself during the war years, but in its origins and much of its writing, *Daughter of the Hills* is a novel of the thirties.

Page expected to publish the novel with Viking Press. But in the late forties, the inquisitions and blacklists of the McCarthy era began to take their toll on American life and culture. Many publishers chose not to publish the works of writers who had been named in the hearings or in publications such as *Red Channels* as Communists and fellow travelers. Myra Page had been named; Viking returned her contract. *With Sun in Our Blood* was subsequently published by Citadel Press, with funds raised by a small group of progressives.[3]

Myra Page has lived in many ways the paradigmatic experience of American leftists: an early sense of outrage at perceived injustices; an engagement in work for social change; a deepening radicalism in the twenties and thirties that frequently in those years meant affiliation with or sympathy for the Communist party; loss of livelihood and harrassment of self and family during the McCarthy years; an attempt, in the fifties, to maintain one's vision and integrity in a time of persecution from the Right and dissaffiliation from the Old Left.[4] One would hardly have predicted such a life on the basis of Page's origins; her Southern middle-class parents wondered aloud how she had gotten into such company.

Born October 1, 1897, in Newport News, Virginia, to Willie Alberta Barham Gary and Benjamin Roscoe Gary, the author was christened Dorothy Page Gary. Myra Page is her pen name, acquired when she began to write politically in the late twenties. Her mother, one of eleven children, had considerable talent as an artist, though she devoted herself primarily to meeting the more traditional obligations of white Southern womanhood, overseeing the home, raising the children, doing her share of visiting and entertaining, and participating in the women's clubs that supported charitable and cultural activity. Her father, a family physician, tended the needs of both whites and blacks, fighting successfully for the inclusion of a wing for black people in the public hospital he helped to found. Page's grandfather on her father's side had fought with General Lee's raiders. He taught her a song that she humorously interpreted as an endorsement of rebellion: "I'm a good old rebel, and that's just what I am; for all those blank blank Yankees, I do not give a blank." (One could not, of course, say "damn" in polite circles.) Her mother, more conventional, conservative, and aristocratic than the young farmer's son she married, was nevertheless, like her husband, a great reader, and Page grew up in a home full of books—Hugo, Scott, Eliot, Thackeray, and Dickens, a family favorite. In the Newport News library, Page discovered Chekhov, Tolstoy, Gorky, and Balzac—"my tutors," she calls them now.

Page's unpublished autobiographical novel, *Sounding*, reconstructs her childhood and youth.[5] Laura, her fictive alter ego, active, intelligent, and strong-willed, wants fiercely to become a doctor like her loved and admired father, and is devastated by the unassailable conviction of her entire family that such ambitions have no place in the dreamings of a girl. The novel testifies also to Page's ambivalence toward her mother, who, with an ambivalence of her own, struggled to socialize her recalcitrant daughter into the ways of proper Southern womanhood, all the while half-cherishing and sometimes openly supporting Dorothy's efforts to escape the constrictions of this life. Willie Alberta Gary wanted her daughter to grow up decorously, to marry well, and to settle down near home and rear a family; yet it was she who supported Dorothy's wish to go north to graduate school, a decision that meant she would never fully go home again, though she returned regularly to the South and to her family over the years. In her mother and her mother's sisters, each gifted with artistic or musical talent, Page came to see the waste of women's talents in a society that relegated those talents to dilettantism—a waste these women themselves questioned without openly challenging its systemic dimensions. Page's feminism is both a reaction against and a legacy of this contradictory heritage.

As a girl Dorothy occasionally accompanied her father on his rounds with the horse and buggy; sometimes their way led to Rockets, the black section of town, and she began to learn something about the ecology of racial segregation in the abrupt absence of paving, sewers, and schools. Her sense of injustice about racial issues, though, developed most immediately from her relationship to Belle Franklin, the family maid. Outwardly compliant, Belle sometimes let Dorothy glimpse her rage and grief at having been born black and female in the South. The two seem to have colluded in a kind of limited rebellion against the strictures of their respective roles, though Belle clearly knew that for her there was no escape. In *Sounding*, Belle ultimately lets herself be kept by a white man to whom she is indifferent, hoping to give her children a chance to get away from the South. Laura learns the details of Belle's fate only through eavesdropping on fragments of conversation—black street-corner talk, white parlor talk, repressed allusions to the taboo subject of interracial sexuality—which Page interprets as a kind of sexual/racial economy. In another incident in the novel, also based on Page's recollections of her own life, Laura and her brother are forbidden to play any more with the black boy who has been their companion during their summer holidays on the family farm. Her bewilderment at this loss teaches her an early first lesson in the absolutism of segregation. One way or another, all Page's novels, including *Daughter of the Hills* in the story of Elijah and Sarah, deplore the sheer human wastefulness of racism.

The young Dorothy enjoyed the freedom small-town Southern life allowed its preadolescent females; she roamed the woods and riverbanks, the docks and the shantytowns that grew up near them, making friends among the shipyard workers' children. Mary Frederickson, in an article on Page in *Southern Changes*, writes of this aspect of her experience:

> In the years before World War I, Newport News was a bustling town dominated by the noise of a shipyard filled with crews which built ships twenty-four hours a day. . . . Black longshoremen in Newport News formed a union during this period, and then helped organize their white counterparts. . . . The two groups worked together and added a different chapter to the long history of craft unionism in the shipyard. Page's father supported organized labor, many of his patients were union members, and with them he viewed labor's platform as one antidote to the high rate of industrial accidents that plagued workers in Newport News.[6]

Page's cross-class friendships with children of the dock workers and her observation of the workers' struggles for better working conditions figure prominently in *Sounding*. Her subsequent engagement with the radical labor movement, then, is rooted after all in her own childhood, in the day-to-day problems she saw and heard about, as well as in her father's humanitarian liberalism.

After high school, Page attended Westhampton College, a division of the University of Richmond that offered liberal arts for women. At Westhampton, she became friends with several young women who shared her liberal views. Pacifists in the increasing patriotic fervor at the onset of World War I, and, one or two of them, integrationists in a rigidly segregated world, they supported one another in their disaffection from dominant belief. She also became active in the YWCA, attending summer conferences that included some students from black colleges. She and a friend invited a black YWCA spokeswoman to their campus; according to Frerickson this was the first such integrated meeting in the college's history.[7]

After college, Page taught in a junior college for a year and then went north to Columbia University. There, she took classes with Franklin Henry Giddings, Franz Boas, and John Dewey. She also joined a social studies group that focused on nationalism as one of its topics. One of her friends in the group was a radical Jewish student from the East Side whose politics of class struggle began to influence her. After receiving her MA in sociology, Page went to work for the YWCA, impressed by its efforts to improve the lives of working women.[8] She joined the Y's Industrial Department and returned to the South in 1920, this time to Norfolk, as YWCA industrial secretary. Ostensibly, she would organize clubs for the female operatives of the textile mills and "bring them a little culture," as she says today. Actually, she hoped to encourage the women workers to unionize. But she found that since her presence in the mills depended on approval by management, working women regarded her and her union talk with suspicion. In addition, she got into trouble with the local YWCA board, one of whose members reminded her, "Your job is to teach them to love God and know their place." After a year, discouraged by the South's resistance to social change, she decided to return to the North for good.

This time she went to Philadelphia, selling books at Wanamakers during the Christmas rush. Then she worked for a year as a factory hand in the garment industry, eventually joining the Amalgamated Clothing Workers Union and helping to organize new locals in non-union shops. She developed an important friendship there with the working-class organizer Hilda Shapiro, who became her comrade, roommate, and in many ways her mentor for the next few years, while the two women worked together to set up union shops in Philadelphia and St. Louis. Page recalls that "Hilda was a real feminist," less interested in the internal debates between the left and the right in the union than she was in on-the-line work with women.

Hilda Shapiro had attended Bryn Mawr's School for Working Girls, and she encouraged Page's interest in workers' education. When the opportunity offered, Page took a graduate student teaching fellowship in sociology at the University of Minnesota. Within a year she had met and married John Markey, a graduate teaching fellow in social psychology, who went on to work as a university teacher and a researcher in economics and statistics until the blacklists intervened. Page says today that in one way *Daughter of the Hills* is autobiographical: In narrating Dolly's love for John Cooper, she celebrated the depth and endurance of her own love for John Markey. Their marriage has lasted now for more than sixty years.

At the University of Minnesota, Page taught a variety of courses, including a course on social reform movements, for which she sent her students to the Twin Cities offices of the Central Trade Union Council, the Farmer-Labor party, the Wobblies, the Cooperative movement, and the Socialist and Communist parties among others. She became active in the teachers' union and in the St. Paul labor movement, teaching a course in St. Paul on women in trade unions. In 1927, the year before she received her doctorate, she was appointed by the Minnesota State Federation of Labor to head its Education Department (a volunteer post). She organized classes in union history, conferences on topics such as unemployment and imperialism in Nicaragua, and education committees elsewhere in the state. In the late twenties, like many other progressives, she found in the apparently successful young revolution in the Soviet Union an alternative to the exploitive economics of capitalism.

Her study of Marxism and the effort to apply it to conditions in the United States pervade much of her writing. In 1929, she published a long essay, "The Developing Study of Culture," a rather sophisticated critique of the dependence on behaviorism and empiricism of bourgeois social science and a spirited defense of historical materialism as a methodology for cultural study.[9] In the same year she published a book based on research for her dissertation, *Southern Cotton Mills and Labor.* As its title implies, her work for her thesis drew her back to the South, this time to a mill community in South Carolina, and back to the issues first raised when she had gone as a YWCA organizer into the textile mills of Norfolk. According to Frederickson, Page wanted to analyze the prospects for building a union movement in the South. She acknowledged the history of spontaneous strike efforts among the textile workers, efforts usually limited by the ruthless opposition of the textile companies, by the racial antagonisms between white and black workers, and by the failure of the American Federation of Labor to build integrated locals and to support local strikes early enough and long enough. She argued for the necessity of organizing black and white workers equally in industrial unions and uniting them in struggles for "full economic, political and social rights," and for the collective ownership and operation of the Southern mills.[10]

In the early thirties, Page traveled throughout the South, reporting on labor issues and struggles in the textile industry, among sharecroppers, among miners in the hills, and among

254

steelworkers in Birmingham. Her reportage is militant, tough, vivid, polemical—characteristic of the journalism of that era. In 1932, Page published her first novel, *Gathering Storm: A Story of the Black Belt* with International Publishers. One of six novels based on a 1929 strike in the Loray textile mills of Gastonia, North Carolina, four of them by women,[11] *Gathering Storm* tells the story of a Southern sister and brother who become involved in the strike and subsequently in the larger movements of radical labor in the thirties. One of the novel's more interesting dimensions is the parallel between Marge, the white millworker whose developing consciousness figures prominently in the novel, and Martha, the black woman whose rape and murder by the millowner's son reminds Marge that Martha's vulnerability exceeds her own.

Page today is critical of the novel. "I tried to put everything I knew into it," she says. *Gathering Storm* received few reviews, and even leftist critics regarded it as better ideologically than artistically.[12] The contributions of left-wing writers of the thirties to American literature have been undergoing an important revaluation in recent years, not least in the scholarly work for this Feminist Press series.[13] These recuperative readings need not blind sympathetic critics to the weaknesses of some of that literature. *Gathering Storm* has some of the flaws commonly associated with the "proletarian novels" of the period: too much rhetoric, too little depth of characterization, too determined a "revolutionary optimism"—though the optimism in this era of struggle and change seemed justified by the real successes of mass organizing. The novel's conclusion at a Communist party conference in Cleveland, based on the first mass congress of William Z. Foster's Trade Union Unity League, was intended to remind readers that the winning or losing of one strike matters little in the movement of history toward a classless and racially united society.

Yet it is all too easy to parody such plots. Candida Lacey, in a doctoral dissertation on women's proletarian fiction, provides a more productive method for reading this and related novels. Lacey applies a kind of feminist deconstruction to these novels, looking for the ruptures, displacements, and silences in their ostensible narrative projects. As Lacey suggests, proletarian novels consciously assert the essential unity and ultimate victory of the working class in its struggles against capital. Yet *Gathering Storm*, and especially its first half, raises many issues specific to women—the anxiety over sex, the fear of rape, the unwanted pregnancies, the desperate abortion attempts. It begins by developing a supportive cross-generational relationship between Marge and her grandmother, who tutors her in resistance. These issues and relations are displaced by a narrative that increasingly focuses less on Marge and the millwomen than on her brother Tom, a labor organizer. Lacey sees in these dislocations the inability of the author to acknowledge fully the very subversiveness of the women's issues raised. They are subversive not only of the dominant culture's sex-role ideologies but also of the Left's insistence on the seamlessness and unity of the working class. Working-class unity, in the narrative, that is, can come only at the price of marginalizing the disruptiveness of a distinctly female experience—an experience female authors of these novels are far more likely to incorporate than male authors working in the same genre, though the women do not always know how to integrate this experience into the ideological structure of their work.[14] Such a reading does not deny the aesthetic flaws of *Gathering Storm*, but it does suggest the novel's significance to readers interested in the complex intersections of literature, gender, and political culture.

In the early thirties, too, Page visited Moscow twice, once on a teachers' union tour to Europe and the Soviet Union and once as a reporter. "I was interested in the people and how the revolution had changed their lives," Page says today. "I asked everyone I met, What were you doing before the revolution and what are you doing now?" In 1935, she published *Moscow Yankee*, a novel about an American auto worker with little political consciousness who, at the height of the Depression, travels to the Soviet Union for a factory job, falls in love with a Russian woman, gradually becomes persuaded of the superiority of communism especially in its transformation of workers' lives in Russia during the Five-Year Plan, and finally decides to stay in Russia. This summary makes the novel sound like tedious propaganda; in fact it offers a detailed and still interesting rendition of the processes and problems of life and work in a postrevolutionary society still a long way from utopia.

In the mid-thirties, living in Manhattan, Page participated actively in the League of American Writers, a Popular Front organization that drew hundreds of writers from every sector of the Left to its first congress in 1935. She served on the board of the League and taught short story classes for its writers' school. (One of her students, then a young refugee from Germany, was feminist historian Gerda Lerner.) Page remembers with pleasure her collaborative relationship particularly with other women on the board—Aline Bernstein, a Broadway-theater designer, in whose home many of the board's meetings were held; Dorothy Brewster, a writer and English professor at Columbia University; Lillian Barnard Gilkes, Brewster's associate; poet and Sarah Lawrence professor Genevieve Taggard.[15]

Page's first child, May, was born in April 1935. Four months later Page and her husband went to teach at Commonwealth College in Arkansas, "a campus that might easily be mistaken for a little farm settlement in the southmost range of the Ozarks."[16] Commonwealth, founded thirteen years earlier as an experimental college designed "to share culture with the underprivileged," became in that era a united front labor college, drawing sharecroppers, miners, immigrant workers, and farmers to study Marxist thought, labor history, organizing strategy, current events, and English. At Commonwealth, Page taught a course on proletarian literature and writing, continuing to report on the labor struggles of sharecroppers and tenant farmers in Arkansas and Mississippi. It was here that Page first met Dolly Hawkins Cooper, worked with her in the college's fields, and heard the story that became *Daughter of the Hills*. *Daughter of the Hills* took shape too from Page's experiences in 1938 and 1939 when she taught classes and workshops at Highlander Folk School, near Chattanooga in Tennessee. There, she visited mining communities in the Cumberland Mountains, getting to know other members of the Hawkins family, getting a feel for the region and the details of its landscape.

Myra Page and John Markey today live in Yonkers, New York, in a home they purchased in 1943, after the birth of their second child, John Roscoe. Page has never lost her commitment to social change or her view of history as an evolution toward a more just society. She has remained active over the years, participating in the civil rights, antiwar, and women's movements. Page participated for several years during the seventies in a left-feminist study group that has included such well-known feminist scholars as Alice Kessler-Harris, Joan Kelly, Blanche Wiesen Cook, Amy Swerdlow, and Bell Chevigny, as well as Page's old friend, literary critic Annette Rubenstein. In 1978, Westhampton College honored her as Distinguished Alumna of the Year. Mary Frederickson tells the story of Page's visit to Newport News in June 1980, at the request of the United Steel Workers, whose interracial local of shipyard workers had just won recognition after an eleven-week strike.[17] Now eighty-eight, Page is polishing the draft of *Sounding* for publication.

II

In its unprogrammatic realism, its powerful evocation of locale, and its incorporation of folklore and legend, *Daughter of the Hills* belongs as much to the tradition of women's literature we associate with such writers as Mary Wilkins Freeman, Sarah Orne Jewett, Zora Neale Hurston, or Harriette Arnow (especially the Arnow of the 1936 novel *Mountain Path*, whose schoolteacher protagonist could be the sister of *Daughter of the Hills'* Mary) as to the more recent tradition of proletarian fiction. The novel captures that strong sense of place that critics have called "regionalist" or "local colorist," when the place is sufficiently different from the urban Northeast. The mountains, the hollow, the creek, and the tipple acquire a kind of palpability: The air smells of pine and coal dust, the atmosphere is charged with the anticipation of the young before a square dance, or with the anxiety of the women as their fathers, sons, and husbands enter the mines.

The novel is "realist" in yet a more literal way, for it does indeed, as Page says in her preface, tell a true story about characters who bear their own real names and recount their real familial legends. In a way, then, it is almost as much oral history as novel. Yet it would be a mistake to conflate either its veracity or its verisimilitude with the absence of craft. Its obvious eloquence and apparent simplicity are a genuine achievement. It is as though, having struggled noticeably in two other novels to find a structure and language expressive of her political vision, she relaxes into a narrative strategy so well adapted to the task that it hardly seems like a strategy at all. Yet the novel's form unpretentiously encompasses love and work, domesticity and political struggle, desire and history.

Much of its success derives from the coherence of Dolly's first-person narration. Page hears regional dialects well, and in the Irish back-country rhythms and locutions of Dolly's voice, she gives us not only authenticity but also lyricism. The novel has some of the qualities of a narrative poem, something between ballad and epic. Its refrain comes in Dolly's repeated visits to High Top; in the mountain Page finds both setting and symbol. Here Dolly has played as a child; here her parents are buried, side by side at last; here Dolly comes to confront her past and decide her future; here she and John walk home together over the mountain; here they come to celebrate and consummate their marriage; here, too, John is buried at the end. The mountain becomes the meeting ground of past and present, the axis linking the natural with the human, time with place, love with loss, individual consciousness with family and society.

Perhaps what moves contemporary readers most in the novel is the quality of feeling between Dolly and John Cooper, particularly the slow transformation of Dolly's sexual anxiety and tension into trust and love. Page's other novels also touch on a young girl's deep fear of sexuality—Marge's in *Gathering Storm*, Laura's in *Sounding*—a fear often associated with a knowledge of men's violence. Dolly Hawkins fears the force of John Cooper's desire as well, wishing (and not wishing) him back in Kentucky. Her fears grow partly from her knowledge of the devastation sexual passions can leave in their wake—her loved father's philandering with Parasidy LaRue has cost her mother her peace of mind and Jim Hawkins, finally, his life, disrupting forever the safe familial order of Dolly's earlier years. Yet Page makes it plain from their first encounter how deeply Dolly is drawn to John. Dolly, describing John, gives herself away in every word, for her language is the language of desire—the vitality of him, the laughing eyes, the chestnut hair "waving like a kind of signal over his forehead and eyes." She is drawn to him both in his phallic difference and in his familiarity: "big as my Dad had been . . . by the bits of coal pockmarking his neck and cheeks, I knew him a miner, like my own kinfolk." In Dolly's assessment of John we hear at once the acknowledgment of class solidarity, the longing for the absent father of the edenic past, and the attentiveness of sexual curiosity. Page captures in these early encounters between Dolly and John all the strange mixture of fear and arousal, combativeness and comfort, that foretell a relationship both passional and enduring.

Nancy Schrom Dye, reviewing the 1977 reprint of *Daughter of the Hills* for *Mountain Heritage*, observes that Page weaves two narratives throughout the novel: the story of Dolly's childhood in the late nineteenth century as she participated vicariously in the miners' battle against convict labor, a battle her father helped lead; and the story of Dolly's adulthood in the boom years of World War I and the hard years of the twenties, encompassing her courtship by and marriage to John Cooper, her hopes for their children, her struggles for survival after John loses his leg, and her militance about working conditions in the mines and homes of Toewad.[18] Page weaves this texture of past and present through the juxtaposition of event and memory. In fact, though, the two stories are really one story: a narrative of the life of a woman who interprets her experience as one of continuity with the past, as well as one of connection with her people. In her marriage to John, Dolly imagines herself able to set right what has gone wrong in the past between her own parents, to love as they did, but better. In her father's militancy in the past, she finds an inspiration for her own militancy in the present. Even in her young son's descent into the mines, a fate she and John have fought against since his birth, she is able to take some pride and comfort from the sense of continuity with previous generations. For Page makes clear that these mountain people, for all their suffering, for all their exploitation, have also lived lives of considerable depth and pleasure. They are part of a specific and cohesive community, and Dolly's sense of connection with others in that community, living and dead, makes her one of the least alienated of American protagonists.

Much of the sense of continuity, of course, takes the form of a continuity of struggle. As Dolly reconstructs it, the story of the miners' insurrection against the convict-leasing system acquires a legendary dimension. The story she remembers stays remarkably true to the actual events of the Cumberland miners' actions. A system in which the state leased convicts to private companies had grown up throughout the South in the years after the Civil War; more than half the "penitents" were black.[19] The system saved money for the states, sparing them the costs of incarceration; for the companies, it not only low-ered wages but also provided what amounted to a slave labor force that could be expanded to replace the free miners when-ever they became restive about conditions at work and in the company-owned towns.

In 1891 miners at the Tennessee Coal Mine Company in An-derson County refused to sign a contract, protesting against the absence of a miners' representative at the tipple where coal was weighed; against the exorbitant prices in the company store, where their families were forced to shop since they were paid (illegally) in scrip; and against no-strike clauses in the new con-tract. When the company brought in forty convicts to replace the stubborn miners, three hundred of them marched on the stockade, took the guards and the convicts prisoner, marched them several miles to Coal Creek, and took them by train to Knoxville. There they met with Governor John B. Buchanan, who subsequently went into the mining towns to ask the min-ers to abide by the law until it could be changed. The miners were not satisfied, but they had initiated a process that would finally end the convict-leasing system. This first revolt had been accomplished, according to the Knoxville *Journal*, "with-out the slightest outward excitement, animosity, or ill-feeling or intoxication, but with the resolute determination of East Tennesseans armed to fight for a just cause."[20] This was the first in a series of insurrections throughout eastern Tennessee in 1891 and 1892.

The description of another such uprising clearly corresponds to the second incident in *Daughter of the Hills*, in which the miners free the convicts and clothe them in street dress:

> About nine o'clock on the evening of October 31, lights were sighted from the hill tops surrounding the Tennessee Coal Mine; shortly afterwards the miners filed up to the stockade and demanded the release of the convicts. After a conference the officials turned over the convicts to the miners, who told them to "get out of here." The 163 convicts scattered over the

valley, casting off their "stripes" and putting on other clothing, for which the store of Captain John Chumley was raid-
ed. The miners set fire to the stockade and to the other
buildings, leaving only the chimneys standing.[21]

In 1893, the Tennessee legislature passed an act providing for a
new penitentiary and for abolishing the lease system when the
state's lease contract expired in 1896. In 1896, the state com-
missioner of labor wrote in his report:

> The convict lease system in Tennessee, so far as it pertains to
> mining, is a thing of the past; all convicts have been removed
> from Tracy City and Coal Creek; their places will be filled by
> free miners. The long sought for event in the history of min-
> ing in this state occurred January 1, 1896, at the expiration of
> the lease with the Tennessee Coal, Iron and Railroad
> Company.[22]

Page integrates these events—the materials of history, and
for Dolly, the materials of memory—at critical moments in the
narrative structure. Dolly recalls part of the story, the story of
the first insurrection, when she has gone up the mountain to
resolve her feelings about John, to decide whether or not to accept him as a mate. Her recollection of this struggle and of her
father's role in it balances her pain at his sexual betrayals: She is
able to see him whole. This is a moment, then, of personal re-
newal: "I knew my fear was passing from me, and what I lost
with my Dad's going, my joy in the rightness of things, acoming
back. Lying with the cleanswept earth under me, I felt things
deep down taking fresh root." The memory also renews her
sense of connection with community, with history. Her decision to accept John means embracing both an adult sexuality
and an adult place in the life of "our Hollow": "I had passed from
my girl-hood and become a woman."

The second time Dolly reconstructs her father's role in the
mining rebellions occurs after John's accident, when he has lost
his leg and his will. Through this structure, Page enables Dolly

to tell an exemplary tale, one she hopes will rekindle John's vitality. The telling also suggests that Dolly herself has assumed the same capacities for leadership and inspiration that characterized her father. Shortly afterward, the miners come to her and ask her to speak at a gathering to protest the terrible absence of minimal safety standards in the mine. She knows she will: "Shades of our dead fathers routing penitents from the hills would rise and speak to us. And Seth's Dad and Elijah [the black miner once ostracized, finally accepted by the community], and gentle-voiced Jake Valitsky, buried under coal." So Dolly becomes a spokesperson for her community, living and dead; now it is not only her father, but "our fathers" who will speak through her. Other mining communities come to ask her to speak: "They'll listen to Jim Hawkins's daughter. . . . We never had anybody the likes of you. Not since Ma Jones, God rest her soul." The allusion to Mother Jones suggests that Dolly too can have a life as speaker, organizer, and "community mother" after John's death.

The last events in the novel are John's burial on High Top; a community gathering to celebrate the installation of the new water pump and the building of the new first aid station: and Dolly's preparation for a journey to speak at yet another mining town. In her son she recognizes the strong will of his forebears; Page transforms the image of his "digging" in the earth into a metaphor for a communal search for "the truth to set men free." The themes of continuity and change, of love and loss, of suffering and struggle in these last chapters emerge organically from the texture of familial and community life woven through the novel as a whole.

If one looks in this novel for the silences, the dislocations, that reveal the pressures of the unsaid against the boundaries of the overt narrative project, one will of course find them. Contemporary feminists will observe that though Dolly in her love for John seeks out and finds in him a worthy successor to her father, it is *she* who finally becomes the activist, the spokesperson. Neither she nor Page seems especially aware of the extent to which she mothers John. She not only takes on the burden of familial support when he is incapacitated, she hides the washing from him so that he will not be hurt by the knowledge. When she goes to speak at the meeting, she returns to find him tossing feverishly, calling out her name, and knows she must never leave him again while he is ill. Indeed, it is John's sickness and death that lead to, or at least enable, Dolly's emergence as a speaker. In some ways, then—but in ways that the text subdues and represses—Dolly joins the ranks of female protagonists who restrain their own capacity or redirect it in order to support their men and to hide from them the knowledge of their own weakness. Here there is no resentment, indeed no real acknowledgment, by Dolly or by Page, of this contradiction. An earlier and a later generation of feminists made this repressed text, and women's resistance to it, a conscious narrative project.[23] *Daughter of the Hills,* like much of the political literature of the thirties, tends to submerge the more painful differences of gender in the commonalities of class. Nor does Page develop the tension between women's capacity for activism and women's and men's capacity to enjoy heterosexual love. In that regard, she creates an enviable world, though one that may seem conservative to contemporary feminists in its unquestioning valorization of marital love.

The novel's hopefulness, sadly, may belong to another era. But *Daughter of the Hills* makes a significant contribution to our literary heritage. Like other women's fiction of the thirties it calls into question facile generalizations about pro-communist writers' "contempt for the aspects of experience that could not be contained by a narrow political utilitarianism."[24] And Page succeeds in infusing her characters' lives with a larger significance. The heroism of Dolly Hawkins lies both in her resistance to exploitation and in her sheer love of life—her capacity to live it fully even in the face of deprivation and loss. This is a text that refuses to sever sexuality and work, love and social protest. *Daughter of the Hills*, in fact, is both a heterosexual love story and a novel of social protest. The combination is curiously rare in American literary history.

Deborah S. Rosenfelt
San Francisco State University

NOTES

1. For the details and contours of Page's life, I am indebted to four sources: a five-hour interview with Page that I conducted on February 13, 1986; Page's comments on the first draft of this essay; the unpublished closely autobiographical novel, *Sounding*; and a biographical essay by historian Mary Frederickson, "Myra Page: Daughter of the South, Worker for Change," *Southern Changes* 5, no. 1 (January/February 1983): 10–15. I have acknowledged specific references to *Sounding* and to the Frederickson essay, but I owe to the Frederickson piece a more general debt than I can acknowledge in a single note, especially for matters of chronology.

2. "The March on Chumley Hollow," in William Kozlenko, ed., *One Hundred Non-Royalty Radio Plays* (New York: Greenberg, 1941).

3. Page writes, "But for the devoted work of these friends, led by Ida Bermin and Irwin and Fran Corey, this novel might have disappeared like so many in this period." Letter to Deborah Rosenfelt, April 1986.

4. Works on the life stories of Americans in the Old Left include Peggy Dennis, *The Autobiography of an American Communist* (Westport, Conn.: Lawrence Hill, 1977); Vivian Gornick, *The Romance of American Communism* (New York: Basic Books, 1977); Elinor Langer, *Josephine Herbst: The Story She Could Never Tell* (Boston: Little, Brown, 1983); Al Richmond, *A Long View from the Left* (New York: Delta, 1972); Deborah Rosenfelt, Commentary on *Salt of the Earth*, in Michael Wilson, *Salt of the Earth* (Old Westbury, N. Y.: The Feminist Press, 1978), pp. 93–168; Deborah Rosenfelt, "From the Thirties: Tillie Olsen and the Radical Tradition,"

Feminist Studies 7, no. 3 (Fall 1981): 371–406; David Talbot and Barbara Zheutlin, *Creative Differences: Profiles of Hollywood Dissidents* (Boston: South End Press, 1978); and of course other essays for this Feminist Press series. Obviously, not all the leftists described in these works lived lives corresponding in every way to the paradigm I have described; unlike Page, for example, many of them were born into radical families.

5. Because *Sounding* is as much a reminiscence as a novel, though written in the third person, and because Page has tried hard in it for historical accuracy, I have felt justified in making the usually dangerous equation between its protagonist and Page herself.

6. Frederickson, p. 11.

7. Ibid. According to Frederickson, Page "became active in the YWCA in order to give substance to New Testament concepts of brotherhood and peace."

8. The YWCA in those years expended most of its funds on recreation and housing for women in the mills and factories, according to Lois W. Banner, *Women in Modern American History* (New York: Harcourt Brace, 1974), 97–98.

9. In George A. Lundberg, ed., *Trends in American Sociology* (New York: Harper, 1929), pp. 172–220.

10. Frederickson, p. 14.

11. The other three by women are Fielding Burke, *Call Home the Heart* (London: Longmans, Green, 1932; reprinted by The Feminist Press with Afterwords by Anna W. Shannon and Sylvia J. Cook, 1983); Grace Lumpkin, *To Make My Bread* (New York: The Macauley Company, 1932), and Mary Heaton Vorse, *Strike!* (New York: Horace Liveright, 1930). Sherwood Anderson and William Rollins also wrote novels inspired by the strike.

12. Candida Ann Lacey, "Engendering Conflict: American Women and the Making of a Proletarian Fiction," doctoral dissertation, University of Sussex, 1986, pp. 164–65. Lacey says that the publication of *Gathering Storm* was ignored by all but the *New Masses* reviewer, Esther Lowell, who praised its Marxist understanding of class conflict. She cites correspondence by Sherwood Anderson, who supported Page's aims but felt himself too critical to write the review *New Masses* had requested of him; she finds in his refusal a reflection also of his own ambivalence toward the Communist party and its sponsorship of proletarian fiction.

13. The fullest study of radical fiction in the thirties remains Walter B. Rideout's *The Radical Novel in the United States, 1900–1954* (New York: Hill and Wang, 1956). More recent work on the literature of the period includes Cook and Shannon on Fielding Burke (Olive Tilford Dargan); Langer on Herbst; Rosenfelt on Olsen; and Lacey, all cited above; Elaine Hedges, Introduction and editorial comments, in Meridel Le Sueur, *Ripening: Selected Work, 1927–1980* (Old Westbury, N.Y.: The Feminist Press, 1982); Alice Kessler-Harris and Paul Lauter, in their Introduction to The Feminist Press's thirties series; Paul Lauter, "Working-Class Women's Literature: An Introduction to Study," in Joan E. Hartman and Ellen Messer-Davidow, eds., *Women in Print* (New York: Modern Language Association, 1982), pp. 100–133; David Madden, ed., *Proletarian Writers of the Thirties* (Carbondale: Southern Illinois University Press, 1968); David Peck, "Joseph North and the Proletarian Reportage of the 1930's," *Zeitschrift für Anglistik und Amerikanistik* 3 (1985): 210–20; Lawrence H. Schwartz, *Marxism and Culture: The CPUSA and Aesthetics in the 1930's* (New York: Kennikat, 1980); and Janet Sharistanian, Afterword to Tess Slesinger, *The Unpossessed* (Old Westbury, N.Y.: The Feminist Press, 1983). A collection less sympathetic to the literature of the "Stalinist" Left is Ralph F. Bogardus and Fred Hobson, eds., *Literature at the Barricades: The American Writer in the 1930's* (University: University of Alabama Press, 1982).

14. Lacey analyzes the four novels written by women in response to the Gastonia strike as well as work by Tillie Olsen, Meridel Le Sueur, and Tess Slesinger.

15. This recollection is expressed in a 1983 letter to Alice Kessler-Harris, Paul Lauter, and Amy Swerdlow, in which Page claims a more extensive role for women of the Left in the thirties than she felt they acknowledged.

16. Myra Page, "Sharecroppers Go Back to School," *American Spectator* (May 4, 1936); I read a draft version in Page's files.

17. Frederickson, p. 15.

18. "*Daughter of the Hills*: A Book Review," *Mountain Heritage* (May 1978): 26.

19. Stanley Folmsbee et al., *Tennessee: A Short History* (Knoxville: University of Tennessee Press, 1969), pp. 404–5.

20. Cited in A. C. Hutson, Jr., "The Coal Miners' Insurrections of

1891 in Anderson County, Tennessee," *Publications of East Tennessee Historical Society* 7 (1935): 111.

21. A. C. Hutson, Jr., "The Overthrow of the Convict Leasing System," *Publications of East Tennessee Historical Society* 8 (1936): 87.

22. Cited in Hutson, "Overthrow," p. 101.

23. I am thinking of earlier texts such as Kate Chopin's *The Awakening*, and Charlotte Perkins Gilman's *The Yellow Wallpaper*, and of many women's texts contemporaneous with the women's liberation movement: Margaret Atwood's *The Edible Woman* and *Surfacing*, Erica Jong's *Fear of Flying*, Marge Piercy's *Small Changes*, and others.

24. Irving Howe, "The Thirties in Retrospect," in *Literature at the Barricades*, p. 27.

The Feminist Press at the City University of New York offers alternatives in education and in literature. Founded in 1970, this non-profit, tax-exempt educational and publishing organization works to eliminate sexual stereotypes in books and schools and to provide literature with a broad vision of human potential. The publishing program includes reprints of important works by women, feminist biographies of women, and nonsexist children's books. Curricular materials, bibliographies, directories, and a quarterly journal provide information and support for students and teachers of women's studies. In-service projects help to transform teaching methods and curricula. Through publications and projects, The Feminist Press contributes to the rediscovery of the history of women and the emergence of a more humane society.

FEMINIST CLASSICS FROM THE FEMINIST PRESS

Antoinette Brown Blackwell: A Biography, by Elizabeth Cazden. $19.95 cloth, $9.95 paper.

Between Mothers and Daughters: Stories Across a Generation. Edited by Susan Koppelman. $8.95 paper.

Brown Girl, Brownstones, a novel by Paule Marshall. Afterword by Mary Helen Washington. $8.95 paper.

Call Home the Heart, a novel of the thirties, by Fielding Burke. Introduction by Alice Kessler-Harris and Paul Lauter and afterwords by Sylvia J. Cook and Anna W. Shannon. $8.95 paper.

Cassandra, by Florence Nightingale. Introduction by Myra Stark. Epilogue by Cynthia Macdonald. $3.50 paper.

The Changelings, a novel by Jo Sinclair. Afterwords by Nellie McKay; and by Johnnetta B. Cole and Elizabeth H. Oakes; biographical note by Elisabeth Sandberg. $8.95 paper.

The Convert, a novel by Elizabeth Robins. Introduction by Jane Marcus. $6.95 paper.

Daughter of Earth, a novel by Agnes Smedley. Afterword by Paul Lauter. $7.95 paper.

A Day at a Time: The Diary Literature of American Women from 1764 to the Present, edited and with an introduction by Margo Culley. $29.95 cloth, $12.95 paper.

The Defiant Muse: French Feminist Poems from the Middle Ages to the Present, a bilingual anthology edited and with an introduction by Domna C. Stanton. $29.95 cloth, $11.95 paper.

The Defiant Muse: German Feminist Poems from the Middle Ages to the Present, a bilingual anthology edited and with an introduction by Susan L. Cocalis. $29.95 cloth, $11.95 paper.

The Defiant Muse: Hispanic Feminist Poems from the Middle Ages to the Present, a bilingual anthology edited and with an introduction by Angel Flores and Kate Flores. $29.95 cloth, $11.95 paper.

The Defiant Muse: Italian Feminist Poems from the Middle Ages to the Present, a bilingual anthology edited by Beverly Allen, Muriel Kittel, and Keala Jane Jewell, and with an introduction by Beverly Allen. $29.95 cloth, $11.95 paper.

The Female Spectator, edited by Mary R. Mahl and Helene Koon. $8.95 paper.

Guardian Angel and Other Stories, by Margery Latimer. Afterwords by Nancy Loughridge, Meridel Le Sueur, and Louis Kampf. $8.95 paper.

I Love Myself When I Am Laughing... And Then Again When I Am Looking Mean and Impressive, by Zora Neale Hurston. Edited by Alice Walker with an introduction by Mary Helen Washington. $9.95 paper.

Käthe Kollwitz: Woman and Artist, by Martha Kearns. $7.95 paper.

Life in the Iron Mills and Other Stories, by Rebecca Harding Davis. Biographical interpretation by Tillie Olsen. $7.95 paper.

The Living Is Easy, a novel by Dorothy West. Afterword by Adelaide M. Cromwell. $8.95 paper.
The Other Woman: Stories of Two Women and a Man. Edited by Susan Koppelman. $8.95 paper.
Mother to Daughter, Daughter to Mother: A Daybook and Reader, selected and shaped by Tillie Olsen. $9.95 paper.
Portraits of Chinese Women in Revolution, by Agnes Smedley. Edited with an introduction by Jan MacKinnon and Steve MacKinnon and an afterword by Florence Howe. $5.95 paper.
Reena and Other Stories, selected short stories by Paule Marshall. $8.95 paper.
Ripening: Selected Work, 1927–1980, by Meridel Le Sueur. Edited with an introduction by Elaine Hedges. $8.95 paper.
Rope of Gold, a novel of the thirties, by Josephine Herbst. Introduction by Alice Kessler-Harris and Paul Lauter and afterword by Elinor Langer. $8.95 paper.
The Silent Partner, a novel by Elizabeth Stuart Phelps. Afterword by Mari Jo Buhle and Florence Howe. $8.95.
Swastika Night, a novel by Katharine Burdekin. Introduction by Daphne Patai. $8.95 paper.
These Modern Women: Autobiographical Essays from the Twenties. Edited with an introduction by Elaine Showalter. $4.95 paper.
The Unpossessed, a novel of the thirties, by Tess Slesinger. Introduction by Alice Kessler-Harris and Paul Lauter and afterword by Janet Sharistanian. $8.95 paper.
Weeds, a novel by Edith Summers Kelley. Afterword by Charlotte Goodman. $7.95 paper.
A Woman of Genius, a novel by Mary Austin. Afterword by Nancy Porter. $8.95 paper.
The Woman and the Myth: Margaret Fuller's Life and Writings, by Bell Gale Chevigny. $8.95 paper.
Women and Appletrees, a novel by Moa Martinson. Translated from the Swedish and with an afterword by Margaret S. Lacy. $8.95 paper.
The Yellow Wallpaper, by Charlotte Perkins Gilman. Afterword by Elaine Hedges. $4.50 paper.

OTHER TITLES FROM THE FEMINIST PRESS

Black Foremothers: Three Lives, by Dorothy Sterling. $8.95 paper.
All The Women Are White, All The Blacks Are Men, But Some of Us Are Brave: Black Women's Studies. Edited by Gloria T. Hull, Patricia Bell Scott, and Barbara Smith. $12.95.
Complaints and Disorders: The Sexual Politics of Sickness, by Barbara Ehrenreich and Deirdre English. $3.95 paper.
The Cross-Cultural Study of Women. Edited by Margot I. Duley and Mary I. Edwards. $29.95 cloth, $12.95 paper.
Feminist Resources for Schools and Colleges: A Guide to Curricular Materials., 3rd edition. Compiled and edited by Anne Chapman. $12.95 paper.
Household and Kin: Families in Flux, by Amy Swerdlow et al. $8.95 paper.
How to Get Money for Research, by Mary Rubin and the Business and Professional Women's Foundation. Foreword by Mariam Chamberlain. $6.95 paper.
In Her Own Image: Women Working in the Arts. Edited with an introduction by Elaine Hedges and Ingrid Wendt. $9.95 paper.
Integrating Women's Studies into the Curriculum: A Guide and Bibliography, by Betty Schmitz. $9.95 paper.
Las Mujeres: Conversations from a Hispanic Community, by Nan Elsasser, Kyle MacKenzie, and Yvonne Tixier y Vigil. $8.95 paper.
Lesbian Studies: Present and Future. Edited by Margaret Cruikshank. $9.95 paper.

Moving the Mountain: Women Working for Social Change, by Ellen Cantarow with Susan Gushee O'Malley and Sharon Hartman Strom. $8.95 paper.

Out of the Bleachers: Writings on Women and Sport. Edited with an introduction by Stephanie L. Twin. $9.95 paper.

Reconstructing American Literature: Courses, Syllabi, Issues. Edited by Paul Lauter. $10.95 paper.

Salt of the Earth, screenplay by Michael Wilson with historical commentary by Deborah Silverton Rosenfelt. $5.95 paper.

Witches, Midwives, and Nurses: A History of Women Healers, by Barbara Ehrenreich and Deirdre English. $3.95 paper.

With These Hands: Women Working on the Land. Edited with an introduction by Joan M. Jensen. $9.95 paper.

Woman's "True" Profession: Voices from the History of Teaching. Edited with an introduction by Nancy Hoffman. $9.95 paper.

Women Have Always Worked: A Historical Overview, by Alice Kessler-Harris. $8.95 paper.

Women Working: An Anthology of Stories and Poems. Edited and with an introduction by Nancy Hoffman and Florence Howe. $8.95 paper.

For free catalog, write to The Feminist Press at the City University of New York, 311 East 94 Street, New York, N.Y. 10128. Send individual book orders to The Feminist Press, P.O. Box 1654, Hagerstown, MD 21741. Include $1.75 postage and handling for one book and 75¢ for each additional book. To order using MasterCard or Visa, call: (800) 638-3030.